Yorath Yewbeam
b.1850
Shape-shifter.

m.

Vera Kuragina
b.1862
Hypnotist.

Gra... B...or
...85
Painte... ...nen...wed.
Lived ... ...her ...n and
grands... ...aton until
she di... ...ged ...ighty.

m.

Manley
b.1884
Soldier. Killed in 1918
in the Great War.

Yolanda
b.1900
Shape-shifter.
Inherited her father's
castle. Never married.

Henry
b.1905
Disappeared when
he was eleven.
Unendowed.

Daphne
b.1908
Clairvoyant. Died
f diphtheria in 1916.

James
b.1910
Unendowed.
Historian.

m.

Solange Sourzac
b.1912
French actress. Fell and broke
her neck in mysterious
circumstances while visiting
Yolanda's castle in 1964.

Monty Bone
b.1937
Pilot. Died 1963.

m.

...izelda
b.1937
...nendowed.

Lucretia
b.1942
Matron.
Unendowed.

Eustacia
b.1947
Clairvoyant.

Venetia
b.1952
Designer
of magic
clothes.

Paton
b.1957
Power-
booster.

Amy Jones
b.1967
Store assistant.

m.

...
b...
Piani...
Disappeared in
1994.

Note:

When James Yewbeam's wife,
Solange, died, his four
daughters went to live with
their evil great aunt,
Yolanda, who turned them
... their father. Yolanda
...ed to steal Paton, but
James resisted her.

Cha...
b.19...
Pict...
trave...

Charlie Bone

AND THE
RED KNIGHT

Also by Jenny Nimmo

Midnight for Charlie Bone
Charlie Bone and the Time Twister
Charlie Bone and the Blue Boa
Charlie Bone and the Castle of Mirrors
Charlie Bone and the Hidden King
Charlie Bone and the Wilderness Wolf
Charlie Bone and the Shadow of Badlock

The Rinaldi Ring
The Snow Spider trilogy
Secret Creatures

For younger readers
Matty Mouse
Farm Fun!
Delilah

Charlie Bone

AND THE
RED KNIGHT

Jenny Nimmo

EGMONT

To Alice and Corwine, with love

www.charlie-bone.com

EGMONT
We bring stories to life

Charlie Bone and the Red Knight first published in
Great Britain 2009
by Egmont UK Limited
239 Kensington High Street
London W8 6SA

Text copyright © 2009 Jenny Nimmo
Cover illustration copyright © 2009 Sam Hadley

The moral rights of the author and illustrator have been asserted

ISBN 978 1 4052 4823 5

1 3 5 7 9 10 8 6 4 2

A CIP catalogue record for this title is available from the British Library

Typeset by Avon DataSet Ltd, Bidford on Avon, Warwickshire
Printed and bound in Great Britain by the CPI Group

Contents

The children of the Red King, called the endowed

Manfred Bloor

Talents Master at Bloor's Academy. Previously head boy. A hypnotiser. He is descended from Borlath, eldest son of the Red King. Borlath was a brutal and sadistic tyrant.

Naren Bloor

Adopted daughter of Bartholomew Bloor, Naren can send shadow words over great distances. She is descended from the Red King's grandson who was abducted by pirates and taken to China.

Asa Pike

A were-beast. He is descended from a tribe who lived in the Northern forests and kept strange beasts. Asa can change shape at dusk.

Billy Raven

Billy can communicate with animals. One of his ancestors conversed with ravens that sat on a gibbet where dead men hung. For this talent he was banished from his village.

Lysander Sage

Descended from an African wise man. He can call up his spirit ancestors.

Tancred Torsson

A storm-bringer. His Scandinavian ancestor was named after the thunder god, Thor. Tancred can bring rain, wind, thunder and lightning.

Gabriel Silk

Gabriel can feel scenes and emotions through the clothes of others. He comes from a line of psychics.

Emma Tolly

Emma can fly. Her surname

derives from the Spanish swordsman from Toledo, whose daughter married the Red King. He is therefore an ancestor to all the endowed children.

Charlie Bone	Charlie can travel into photographs and pictures. Through his father he is descended from the Red King, and through his mother, from Mathonwy, a Welsh magician and friend of the Red King.
Dorcas Loom	Dorcas can bewitch items of clothing. Her ancestor, Lola Defarge, knitted a shrivelling shawl whilst enjoying the execution of the Queen of France in 1793.
Idith and Inez Branko	Telekinetic twins, distantly related to Zelda Dobinsky, who has left Bloor's Academy.

Joshua Tilpin Joshua has magnetism. He is descended from Lilith, the Red King's oldest daughter, and Harken, the evil enchanter who married her.

Una Onimous Mr Onimous's niece. Una is five years old and her endowment is being kept secret until it has fully developed.

Olivia Vertigo Descended from Guanhamara, who fled the Red King's castle and married an Italian Prince. Olivia is an illusionist. The Bloors are unaware of her endowment.

Dagbert Endless Dagbert is the son of Lord Grimwald who can control the oceans. His mother took the gold from drowned men's teeth, and made them into charms to protect her son. Dagbert is a drowner.

Eric Shellhorn   Eric can animate stone carvings.

The endowed are all descended from the ten children of the Red King: a magician-king who left Africa in the twelfth century, accompanied by three leopards.

Prologue

The Red King arrived in the North nine hundred years ago. He was an African magician and each of his ten children inherited a small part of his power. These powers were passed down, through their descendants, to the inhabitants of an ancient city. But not all the inheritors use their powers wisely. Some of them are bent on evil, and Charlie Bone strives constantly to thwart them.

Charlie's parents are on their second honeymoon. They have been away for more than a month. Postcards arrive for Charlie, describing his parents' wonderful adventures on the world's oceans. Although Charlie is happy for them, he wishes they would return. The city is becoming a dangerous place for him and his friends. One of them was almost drowned and their favourite meeting place, the Pets' Café, has been closed. Charlie is afraid that the Red King's old enemy, Count Harken,

will try and enter the city once again. The count, an enchanter, has already abducted the orphan, Billy Raven, and now keeps him in Badlock, a world that exists in the far distant past.

If only the Red King could return to keep the city safe. But that is too much to hope for. And yet, deep in the ruins of the Red King's castle, a heart still beats within a tall red tree. The king can watch with the eyes of birds that settle on his branches; he can listen with the ears of creatures that graze beside him; sometimes he can even move. But he who was once mighty is now powerless to help the children who need him. His last spell has been cast. He can only hope that his cloak and sword will protect the man who has chosen to take his place. One thing is certain: the white mare that was once the king's beloved queen will do all in her power to carry their champion to victory.

The enchanted sword

To the small man hurrying through the city, the dark buildings that rose about him had never appeared so menacing.

'Menaced,' muttered Orvil Onimous. 'That's what we are, my dears, menaced.' He was speaking to three cats that paced about him, magnificent creatures with fire-bright coats, from the deep copper of the cat that leapt ahead, to the flame orange and starry yellow of the two that ran on either side of him.

'You are a comfort, Flames,' sighed the little man, 'you know that, don't you?'

They turned off the High Street and made their way down Frog Street, a narrow alley that led to the ancient city walls. It was

a cold, damp night and the cobblestones were wet with melting frost. Every step the small man took became more laboured. He rounded a corner and came within sight of an unusual-looking shop, built into the very fabric of the old walls. Above a large, latticed window, the words 'The Pets' Café' could just be made out on a sign filled with the paintings of animals.

Mr Onimous seemed unable to continue. He hung his head, gasping for air. With his whiskery face and furry brown head he resembled a large vole in an ill-fitting tweed coat.

The cats gathered round him, mewing encouragement, but Orvil Onimous let out a mournful sob and pointed to a sheet of paper nailed to the green painted door.

These premises are closed, said the notice, *by order of the city councillors, in accordance with Section 238 of the Public Health Act.*

The cats could not read the notice but they were well aware of its meaning. Their friend's livelihood had been stolen from him. The Pets' Café, where every customer was obliged to bring a pet, was now closed. The joyful twittering, the braying, barking and mewing

that once had welcomed every visitor was now gone, leaving only a bleak silence.

Inside the café, chairs were piled on empty tables, the lights were out in the coloured lanterns hanging from the ceiling, and in the kitchen Mrs Onimous endlessly filled the stove with cakes and cookies that no one would eat.

Thinking of his wife, Mr Onimous took a firm step towards the green door, and then hesitated. A sound at the far end of the alley made him peer cautiously round the corner.

A figure came striding towards him.

'We're closed,' called Mr Onimous. 'It's no use coming down here. Besides,' he added sadly, 'you haven't got a pet – unless it's in your pocket. Go away.'

The stranger paid no attention. He marched purposefully closer. A boy, thought Mr Onimous, noting the slim build and youthful stride. A yellow scarf covered the lower half of the boy's face, and the hood of his blue coat was pulled well down over his forehead.

Mr Onimous backed nervously round the corner. His heart was beating rather fast, but his gloomy mood had been replaced by resentful anger. Who was this silent

stranger, marching towards him when he had expressly told him to go away?

The cats were usually quick to defend Mr Onimous but they stood in the alley with their tails erect, sniffing the air and mewing expectantly.

A strong breeze accompanied the stranger – a sinister breeze in Mr Onimous's opinion. Can't be one of the kids, he thought. Can't be one of the endowed. It's Wednesday night. They're all at school and in bed most likely. He ran across to the green door and, pulling a key from his pocket, shakily inserted it into the lock.

'Mr Onimous!' The voice was a harsh, urgent whisper.

The little man turned fearfully, and looked into a pair of familiar sky-blue eyes. 'Tancred Torsson!' he cried.

'Sssh!' Tancred put a finger to his lips.

'Oh, my dear, dear fellow.' Mr Onimous clasped both Tancred's hands and squeezed them tight. 'Oh, you can't know how you've lifted my spirits. We thought you were dead.'

'I am dead, Mr Onimous,' whispered Tancred. 'Dead to THEM at least. Can I come in? I'll explain everything.'

'Of course, of course.' Mr Onimous unlocked the

door and drew Tancred into the empty café. The three cats bounced swiftly after them and Mr Onimous locked and bolted the door.

Tancred pulled down his scarf and gazed at the upturned chairs with their legs pointing desolately at the darkened ceiling. 'This is so sad, Mr Onimous,' he said. 'We must do something about it.'

'Course we must, but it's too much for my poor old brain to sort out.' Mr Onimous led the way round the counter at the back of the café, and into the bright kitchen beyond.

An exceptionally tall woman with a long melancholy face was spooning jam into some rather pale-looking tarts. There were several plates of them spread across the kitchen table, and if it hadn't been for Mrs Onimous's desolate expression, you would have thought she was preparing for a party.

'Don't say it,' murmured Mrs Onimous, without looking up. 'Who's going to eat a hundred tarts? I couldn't help myself, Orvil. What else am I to do?'

'Onoria, my darling,' Mr Onimous failed to keep a squeak of excitement out of his voice. 'We have a visitor.'

She looked up, opened her mouth, screamed, staggered backwards and collapsed into an old armchair. 'Tancred Torsson!' she gasped. 'You're dead!'

'Not so, Mrs Onimous.' Tancred pulled back his hood, revealing a mop of thick corn-gold hair. 'As you see, I am very much alive.'

'The news is all round the city. They said you had drowned.' Two fat tears rolled down Mrs Onimous's cheeks. 'A terrible accident, they said it was, but we guessed it was that evil boy Dagbert Endless who had drowned you.'

'Well, he did, in a sense,' Tancred agreed. 'I was just about gone when Emma rescued me. And then, soon after my father had carried my lifeless body home, we had visitors.' Tancred sat at the table and stroked the head of the yellow cat, Sagittarius, drawing a deep purr from his silky throat. 'I thought you had sent them.'

'The cats!' cried Mr Onimous, clapping his hands. 'I should have known it. But they lead a mysterious life. I never know where they are off to.'

'They saved your life too, Orvil,' said his wife, pouring tea for their visitor. 'It's a miracle how they

always know when a child of the Red King is in trouble.'

'I'm no child,' chuckled Mr Onimous, lifting orange Leo into his arms.

'You're a descendant; that's good enough for them.' Onoria smiled as Aries, the copper cat, wound himself round her legs.

'They sat on my bed all through the night.' Tancred's eyes took on a faraway gleam as he began to describe the warmth and comfort the cats had brought to his aching limbs, and how their voices had soothed the pain in his head and steadied his faltering heart.

'I know, I know.' Mr Onimous thought of his own miraculous recovery.

Mrs Onimous sat down and pushed same tarts across to Tancred. 'Empty the plate, there's a good boy,' she said. 'And take some home to your mother. We don't see enough of her down here.'

'She doesn't have a pet,' said Tancred through a mouthful of tart. 'She's tried dogs and cats, guinea pigs and rabbits, even a pony, but they all ran away. They couldn't take my dad's thunder.'

Tancred's father was known as the Thunder Man, on

account of the violent weather that constantly attended him.

'Does Charlie Bone know that you survived?' asked Mr Onimous, biting into one of his wife's tarts.

Tancred nodded vigorously. 'So do the others: Lysander, Gabriel and co, but no one else must know. I can do more to help them if Dagbert and the Bloors think that I'm dead.'

'We won't tell a soul.' Mr Onimous lowered his voice as though the Bloors might be outside the door that very moment. 'I feel so sorry for poor Charlie. His parents have been away for more than a month now, and although I don't like to criticise a fine person like Lyell Bone, it's a long time to leave your only child when you've already been apart for more than ten years.'

'I agree,' said Tancred, 'but Charlie's such a great –' A loud knocking caused him to stop mid-sentence and stare over his shoulder.

'Whoever can it be?' Mr Onimous opened the kitchen door and stared across the café at a large figure framed in the window. 'Bless me, it's Norton. I'll –'

'NO, Mr Onimous!' Tancred leapt up and pulled the little man back into the kitchen. 'Charlie asked me to

warn you. That's why I came. Norton Cross has betrayed you, Mr Onimous.'

'What?' Mr Onimous frowned at Tancred in disbelief. 'How can you say such a thing? Norton? He's the best doorman we've ever had.'

'You have to believe me, sir,' said Tancred in a low voice. 'He's been seen in the company of the Witch Tilpin and others. Some of the villains from Piminy Street, in fact.'

'Norton?' Clutching the edge of the table, Mr Onimous sank on to a chair. 'What's the world coming to?'

'Well, at least we'll be on our guard, Orvil,' said his wife. She shook her head. 'Who can have turned our dear Norton to wickedness?'

No one could answer her.

The knocking had ceased at last and, peering into the dark café, Tancred caught a glimpse of two figures walking down the alley. Norton was unmistakable, his bulky form clad in a green padded jacket printed with yellow elephants. His companion was shorter and wore a black cloak and a hat with a drooping feather. The hat was an odd shape, soft and velvety. It reminded

Tancred of another hat he'd seen. Was it in a book or in a painting? He couldn't yet place it.

'Think I'd better be going now,' Tancred told the Onimouses.

'Do take care, my dear.' Mrs Onimous came and gave him a hug. 'You're young to be out alone on such a dark night.'

Tancred was fourteen and accustomed to being out alone on dark nights. His endowment was the only protection he needed, or so he thought. A bolt of lightning or a blast of gale-force wind had always been enough to deter any would-be assailant. 'I can look after myself,' he said, extricating himself from Mrs Onimous's embrace.

A violent gust of wind blew through the kitchen and the cups hanging on the dresser rattled and clinked in a wild tune.

'All right, Weather-boy, you don't have to prove it,' chuckled Mr Onimous.

Tancred walked briskly through the café, calling, 'Goodnight, Onimouses. Keep safe!'

Stepping into the alley, he closed the café door and stood listening for a moment. Footfalls could be heard

turning right on to the High Street. Pulling up his hood, Tancred tiptoed swiftly up the alley and looked round the corner.

The two figures were walking briskly in the direction of Bloor's Academy. Tancred drew his scarf over the lower part of his face and hurried after them. At first, Norton and his companion seemed unaware of their stalker, but all at once the man in the black cloak swung round. Tancred leapt into a doorway. He stood with his back against the door, breathing heavily.

He must have seen me, thought Tancred, for I saw him.

It was a face Tancred had instantly recognised. Framed in shoulder-length black curls, the stranger's pale features were dominated by large dark eyes and heavy arched eyebrows. He had a small pointed beard and the tips of his fine moustache curled up to each cheek.

If the man had seen Tancred he was apparently unconcerned, for the footsteps resumed their brisk walk.

It was several minutes before Tancred could bring himself to move again and, by the time he emerged on to the High Street, the two figures were nowhere to be

seen. They had evidently taken the side street that led to the Academy.

Keeping close to the buildings, Tancred flew after them. He reached the square in front of the Academy just in time to see Norton climb the steps up to the school.

A cold shudder ran down Tancred's spine. He had spent three years at the Academy and, in spite of the friends he had made, he had always been aware that at any moment old Ezekiel Bloor and the children he controlled might do something irrevocably evil. And then Dagbert-the-drowner had arrived, and the evil had finally shown its hand. Dagbert thought he had drowned Tancred Torsson; indeed, if it hadn't been for the cats' miraculous powers, Tancred would be dead.

He watched Norton climb to the top step, then turn and look back at the fountain in the centre of the square. A circle of swans, their beaks upraised, blew silvery streams into the lamplit air. Tancred pressed himself against a wall, where the light from the street lamps couldn't reach him. Norton made an odd sign with his hand: a sort of thumbs up, with all his fingers. And then, before Tancred realised what was

happening, Norton's hand had twisted round so that his forefinger was now pointing straight at him. Tancred cursed himself for being such a fool. He had forgotten Norton's companion.

The man now emerged from behind the fountain and advanced towards Tancred.

'Who are ye? Give us thy name.' The voice was deep and husky. 'Speak!'

With his back to the wall Tancred shuffled sideways, attempting to slide back into the alley.

'Stop!' roared the man, and Tancred froze as, from beneath the folds of his cloak, the man drew out a gleaming sword. 'Spy! Give thy name!'

Tancred found he couldn't breathe; his legs felt so weak he feared they would give way at any moment. He tried to summon up a wind, to fill the air with hailstones, but in the stranger's presence he could only muster up a damp breeze. The man was almost upon him, his sword slicing the air in shining arcs of light.

'Must I die a second time?' Tancred whispered dismally.

There would be no witnesses. The city seemed deserted, even the noise of traffic had died away; the

only sound that Tancred could hear was a faint
clattering, which he mistook for his own beating heart.
But the clattering grew louder. And now the sound
resembled hoofs cantering on stone, and then a voice
cut through the night, 'ASHKELAN!'

The swordsman whirled round and Tancred blinked
in amazement as a knight on a white horse charged into
the square. The knight was dressed from head to foot in
glittering chain mail; he wore a helmet of polished
metal with a plume of red feathers flowing from its
crown, and a red cloak that billowed behind him like a
sail. In his right hand he wielded a bright sword, the
hilt encrusted with glittering jewels, and the shield
that hung from his saddle was emblazoned with a
burning sun.

'You!' grunted the man called Ashkelan; holding his
sword aloft, he rushed at the knight.

With one blow of his own weapon the knight swept
the sword from his assailant's hand, and it rattled over
the cobblestones. There was a scream of pain, followed
by a roar of anger as the owner of the sword fell to the
ground, clutching his arm.

A stream of mysterious and indecipherable words

issued from the man as he reached for his sword. Tancred had been about to run from the scene but he stood rooted to the spot, scarcely able to believe his eyes. For all at once the fallen sword was in the air and flying towards the knight. Lifting his weapon, the knight parried the blow that would surely have severed his arm, but the enchanted sword came at him again, and again he fought off the blow. An extraordinary duel was taking place and, frightened as he was, Tancred could not bring himself to leave the square.

The knight and his mount seemed almost to be one, for the horse turned in a flash. It leapt high above the fountain and raced around the square, its hoofs moving in a cloud of sparks. The enchanted sword, now a flying streak of light, attacked the knight from every angle. How he managed to fight off such a battery of lightning blows, it was hard to comprehend. And then, at last, came the strike that might have finished him. It fell across his chest, slicing through the chain mail and drawing a deep grunt of pain from the knight. But with a mighty upward thrust he caught the enchanted sword and set it spinning into the sky.

Tancred didn't wait for the sword to fall to earth.

Astounded by what he had seen, he tore down the alley and on to the High Street. Fear and excitement caused great gusts of wind to whistle round his head; his hood blew back and the air above him fizzed with blue and white sparks. He reached Frog Street and ran towards the Pets' Café, calling, 'Mr Onimous, let me in!'

A tall man stepped out of the shadows and Tancred ran straight into him. With a moan of defeat the weather-boy closed his eyes and dropped to the ground.

Lord Grimwald arrives

Charlie Bone had been fast asleep. Now, suddenly, he was not. There were voices in the courtyard below. Charlie got out of bed, crossed the dormitory and looked out of the window. Two men were moving towards the main doors of the Academy. One Charlie recognised as Norton Cross, the doorman at the Pets' Café. He was half-dragging, half-carrying a smaller person in a large hat with a drooping feather at the back.

'Grief!' muttered Charlie. He couldn't see the face of the man beneath the hat, but he was groaning horribly. Charlie opened the window, just a crack, so that he could hear what was going on.

'Ssssh!' hissed Norton. 'You'll wake the whole school, sir.'

The two men climbed the steps to the main doors and Norton rang the bell. A moment later there was a loud rattle and one of the doors opened. Weedon the porter stood on the threshold. He was a bald, stocky man with a sour face.

'I thought he wasn't supposed to go out yet,' said Weedon.

'He wanted to see the city.' Norton dragged his companion through the door.

'What's the matter with him?' asked Weedon, frowning at the sword that danced past him.

The door was closed before Charlie had a chance to hear Norton's reply. But then his attention was drawn to a second arrival. Three women came through the arched entrance and crossed the courtyard. Grizelda Bone's imposing beak of a nose led the way. Grizelda was Charlie's grandmother. Her sisters, Eustacia and Venetia, came close on her heels. All three were tall and lean, their dark eyes small, their black brows thick and heavy. Grandma Bone's hair was a startling white, Venetia's black, Eustacia's somewhere in between.

Charlie watched them climb the steps, his grandmother teetering very slightly in her high-heeled boots. As she rang the bell, Eustacia, for no good reason, suddenly looked up at the window where Charlie stood.

Charlie backed into the shadows. Eustacia boasted that she was clairvoyant, though Charlie was not entirely convinced. Her power could wax and wane. Tonight it appeared to be waxing.

To complicate matters the dormitory door was suddenly flung open and Charlie was caught in a strip of light from the passage. The matron, Grandma Bone's third sister, Lucretia, stood silhouetted in the doorway. 'What are you doing out of bed?' she demanded.

'Er, getting some air,' Charlie said feebly.

'Air? There's enough air in here to fill the lungs of a thousand boys, let alone twelve.'

'Is there?' Charlie looked round at the eleven boys sleeping behind him. Not one had woken up, even though the matron had made no attempt to lower her voice.

'Get back to bed!'

Without waiting for Charlie to obey, the matron

closed the door. Her footsteps receded so fast Charlie imagined she must be running down the passage. In the two years he had been at the Academy he had never known his great-aunt Lucretia to run. Tonight she must either be escaping from something unpleasant, or she was late for a very important meeting.

And who would be holding a meeting at such a late hour? Only Ezekiel Bloor, Charlie decided. At a hundred and one years old, Ezekiel made no distinction between night and day. He spent his mornings dozing in his wheelchair and afternoons reading up on unpleasant spells. It was only at night that his malicious mind really came alive, and then woe betide anyone who didn't fit in with his plans.

Charlie was about to close the window when a curious smell drifted up to him: a salty, seaweedy tang that left its taste on the tongue. It was horribly familiar. Looking down into the courtyard he wasn't surprised to see a large figure appear in the archway. The man wore an oilskin coat and long fisherman's boots. He moved over the cobblestones with an odd swaying stride, as though he were on the heaving deck of a ship.

Charlie raced back to his bed. Before he climbed

into it, however, there was a husky whisper from the bed at the end of his row.

'The window. Close the window.'

Charlie pulled the bedclothes over his head. He could hardly bear to look at Dagbert Endless, let alone talk to him. Dagbert kept protesting that Tancred's near-drowning had been an accident. Even the headmaster believed his story. The school had been told that Tancred Torsson had accidentally slipped in the Sculpture room, and been drowned by water pouring from a broken tap. Charlie knew better. Dagbert was a drowner. He even boasted of his power. But neither he nor the Bloors were aware that Tancred had survived. Tancred's friends intended to keep it that way.

'The window. Close the window.' This time the voice was louder. The seaweedy smell from outside mingled with the fishy stench that Dagbert sometimes gave off.

Charlie held his nose and lay still.

'CLOSE THE WINDOW!'

The shout woke half the dormitory. Some of the boys yawned sleepily and turned over, but Bragger Braine,

the bully of the second year, sat up and grunted, 'Who said that?'

'I did,' Dagbert answered in an aggrieved tone. 'Charlie opened the window and he won't close it.'

'Close the window, Charlie Bone,' Bragger commanded.

His ardent follower, Rupert Small, echoed his words in a thin reedy voice. 'Close the window, Charlie Bone.'

Charlie held his breath. He was determined not to obey Bragger Braine or his pathetic crony.

'CLOSE THE WINDOW!' shouted Dagbert.

This shout woke Fidelio Gunn in the bed next to Charlie. 'Stop bellowing, Fish-boy!' he cried, punching his pillow into shape. 'Let normal people get some sleep.'

For a few seconds silence reigned. Charlie smiled to himself in the dark and whispered, 'Well done, Fido!'

The whisper irritated Bragger. If his bed had been beside Charlie's he would have thumped him. But they were half a dormitory apart and a day of thumping other people and starring on the football pitch had exhausted Bragger. He just wanted to go to sleep. The next time Dagbert repeated his demand, Bragger said, 'Close it yourself, Fish-boy!'

Charlie waited for Dagbert to slip out of bed and close the window, but the fish-boy didn't move. Soon the room was filled with the soft rhythmic breathing of heavy sleepers. Charlie turned over and closed his eyes.

Minutes passed. Try as he might, Charlie couldn't sleep. A soft light insisted on creeping through his eyelids. He half-opened one eye. A bluish glow was spreading across the walls; a luminous rippling gleam, like the water in a swimming pool. Charlie screwed his eyes tight shut, trying to wish away the eerie light. This was what happened when Dagbert was nervous or excited. Perhaps he sensed Lord Grimwald's arrival. Charlie knew that Dagbert was afraid of his father; they seldom saw each other, for Lord Grimwald rarely left his gloomy castle in the Northern Isles.

At the far end of Charlie's row a bed creaked, and he heard quick footfalls on the bare floorboards. Someone slammed the window shut but no one woke up. Charlie curled himself up and began to drift into sleep. And then something heavy sank on to his bed, just below his knees, and a voice whispered, 'Charlie, are you awake?'

No. I am asleep, Charlie told himself. He didn't stir.

'Charlie, wake up.'

He could have remained as he was, motionless, his eyes closed, but sudden anger made Charlie sit up and whisper harshly, 'What is it?'

'My father's here,' said Dagbert, his quiet voice husky and urgent. 'I can smell him.'

'And I can smell you,' Charlie grunted. 'Get off my bed.'

'Charlie, I think I might need your help.'

'What?' Charlie exclaimed. '*Me* help *you*, after you drowned my friend?'

'It was an accident.' Dagbert's whisper became a low whine. 'I didn't mean to.'

'Oh, you meant to, all right,' Charlie growled. 'Emma Tolly saw everything. Now get off my bed.' He kicked Dagbert in the back.

Dagbert stood up, but he didn't move from Charlie's side. Charlie could see his rigid form silhouetted against the glimmering blue-green wall. At last a soft grumble of words came tumbling from Dagbert. 'You know our secret, our family curse. You know that my destiny is to die in my thirteenth year – unless my father dies before me. It has to be one of us, and now he's here, unexpectedly, in the night, and I am twelve, Charlie.

So what's going to happen? Find out for me, please. No one else is like you, Charlie. No one else would do it.'

'Do it yourself,' muttered Charlie. Turning his back on Dagbert, he wriggled under the bedclothes.

Seconds passed before Dagbert said dully, 'I'm afraid.'

'Too bad,' Charlie replied.

'But I want to know why my father's here.'

'Well, I don't. Not interested.' Charlie pulled the bedclothes over his head. He waited for Dagbert's response, but none came. Before falling asleep, Charlie opened his eyes briefly and found that the dormitory was in darkness again. Hopefully Dagbert had gone back to bed.

Charlie hadn't been quite truthful with Dagbert. He *was* interested in Lord Grimwald's arrival. In fact, he was very curious about everything that he had seen from the window that night. He just wasn't quite curious enough to risk being caught by some of the school's unpleasant-looking visitors.

In a dark passage leading off the great hall, two highly polished ancient doors opened into a magnificent, but seldom used, ballroom. Tonight the ballroom had been

filled with chairs, and Ezekiel Bloor's visitors sat in rows beneath four glittering chandeliers. The brilliant light reflected in the crystals was rather disconcerting to some of Ezekiel's unwholesome-looking guests. They were people who were happier in shadow: thieves, poisoners, fraudsters, kidnappers, swindlers and even murderers. Most of them lived in Piminy Street, a narrow road in the ancient part of the city. Once it had been inhabited by magicians, sorcerers, warlocks and the like. Indeed, among the villains seated in the ballroom that night, there were those who had inherited the talents of their notorious ancestors. Prominent among them was a clairvoyant named Dolores Slingshot, so named because of her deadly accuracy with a catapult. Dolores was eighty years old and wore a wig of claret-coloured ringlets.

In a corner at the back of the room stood a huge white cube. Even in a corner it seemed to dominate the room. Everyone who entered eyed the cube with surprise and curiosity. As well they might, for it was hard to understand how the great white square had managed to get itself down the narrow passage outside. In fact, it hadn't. Weedon had been forced to open

up the disused doors at the side of the ballroom and push the cube (with the help of four removal men) through the garden and into the room. The whole process had been extremely difficult and exhausting. Even Weedon didn't know what lay beneath the cladding. The visitors wondered if they were about to find out.

The last person but two to arrive was a sickly-looking arsonist called Amos Byrne. When he had taken his place, Weedon closed the doors and all eyes turned to the stage.

The grand piano had been pushed to the back and in its place stood an oval table covered with a purple cloth. At one end of the table an ancient man in a wheelchair sat grinning at the audience. Ezekiel Bloor's white, waxy hair framed a face so gaunt and bony it looked more like a skull than the face of a living person. Next to him, and not smiling at all, his great-grandson, Manfred, sat slightly turned from his neighbour, an ashen-faced woman with strands of grey hair and a nose as blue as a bruise.

At the other end of the table, the headmaster, Dr Harold Bloor, was in the middle of a long, extremely

boring speech when another guest arrived. He was a well-muscled man wearing only a string vest and camouflage trousers. He took a chair at the back, twirled it in one hand and brought it to rest with a loud bang. The headmaster glared at the latecomer and then resumed his speech. It went on for another ten minutes before grinding to a halt, and those of the audience who hadn't fallen asleep were able to applaud.

The applause didn't go on for as long as the headmaster would have liked, however, because the doors suddenly crashed open and a strong salty smell wafted into the room, followed by a large man.

'Lord Grimwald!' Dr Bloor's mouth hung open. 'We didn't expect . . . that is to say we hardly dared to hope that you would arrive today. As you see, your . . . your . . .' he pointed to the cube.

'Sea Globe.' Lord Grimwald smiled at the cube with satisfaction. 'Well, I'm here now, so get on with it.' He swayed down the narrow aisle between the seats as though his legs were of different lengths. His crinkled grey hair was streaked with a seaweedy green and his eyes were an icy aquamarine. The strong, salty smell

that accompanied him caused several people to sneeze and cough.

'We have already covered several issues,' said Dr Bloor, 'but I have not yet introduced –'

'Yes, yes. Go on.' Lord Grimwald climbed the steps up to the stage and Manfred, leaping up, hastily pulled an extra chair between himself and his neighbour.

Lord Grimwald sat down heavily on the empty chair. 'Grimwald,' he said, extending his hand to the woman on his left.

She took the eel-like fingers with a barely concealed look of distaste. 'Titania Tilpin,' she said, rising to her feet. 'I am about to speak.'

Everyone in the room appeared to know Titania and wild applause broke out. She gave her audience a gratified smile and said, 'I know what you are expecting and I shall not disappoint you.'

More applause. The headmaster frowned. He had not received such generous applause. 'Allow Mrs Tilpin to speak,' he said.

The woman smiled and drew from the folds of her sparkling black cloak a round mirror set in a jewelled frame. The mirror glass blazed so brilliantly some of the

visitors had to cover their eyes. And then, with blissful sighs, the spellbound audience fell silent.

'The Mirror of Amoret,' announced Mrs Tilpin. 'Most of my audience have seen it already, but for your benefit, Lord Grimwald, this mirror was made by the Red King for his daughter Amoret. It is nine hundred years old.'

'And is an aid to travel,' Lord Grimwald interrupted in a bored tone. 'Yes, I've heard of it.'

'Much more than an aid,' Mrs Tilpin said indignantly. 'I have only just begun to understand its many properties. Formerly I have used it to bring my ancestor, the enchanter Count Harken, into the city. He was eventually driven back into his own world – I won't go into detail – but I have hopes that he can return again. Now, I have something to show you all.' She turned and, tossing back her sequinned cloak, held the mirror so that its radiant light was beamed on the wall behind her.

A glowing circle appeared on the wall. It grew to the size of a small table. And then, within the circle, the fuzzy contours of plants and trees appeared. As a green jungle came into focus, a boy could be seen, wandering

through the trees with a tiger at his side. The boy had snow-white hair and thick-lensed spectacles. Unfortunately a jagged line ran diagonally across the scene, cutting it in two.

'Your mirror is flawed,' Lord Grimwald observed.

'Charlie Bone did it,' snapped Mrs Tilpin. 'Infernal boy. I had a promise from Ezekiel here that he would help to mend it. But, so far, his promises have come to nothing.'

'I am old, Titania,' Ezekiel protested. 'My magic is waning and I must conserve my strength. I told you to consult Dorcas Loom. She can do it, I am certain.'

'It is of no consequence,' Lord Grimwald said with a yawn. 'We can see the boy well enough. Continue, Mrs Tilpin.'

'Of no consequence!' Mrs Tilpin glared at Lord Grimwald. She shook her shoulders like a hen ruffling her feathers and the black cape sparkled. 'My mirror is of great consequence.'

'Of course, of course, Titania,' said the headmaster. 'Tell us more – our audience is waiting.'

With a defiant look at Lord Grimwald, Mrs Tilpin pointed to the white-haired boy. 'Billy Raven,' she said,

'and a tiger that is not a tiger – an illusion conjured up by the enchanter to entertain the boy.'

Ezekiel gave a sudden cackle. 'How delicious to see the little wretch trapped in Badlock, never to return. Never to claim his inheritance. There's a will, you see, my friends.' He wheeled himself to the front of the stage and addressed the audience directly. 'That's where you come in. The document is signed by my great-grandfather, Septimus Bloor. It leaves all his land, his treasures and even this house, to his oldest daughter, Maybelle, and her heirs. Her only remaining descendant is Billy Raven,' Ezekiel turned his chair and pointed to the wall, 'still strolling through the enchanted jungle. Billy is unaware, you see, and only I know the truth because it was told to me by my great-aunt Beatrice, a witch, who poisoned Maybelle and forged a false will leaving everything to my side of the family. But the real will still exists.' Ezekiel banged the arm of his wheelchair with surprising vigour. 'And I believe that Lyell Bone, father of Charlie, has hidden it.'

At this point Manfred stood up and, leaning over the table, declared, 'It must never be found by anyone outside this room. Do you understand?'

A low murmur broke out. There were enthusiastic nods and cries of, 'Never!' and 'We'll see to it!'

'See to it you must,' said Manfred, his dark, hypnotic gaze travelling over the assembled villains. 'Find it you must. Destroy it we must. Lyell Bone is at sea, hopefully never to return.' He glanced at Lord Grimwald. 'But he might have passed a hint, a clue to his son Charlie. We will deal with the boy. You must find the will.'

'Carefully, mind,' said Dr Bloor. 'Nothing violent. We don't want to cause suspicion or alert the law. The Pets' Café is a good place to start. Councillor Loom and Norton Cross,' he looked at Norton in the front row and Norton gave a nod, 'they have helped us to close the place. Once the owners are evicted you can search the café. There may be a tunnel that leads to the castle ruins. Find it! Investigate!'

'I'll do it,' said Amos the arsonist.

'And me,' called the man in the string vest. 'I'm very nimble, me.'

'Don't cause suspicion,' warned Dr Bloor.

'Rewards?' piped up Dolores, tossing her red ringlets. 'What do we get for helping you?'

'Money,' said Ezekiel. 'Lots of it. What else would you want?'

'Money'll do,' said Dolores. 'Ten thousand if I find the will.'

Ezekiel scratched his long nose, wondering if he could eventually go back on his word. 'Ten thousand,' he agreed, somewhat reluctantly.

'A thousand for trying!' demanded a white-haired man in a purple suit; an illusionist by the name of Wilfred Coalpaw.

Dr Bloor shook his head. 'Just for trying? It's rather –'

'Agreed!' cried Ezekiel, who had decided that going back on his word wouldn't be too difficult. 'A thousand for each of you. There'll be plenty to go round if we find where Septimus hid the rest of his treasure. You can go now.' He waved his hand dismissively.

There was a great deal of scraping, stamping and shuffling as the audience rose from their seats and made for the door. A few of them cast curious glances at the white cube. A sound came from it. Waves perhaps. There was the faint rustle of a tide rolling on to a stony shore.

'By the way,' called Manfred, as though to distract

them, 'Ingledew's Bookshop. Keep an eye on it. Get in there if you can. Old tomes make good hiding places.'

The guests murmured among themselves and left the room.

Six people remained sitting in the front row: Grizelda Bone and her three sisters on one side of the aisle, Norton Cross and the swordsman on the other.

'Bring us some tea!' Dr Bloor demanded when Weedon poked his head round the door.

'And biscuits,' added Ezekiel. 'And cake!'

'For all of you?' asked Weedon, counting heads.

'All,' said Dr Bloor. 'Eleven, to be precise.'

With a bad-tempered mutter, Weedon withdrew his head and closed the doors.

'At last, the elite.' Ezekiel beamed down at his six remaining guests. 'Now we can discuss things more . . . comprehensively. Ashkelan Kapaldi, welcome!'

The swordsman stood and bowed deeply, first to the stage and then to Grandma Bone and her three sisters. He was a very colourful figure with his wide lace collar and emerald-green tunic, embroidered with gold. His cuffs were made of lace too, and his breeches were green velvet. Wide leather boots reached almost to his

thighs, and a scarlet cummerbund encircled his waist. A broad leather belt hung diagonally across his chest from his shoulder to below his waist, and attached to this was a dark green scabbard.

'In the seventeenth century,' Ezekiel announced, 'Ashkelan Kapaldi was the greatest swordsman in Europe.'

'Swordsman?' questioned Grandma Bone.

'Seventeenth . . .?' murmured her sister Eustacia.

'I did it,' said Mrs Tilpin. 'That is to say, I did it with the help of the mirror and my son Joshua, who is endowed with magnetism. Together,' she made a small circular motion with her hand, 'they drew Asheklan from his painting. And here he is . . . and his sword!'

At this Ashkelan withdrew his sword from its scabbard and sent it skimming towards the four sisters. They rose, as one, with loud shrieks and exclamations, and the sword came to a halt, swaying gently on its point. A deep scratch on the polished floor left no doubt as to the sword's effectiveness.

'Fear not, ladies,' said Ashkelan as the sword swept back to him. 'See, it is under my command.' He grabbed the sword and limped closer to Ezekiel. 'I have

been told, good sire, that every endowed child in this part of the world is within these walls of a weekday.'

'That is so,' said Dr Bloor.

'Not so,' stated Ashkelan. 'I can sense the endowed and I have seen one, not one hour since, in the very courtyard before your establishment. A boy of medium height; a creeping, prying, nasty boy. And he is protected, sir, by none other than the Red Knight.'

'Red Knight,' breathed Ezekiel, leaning towards Ashkelan. 'A *Red* Knight, you say?'

'Aye. His mount is a white mare,' said the swordsman, 'his cloak all red, the helmet's plume a fluttering scarlet. And he *wounded* me, good sirs and ladies. He *wounded* me and I cannot let that pass.'

'Of course not, sir!' Ezekiel was now bent almost in half, his breath rattling in his chest. 'Whoever this knight may be, we shall put an end to him.'

'First the boy,' said Manfred coldly. 'We can't have an endowed boy wandering the streets without our knowledge.'

A family tree

Tancred got to his feet. Had he known it was Charlie's Uncle Paton standing there in the dark, he wouldn't have taken fright. He brushed the knees of his jeans, feeling rather foolish. 'Sorry, sir,' he said.

'On the contrary, Tancred,' Paton said in a low voice, 'it is I who must apologise. My wretched affliction compels me to walk in the shadows. I'm afraid I've already distressed at least three other people tonight.'

'There's a man with a sword . . . a sword that . . .' Tancred hesitated, unsure how to describe the scene that had so unnerved him.

'I know, I saw him too,' said Paton, 'and the knight.'

'I didn't know where to go, what to –'

'Come with me.' Paton took Tancred's arm and hurried him away from Frog Street. 'I was on my way to the bookshop. We can discuss things there. Hurry! And tread softly if you can.'

'Yes, sir.'

They walked together down the High Street, their footsteps light and brisk. Every so often Paton would stop and hold Tancred still so that he could listen for any following sounds. But there were none. And yet something accompanied them. A hoarse whisper seemed to echo down the street, a faint groan came from a shifting manhole cover, and there was a soft whine in the air above them, either from overhead cables or TV aerials. And then there was the smell, strong and salty, that clung to their hair and faces.

'The father of the boy who tried to drown you is here,' murmured Paton.

'I know. I can taste him,' Tancred said.

They reached a row of ancient half-timbered buildings standing in the shadow of the great cathedral. Ingledew's Bookshop was one of a dozen small, rather exclusive shops on a paved walk that ran beside the

cathedral square. There was a lamp post standing immediately outside the window, but the lamp at the top was unlit. The council had given up replacing the bulb as it exploded so frequently. The councillors were all aware of Paton Yewbeam's unfortunate talent, and guessed that he was responsible for the power surges. But none of them could bring themselves to mention it, for fear of being ridiculed. They pretended to believe that the constant shattering of glass was caused by hooligans.

Soft candlelight illuminated the bookshop window, where large, leather-bound books lay on folded velvet. Paton rang the bell and a tall woman appeared so quickly behind the glass in the door it seemed likely that she had been waiting for him. She withdrew the bolts, unlocked the door and opened it, saying, 'Paton, come in.'

There was tenderness in the woman's voice, and the sort of intimacy that made Tancred feel a little uncomfortable. And then she saw him and uttered a little gasp of surprise.

'Julia, it's Tancred,' Paton reassured her. 'I thought it best to bring him here.'

'Sorry, Miss Ingledew,' Tancred mumbled. 'Hope I'm not intruding.'

'Of course not.' She gave him a warm smile and walked down the three steps into her shop.

Tancred followed her while Paton locked and bolted the door again. Miss Ingledew led the way round the shop counter, where three candles in bronze saucers burned with a sudden brightness as the visitors stirred the air.

Behind the counter, a thick velvet curtain hid Miss Ingledew's cosy sitting room. Here, a log fire burned in the grate, and shelves of books lined the walls right up to the ceiling. Tancred was surprised to see Miss Ingledew's niece, Emma, kneeling before the fire. She had her back to him, while she brushed her pale gold hair over her head. Tancred gave a polite cough and said, 'Em?'

The girl tossed back her long hair and stared at Tancred, her cheeks reddening.

'Hello,' she said. 'I've . . . erm . . . got a cold, or a sore throat that might soon be a cold. So I didn't go back to school.'

'Me neither.' Tancred grinned.

'Well, you can't go back, can you?' Emma wrapped a hank of hair around her hand. 'I mean you can't ever, now they think you're dead.'

Paton and Miss Ingledew had disappeared through the door into the kitchen, and the clink of crockery could be heard above the low murmur of their voices.

Tancred eased himself on to the sofa behind Emma. 'I suppose I could turn up and give everyone a fright,' he said.

'Not a good idea.' Emma came to sit beside him, and he noticed that her hair was still damp. It was very fine, silky hair and he had a sudden urge to touch it. This thought made him blush for some reason, and he stared into the flames, not quite knowing how to continue the conversation.

Miss Ingledew saved him the trouble by carrying a tray of tea into the room. She set it down on her desk, every other available surface having been taken over by books and candlesticks.

'I've told Julia about the things you saw tonight.' Paton handed Tancred a mug of tea.

'Thanks, Mr Yewbeam!' Tancred clutched the warm

mug. 'But you saw them too,' he added anxiously. 'You know I didn't imagine it.'

'What did you see?' Emma demanded as she reached for her tea. 'What's been going on?' She turned to Tancred. 'And, come to that, why are you here, in the middle of the night?'

Tancred explained that he had come to warn the Onimouses that Norton Cross, their doorman, could no longer be trusted. He went on to describe the extraordinary events that had followed: the foreign swordsman who seemed to have stepped from the past, the sword that fought on its own and the mounted knight in his scarlet cloak. 'If the knight hadn't turned up, I'd have been done for,' Tancred finished dramatically.

Emma's grey eyes widened. 'Oh, Tancred!'

Tancred glanced at her anxious face and smiled. 'Funny thing is, I recognised the swordsman. I'm sure I've seen him in the school – in a painting, that is.'

'You have.' Paton lowered himself into an armchair by the fire. 'I saw him once, and have never forgotten it. He is one of Mrs Tilpin's forbears. I imagine it was she who brought the man into our world.'

'With the help of a mirror that does not belong to her, no doubt,' Miss Ingledew remarked crisply.

'Charlie's mirror?' said Emma.

'Indeed.' Paton's dark eyes glinted. 'The Mirror of Amoret.'

'But who *is* this mysterious swordsman?' begged Emma.

'Ashkelan Kapaldi,' Paton told her. 'A swordsman of renown, and a magician of sorts. Though, as far as I can tell, it was only his sword that he could bend to his will, and set to killing, all on its own. He was active during the English civil war. How do I know this?' He waved a hand at a bookcase in the corner. It contained ancient, dusty books bound in peeling leather, their yellowed leaves covered in mysterious, faded writing. Tancred had taken a look at one of them, and understood hardly a word.

'He seemed to recognise me,' Tancred said thoughtfully, 'that swordsman. I felt that he knew I was endowed.'

'It's something we have in common,' Paton remarked. 'I can often recognise one of the Red King's descendants. Most of us have a way of knowing each

other. Isn't it the same for you, Tancred?'

Tancred wasn't sure. He certainly wouldn't have known that pretty Miss Chrystal, the former music teacher, was, in fact, a witch of the very darkest nature. He slowly shook his head. 'I didn't know Mrs Tilpin.'

'No,' Paton agreed. 'She was a tricky one.'

Emma slipped off the sofa and knelt in front of the fire again, flicking out strands of her damp hair. 'Why has it all got so ominous?' She looked at Paton, as though he must hold the answer.

Paton was in no hurry to reply. He sipped his tea and then stared into his mug, apparently having forgotten Emma's question. He hadn't forgotten, however. 'Convergence,' he said at last. 'Two things have occurred in these last few months. Charlie's father has reappeared and Titania Tilpin has become the witch she was destined to be. I believe she is the conduit – the channel, if you like – between the present and the distant past; the world of her ancestor, Count Harken of Badlock. And it is Titania who is drawing Harken's minions back into our city. Some of them are present-day villains, descendants of Harken, others are, for now, mere shadows; whispers, rustlings, echoes. But if

Titania and Harken have their way, these shadowy phantoms will soon take on form and substance and then our lives, if we manage to hold on to them, will be changed forever.'

Paton's dreadful prophecy shocked everyone into a long silence. Eventually Emma, scrambling on to the sofa again, said shakily, 'Billy Raven is there, in Harken's world, so Charlie says.'

'I'm sure it's true,' Paton said. 'And I'm equally sure that Charlie will try to rescue him.'

'And what about Charlie's father?' asked Tancred.

'Ah, Lyell.' Paton's frown lifted and he actually managed to smile. 'My recent travels have borne fruit. It's quite incredible what you can turn up these days.'

Tancred and Emma stared at Paton, uncomprehending.

On the other side of the fireplace, Miss Ingledew pulled herself from the depths of a battered armchair, and gave a light, ringing laugh. 'Paton,' she cried, 'they haven't a clue what you're talking about.'

Paton cleared his throat. 'I'll explain,' he said. And he told them of his search for a certain pearl-inlaid box that Billy Raven's father, Rufus, had entrusted to Lyell

Bone. Soon after this, Rufus and his wife were both dead, victims of a supposed traffic accident, and Lyell began ten long years of spellbound forgetfulness, a trance-like state brought about by Manfred Bloor's dreadful hypnotic power.

Paton's deep voice shook with emotion when he spoke of Lyell and Rufus, but his tone became firmer when he described his growing suspicion that Billy Raven was closely connected to these vile crimes. Why, for instance, did Ezekiel Bloor keep the orphan Billy almost a prisoner in the school? And then allow him to be dragged into the past by the enchanter of Badlock?

'I don't have an answer either,' said Paton, looking at the bemused expressions around him.

'So how d'you know about the box?' Tancred ventured.

'Ah, the box. I was coming to that.' Paton stood up and began to pace the room. 'My suspicions led me to search for any of Billy's remaining relatives. I discovered the aunt who cared for him after his parents' deaths, but she would tell me nothing. It was only by chance that she mentioned a certain Timothy Raven, Billy's great-uncle. I could see that she instantly

regretted it, and she wouldn't tell me where he lived. I had to discover that for myself. I now know that she was on Ezekiel's payroll. She didn't even tell me that her own mother was still alive. It was Timothy who told me that. I found him in Aberdeen. He was ailing when I met him and has since died, but he was able to give me an old address of Billy's great-grandmother. And I found her.'

Paton's audience waited breathlessly for his next revelation. He smiled at them with satisfaction and announced, 'Her name is Sally Raven and she lives in a care home on the north-east coast. It seems she had become estranged from her daughter and knew nothing of Billy's fate after his parents had died. But she told me about the box, Maybelle's box she called it, with its beautiful pattern of inlaid mother-of-pearl. It was given to her by her husband's aunt Evangeline, and Sally gave it to her grandson, Rufus, on his wedding day.'

Emma uttered a quiet, 'Ah!' She had been thinking of weddings lately. She looked at her aunt, who smiled.

'The key was lost,' Paton continued, rather hurriedly. 'And there was no way of opening the box. It was just a very beautiful object, Sally said. But in her

heart she knew it contained something special because there were others, on the Bloor side of the family, who desperately wanted it.'

'The Bloors?' said Tancred and Emma.

'Just so,' replied Paton. He turned to Miss Ingledew. 'Shall we show them?'

'I think we had better.' Miss Ingledew went to her desk and unlocked a small drawer at the top. She withdrew a folded piece of paper and carried it over to Tancred. 'Open it out,' she said. 'I call it the Raven Tree.'

Tancred unfolded the paper on his knees, where Emma could see it.

'A family tree!' Emma exclaimed.

'Sally Raven is an extraordinary woman,' Paton told them. 'She has a case full of photos, letters and cards from her family and her husband's. She was able to help me draw up a family tree that goes right back to Septimus Bloor, old Ezekiel's great-grandfather.'

'So Billy is related to Ezekiel?' said Tancred with a frown.

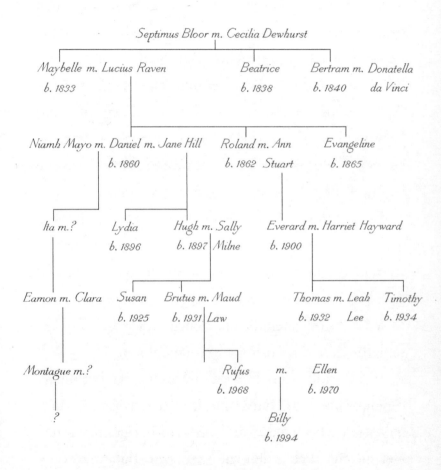

Septimus Bloor m. Cecilia Dewhurst

Maybelle m. Lucius Raven
b. 1833

Beatrice
b. 1838

Bertram m. Donatella
b. 1840   da Vinci

Niamh Mayo m. Daniel m. Jane Hill
b. 1860

Roland m. Ann
b. 1862 Stuart

Evangeline
b. 1865

Ita m.?

Lydia
b. 1896

Hugh m. Sally
b. 1897 Milne

Everard m. Harriet Hayward
b. 1900

Eamon m. Clara

Susan
b. 1925

Brutus m. Maud
b. 1931 Law

Thomas m. Leah
b. 1932   Lee

Timothy
b. 1934

Montague m.?

Rufus
b. 1968

m.

Ellen
b. 1970

?

Billy
b. 1994

Maybelle gave the mother-of-pearl inlaid box to Evangeline.
Evangeline gave it to Hugh and Sally on their wedding day.
Hugh and Sally gave it to Rufus and Ellen on their wedding day.
Rufus gave it to Lyell Bone for safe-keeping.
Daniel Raven's first wife, Niamh, died in childbirth. He then married Jane Hill.

'Distantly,' Paton agreed. 'Billy is descended from Maybelle, who married a Raven. Ezekiel is descended from Maybelle's brother, Bertram, who inherited Septimus's fabulous wealth. But Sally believes that Septimus left his fortune to Maybelle and her heirs. And his original and true will is hidden in that beautiful box. The box she gave to Rufus. The box she believes Rufus entrusted to his dearest friend. And he was Lyell Bone.'

Tancred gave a low whistle. 'What a tangle.' He was about to hand back the family tree when Emma restrained him. She was scrutinising the paper intently.

'There's a line that goes nowhere,' she said, pointing to a name on the far left side of the tree. 'N-I-A-something, and then Ita, and then Eamon.'

'Irish,' said Paton. 'I intend to follow it up, but it may be impossible. Sally told me that her husband had a half-sister who lived in Ireland with her grandparents. Her mother died when she was born. But we're only interested in the line that ends with Billy. If Sally is right then Billy Raven is the heir to Septimus Bloor's fortune.'

Tancred rolled his eyes. 'No wonder they want to get

rid of him. Does Charlie know about this, Mr Yewbeam?'

Paton nodded. 'I managed to fill him in before he left for school on Monday.'

The telephone on Miss Ingledew's desk suddenly gave a sharp ring, and everyone jumped. Miss Ingledew picked up the receiver. The voice at the other end could be heard quite clearly and Tancred leapt off the sofa, crying, 'It's Dad. Oh no, I forgot to ring him.'

Miss Ingledew had to hold the receiver well away from her ear as Mr Torsson's voice thundered into the room, sending pens and papers flying off her desk. Paton took the receiver from her and shouted, 'Torsson!' into the phone. 'Tancred's here, as you no doubt suspected. He's quite safe, but he'd better spend the night in the bookshop. There's a lot going on. We'll talk about it later.'

Mr Torsson's reply was loud but reasonable. He'd managed to get his thunder under control. Tancred took over from Paton and told his father he would be home in the morning. He replaced the receiver with a sigh of exhaustion.

'It's all right to stay the night, is it?' he asked Miss Ingledew, darting a look at Emma.

'We'll make up a bed on the sofa,' Miss Ingledew said with a smile.

Paton decided it was time for him to leave. He wished everyone a good night and reminded Miss Ingledew to lock and bolt the door as soon as he had left. He waited outside the shop while she did this, and then she waved at him through the glass in the door, and he set off.

When he left Cathedral Square, he heard a low muttering of voices that grew louder as he approached the turn to Piminy Street. A group of people were coming up the road towards him. They were an odd bunch, with their heavy topcoats, their furs and their leathers and strangely dated hats. One of them wore a string vest. Paton retreated a few steps and slid into the shadows behind a narrow porch. He watched as they all turned into Piminy Street. There must have been at least a dozen of them. When they had passed the first few houses, Paton felt confident enough to step quietly into the street, but one of the group turned suddenly and stared at him, her eyes glinting in the dark; she was

very small, her face ancient in the lamplight, her hair a deep red. Paton averted his eyes and hurried on.

Not for the first time he wished that Julia Ingledew didn't live so close to Piminy Street. 'On the doorstep of another world,' he said to himself as he walked briskly through the city, avoiding lamp posts where he could. The salty tang on his lips reminded him that Lord Grimwald was in the city once again. At Ezekiel's invitation, no doubt. And Paton thought of Lyell Bone, out on the wild ocean.

As Paton strode down Filbert Street, a black car rolled past him and stopped outside number nine. Grizelda Bone got out of the car and climbed the steps to the door.

'I'll wager she's up to her neck in all this skulduggery,' Paton said to himself.

Gabriel's secret

Gabriel Silk had a secret. He wanted to tell Charlie about it, but there was never an opportunity. They were in different dormitories now, and different classes. The canteen was too public, and out in the grounds they were never alone. There might, however, be a chance when Charlie was on his way to a music lesson.

Gabriel had been waiting in the corridor of portraits, hoping to waylay Charlie as he crossed the hall. He had intended to stand just inside the corridor, but found himself wandering further down, studying the portraits on the wall. He passed them every day but had never really studied them. The subjects were mostly stern-looking men and

women, though occasionally you could find a smiling person. If you knew your history well enough, you could tell by their clothes what century they had lived in. Gabriel had been told that every one of them was descended from the Red King. There was even a Silvio Silk, in a black velvet suit and a white curled wig. He might have been Gabriel's ancestor, but he bore no resemblance to him.

If Gabriel wore someone else's clothes, he immediately knew what sort of person had worn them before. He could sometimes picture them, see what they had done and even hear their voices. But portraits could tell him nothing. 'If I was Charlie, I could go right in and talk to you,' Gabriel whispered to Silvio Silk. 'And you could talk to me.'

Silvio Silk didn't bat an eyelid. He wore the same resigned expression that he had worn when the artist painted him, two hundred years before.

Gabriel wandered further down the corridor. He passed men in sober black suits, in rich red jackets and glittering gold waistcoats; he passed women whose necks were hung with diamonds and pearls, whose hair was garlanded with flowers, and whose shoulders were

draped in velvet and fur. And then he stopped before a full-length portrait of a cavalier. Gabriel's eye was drawn to the sword at the man's side. It had a delicately wrought golden hilt, and the man's gloved fingers rested on it almost lovingly. As Gabriel stared at the intricate gold curves they glinted suddenly, as though the sun had caught them. And then Gabriel found his gaze lifting to the face above the wide lace collar. The man had shoulder-length black hair, and between the black moustache and pointed beard, the fleshy lips had an unpleasant grin.

Gabriel stepped back to get a better view, and now he noticed that the eyes seemed wrong. There was no light in them. It was as if the man's spirit had left the painted face.

A cold shudder ran down Gabriel's spine. It was dark in the passage. There were no lights, no sunlit windows. Had he imagined the sudden bright glint on the gold sword-hilt? Was the lack of light in the man's eyes or merely Gabriel's own shadow? No. There was something different about this painting. The name on the bronze plaque at the base of the frame read *Ashkelan Kapaldi*. The plaque had come loose, it hung at an angle

and there were fingerprints on the shiny surface of the paint. Someone had touched the portrait very recently; pressed and prodded it repeatedly.

'Gabriel Silk, what are you doing?' Manfred's voice came ringing down the corridor of portraits.

Gabriel turned guiltily, although, as far as he knew, he had nothing to feel guilty about. He must make sure that Manfred didn't guess what was on his mind. The Talents Master had been using hypnotism a great deal recently.

'What are you doing here?' Manfred came up to Gabriel and stared at him.

'Nothing, sir.' Gabriel looked away from the narrow black eyes. Beneath his black cape, Manfred was wearing a bright green waistcoat. Surprising for one who was usually so soberly dressed.

'Nothing?' The Talents Master glared at Gabriel, forcing him to look up. 'Nothing?'

Gabriel felt dizzy. 'Going to a music lesson, sir,' he said faintly.

'Go then! And stop hanging about!'

Gabriel was about to turn away when he saw two figures coming down the corridor behind Manfred. One

of them was limping, the other lurching. Gabriel's eyes widened in surprise, for the limping man bore a strong resemblance to the man in the portrait: Ashkelan Kapaldi.

The surprise in Gabriel's eyes caused Manfred to whirl round. 'Go!' he shouted at Gabriel. 'This instant!'

Gabriel walked away quickly, but not so quickly that he didn't hear the Talents Master say, 'It's not wise, sir, for you to leave the west wing during the day. Pupils will recognise you . . . and wonder.'

'Let them wonder.' The stranger's voice had a foreign lilt. 'Let them be amazed . . .'

'It's not the time, Ashkelan.' This second voice had a cavernous, echoing sound. Something in the ebb and flow of it reminded Gabriel of Dagbert Endless. He hastened into the hall, which was full of children on their way to different classrooms. Occasionally someone would whisper to a companion, while glancing anxiously about in case a prefect was watching. Silence in the hall was the rule.

Gabriel spotted Charlie's wild mop of hair. He wore a slight frown and his thoughts were obviously miles away. Gabriel waved, trying to get Charlie's

attention, but Charlie didn't see him. And then Dagbert Endless walked between them. He followed Charlie doggedly across the hall and into the passage that led to Señor Alvaro's music room. Gabriel pursued them.

Safely out of the hall, Gabriel called, 'Charlie!'

Dagbert swung round and snapped, 'What do you want?'

Gabriel was momentarily taken aback by Dagbert's sharp tone. 'I want to speak to Charlie,' he said.

'Hi, Gabe!' Charlie had noticed Gabriel at last. 'What is it?'

Gabriel saw that Dagbert wasn't going to leave them. 'It's nothing,' he murmured. 'I'll catch you later.'

Charlie watched Gabriel slouch away, his shoulders hunched, his hands in his pockets. Obviously he didn't want Dagbert to hear what he had to tell Charlie.

'Why d'you keep following me?' Charlie demanded. 'Shouldn't you be in a lesson?'

Dagbert shrugged. 'I've lost my flute. I thought Señor Alvaro might have it.'

'Why? Mr Paltry teaches flute.' Charlie walked faster, trying to shake Dagbert off.

Dagbert caught up with him. 'OK. The truth is . . . my father's here.'

'I *know*,' said Charlie irritably. 'We've been through that. What d'you want me to do about it?'

'I want you to keep my sea-gold creatures for a while.'

'What?' Charlie stopped dead in his tracks. He could hardly believe his ears. 'Are you seriously asking me to keep something that you almost k–' he quickly corrected himself, 'something that you drowned Tancred for taking?'

'I've told you,' Dagbert said desperately. 'I didn't mean to drown him. It was an accident.' He dug into his pocket and brought out a handful of tiny charms: five golden crabs, a fish and a miniature sea urchin. 'Please, keep them safe for me.' He held the charms out to Charlie. 'My father's looking for them.'

'Why?'

'I can't explain right now.' Dagbert pushed the charms at Charlie.

Charlie stepped back. 'Why me?'

'You're the only person I can trust.'

Charlie found this hard to believe. 'What about

your friends: Joshua, Dorcas, the twins? What about Manfred?'

Dagbert shook his head vigorously. 'No, no, no.' He grabbed Charlie's wrist and attempted to press the charms into his hand. *'Please!'*

'No.' Charlie snatched his hand away and the sea-gold creatures spilled on to the floor. The sea urchin rolled towards Señor Alvaro's door which, at that very instant, began to open.

Señor Alvaro stood in the doorway regarding the sea urchin at his feet. He gave it a small kick.

'No!' Dagbert pounced on the charm as it rolled across the floor. 'You could have broken it.' He hastily gathered up the five crabs and the golden fish as well and shoved them into his pocket.

'What's going on?' Señor Alvaro frowned at the wall behind the boys. It was now a rippling bluish-green; silvery bubbles rose from a shell that floated just behind Charlie's ear, and fronds of seaweed waved gently from the skirting board.

Charlie glanced at the scowling Dagbert. 'It's what happens, sir,' he told the music teacher. 'He can't help it.'

'Can't help it?' Señor Alvaro raised a neat black eyebrow. He was young for a teacher and his clothes were always interesting and colourful. He had permanently smiling brown eyes, a sharp nose and shiny black hair. He didn't appear to be too surprised by the watery shapes on the wall.

As Dagbert shuffled away, the weeds and shells and bubbles gradually faded, and the wall took on its usual greyish colour.

'Come in, Charlie,' said Señor Alvaro.

Charlie always enjoyed his music lessons now. He knew he wasn't talented but Señor Alvaro had convinced him that music could be fun, as long as you blew with conviction and hit the right notes, more or less. Charlie had even managed half an hour's practice the previous evening, and Señor Alvaro was pleasantly surprised.

'Excellente, Charlie!' The music teacher's Spanish accent was soft and compelling. 'I am astounded by your improvement. A little more practice and that piece will be perfect.'

The lesson was at an end but Charlie was reluctant to leave. Señor Alvaro was one of the few teachers at

Bloor's whom Charlie felt he could trust. He had an overwhelming urge to confide in him.

'Do you understand about Dagbert?' he asked as he put his trumpet in its case.

'I know about the boy's father, if that's what you mean, Charlie. I'm aware of the curse placed upon the Grimwald dynasty and I know that Dagbert believes the charms his mother made can protect him.' Señor Alvaro's tone was very matter-of-fact. Charlie was surprised he knew so much.

'Do you know about . . . about . . . my talent?' Charlie was unsure of putting this question and found himself stuttering.

'Of course!' Señor Alvaro gave one of his heart-warming smiles. 'I'll see you on Friday, Charlie. Usual time.'

'Yes, sir.' Charlie left the room.

When he closed Señor Alvaro's door he felt slightly dizzy. Perhaps it was the darkness of the passage, coming so soon after the bright lights in the music room. He closed his eyes for a moment and a rushing, foggy grey seeped behind his lids; it was the sea, and in the churning grey waves there was a small boat bobbing

among the foam. Charlie saw this boat in his mind's eye whenever he thought of his parents, somewhere on the ocean, watching whales. But today he could just make out a name on the side of the boat: *Greywing*.

Charlie opened his eyes. Why had the name come to him so suddenly? Did anyone else know about it? His grandmother Maisie? Uncle Paton? The company that arranged his parents' whale-watching holiday?

'Charlie!'

Gabriel came running down the passage just as the bell went for lunch. 'Can we talk outside, Charlie, after lunch?'

'Why not now?' asked Charlie.

'I can't explain. It's too complicated,' said Gabriel.

'Give us a clue!'

'It's about the Red Knight.'

'Now I'm really interested.' Charlie hurried into the hall where the usual crowd of children were rushing to their cloakrooms: blue for music students, purple for the actors and green for the artists. Gabriel hovered beside Charlie while he washed his hands and then they walked together across the hall and down the corridor of portraits towards the blue canteen. As they

passed Ashkelan Kapaldi, Gabriel nodded at the portrait and whispered, 'I saw him today.'

'I think I saw him last night,' Charlie whispered back.

Gabriel rolled his eyes. 'What's going on?'

Charlie shrugged.

Fidelio had kept two places for them at a corner table. While they ate their macaroni cheese, Charlie bent close to his friend and, as quietly as he could, described the swordsman both he and Gabriel had seen *outside his portrait.*

'I wouldn't be in your shoes,' Fidelio remarked with a grin.

'What do you mean by that?' Gabriel asked in an offended tone. 'This man isn't after me and Charlie particularly.'

'Sorry.' Fidelio often forgot how touchy Gabriel Silk could be. 'But you're both endowed, Gabe. These weirdos are always after you lot; by and large they leave normal people like me alone.'

Gabriel had to admit that this was true. He realised that he would have to take Fidelio into his confidence as well as Charlie. Best friends always stuck together during break.

After lunch the three boys jogged round the grounds. It was one of those dreary March days when the sky is a dark grey slab and the cold air sneaks into your very bones. Sixth-formers were allowed to stay indoors, but the rest of the school, almost three hundred children from eight years old to sixteen, were trying various ways to keep warm.

Some of the boys were playing a rather half-hearted game of football, others were being violently active in an athletic kind of way, and yet more were doing formal exercises, presided over by an enthusiastic outdoor type called Simon Hawke.

Most of the girls were walking around in pairs or large groups. Someone had put up an umbrella, even though the rain wasn't more than a damp mist. It was a very bright umbrella, printed with red and yellow butterflies. The girl beneath it had almost white hair and wore a scarlet coat. She was holding her umbrella high enough to cover the head of a very tall African.

'Is that Lysander?' Gabriel pointed at the boy beneath the umbrella.

'Must be,' said Fidelio. 'Who's the girl?'

'Never seen her before,' said Charlie.

The girl turned towards them and Charlie recognised Olivia Vertigo. He had never seen her as a bleached blonde before. Her hair colour changed frequently from purple to green to indigo – she'd even gone stripy – but never white. He wondered why she and Lysander were together. They were both endowed, but they had little else in common. And then he remembered that their best friends were both missing. Lysander was seldom apart from Tancred Torsson, while Olivia and Emma were practically inseparable.

Charlie waved at Olivia and she leapt forward, catching Lysander's head in her brolly. 'Ow!' he yelled. Olivia flapped her hand at him and came bouncing over the grass in her red fur-tipped boots. Lysander stood looking around for another companion for a moment but, finding none, he followed Olivia over to the group.

Gabriel groaned to himself. Now he would have to tell his story to four people instead of one. It was such a small incident, it might mean nothing or everything. He hadn't wanted to broadcast it this way; in fact, he decided, he probably wouldn't tell anyone at all, because what he had seen wasn't that important. His

mind had simply exaggerated its significance.

'We've been talking about the Pets' Café,' said Olivia, obligingly closing her umbrella, 'and you – know – who.' She glanced at Lysander.

'Shhh!' Lysander looked over his shoulder as the Branko twins passed behind them.

The Branko twins were now lingering just within earshot. They had pale, impassive faces and the fringes of their shiny black hair touched the tips of their long thick eyelashes. The eyes beneath those lashes were dark and inscrutable. If the twins were to get the slightest hint that Tancred was still alive, they would pass the news straight to Manfred, and that would be a disaster. The Bloors would be furious that his survival had been kept a secret, and Dagbert might even make a second attempt on Tancred's life.

'Let's move,' Lysander suggested, nodding at an ancient wall standing at the top end of the grounds.

The massive red walls surrounded a castle built by the Red King nine centuries ago. It had been a vast and beautiful building but today it lay in ruins, its thick walls crumbling, its stone floors lined with moss and weeds, its roofs fallen and its once sturdy beams

mildewed and rotting. But just inside the great arched entrance was a paved courtyard surrounded by thick hedges, and facing the entrance were five smaller arches, each one leading into the castle. Four were like the mouths of dark tunnels. Only one gave a view of the green hill beyond.

'Smells a bit fusty in here,' said Olivia. She planted herself on one of the stone benches placed between the arches.

The others squeezed in beside her, but Fidelio suddenly jumped up and ran to the entrance. He stood beneath the arch where he could get a good view of the rest of the school. 'Don't want any snoops,' he said.

A low grunt came from beneath the bench beside them. Everyone stared at it until a grey paw emerged, followed by a long-nosed, overweight, short-legged dog.

'Blessed!' they cried.

Olivia held her nose. 'I might have known.'

'He can't help being smelly,' Gabriel reproved her.

'He looks so sad,' said Charlie. 'I'm sure he misses Billy.'

At the mention of Billy's name, Blessed waddled over to Charlie, wagging his bald tail. Charlie stroked

the dog's rough head, saying, 'Billy will come back, Blessed, I promise you.'

The dog grunted a couple of times and then waddled away through the arch.

'How are you going to keep that promise, Charlie?' said Gabriel. 'Billy doesn't even *want* to come back.'

'He will.' Charlie looked pointedly at Gabriel. 'You wanted to tell me something, Gabe.'

Gabriel grimaced. 'I said *you*, Charlie, not everyone.'

'We're not everyone, Gabe.' Olivia dug her elbow into his side. 'Or is it just very, very private?'

Gabriel shifted uneasily on the cold stone bench. 'Not private exactly. I mean, I suppose it concerns you as much as anyone, being endowed.'

'Come on, Gabe. I can't bear the suspense,' said Lysander.

Gabriel stared at his hands rather than meeting anyone's eye. 'It's about the Red Knight,' he muttered.

No one spoke. It was as if Gabriel had dropped a spell into the chilly air. He looked up and saw that they were taking him very seriously.

'What about him?' asked Charlie with a catch in his voice.

'I think you're the only one who's seen him,' said Gabriel, playing for time.

'I've seen him,' Olivia said quietly.

'Oh, yes. I forgot.' Gabriel had seldom seen such an earnest expression on Olivia's face. It was encouraging. 'As you know,' he continued, 'my family inherited the Red King's cloak. It was kept in a chest under my parents' bed and, as I told you before, the cloak disappeared just before the knight was seen.'

Charlie nodded. 'He was on the iron bridge, and he saved Liv and me from drowning. He's saved my life twice now.'

'The cloak was billowing all around him, like a great red cloud,' Olivia said, elegantly demonstrating with her arms, 'but we couldn't see his face because of the helmet and the visor. We thought it might be the Red King himself, or his ghost.'

'No,' said Gabriel. 'It wasn't. I've thought and thought about it. I've gone over it in my mind, trying to remember every little detail –'

'Buck up, Gabe,' said Fidelio. 'Some of the others are leaving the grounds. It's nearly the end of break.'

Fidelio's interruption flustered Gabriel. He frowned

with concentration while the others waited for him to continue.

'It was one morning,' Gabriel began, 'very early, still night really, because the moon was up. Something woke me, I don't know what. I went to the window to see if a fox had crept in and got one of our chickens. And I saw this figure in our yard in the moonlight. He was wearing a navy duffel coat with the hood up, so I couldn't see his face. The funny thing was my dad was down there, talking to him in a very low voice, almost whispering really. And then my dad handed the man a parcel. Quite a big parcel, tied up with string. And then the man left. He crossed our yard and when he reached the gate, he gave my dad a wave, and then he was gone. And the next day I found that the cloak had disappeared, and I thought it must have been the man in the duffel coat who took it. And if my dad *gave* it to him, he must have trusted him.'

'Or he was under some kind of spell,' muttered Charlie.

'It might not have been the king's cloak, Gabe,' said Lysander, standing up and rubbing his cold bottom. 'I mean, we know your dad writes thrillers. It could have

been a manuscript or a load of books.'

Gabriel shook his head. 'It was the cloak.'

'What makes you so sure?' asked Lysander.

'Because the horse was there,' said Gabriel, 'the white mare: Queen Berenice. She was standing just beyond the hedge, waiting for the man, whoever he was.'

The others stared at him for a moment, and then Lysander said, 'Come on, we'd better get going.'

They left the castle courtyard and began to run across the grass towards the school door. Just before they stepped into the hall, Charlie said, 'Did you ask your dad about the stranger, Gabe?'

'He told me I'd been dreaming,' Gabriel said.

Fire in the tunnel

Charlie had often wondered about the Branko twins. He knew where all the other endowed children lived; he even knew about their parents, although he hadn't actually met them all. But the Brankos were a mystery. This was because they ran a shop called 'Fine and Fancy'; the sort of shop that Charlie generally avoided.

Mr and Mrs Branko prided themselves that almost anything at all could be purchased in their shop, as long as it wasn't a live animal, and you didn't mind your food in a tin. The Brankos didn't like animals.

Mrs Branko looked like a large, tired version of her daughters. Before she was married she had been Natalia Dobinsky, a

77

woman renowned for her telekinetic powers and a few other, more peculiar talents. Not only could she move things with her mind, she could also produce anything – from tins of Peking duck to breadfruit, boiled cauliflower and curried spiders.

Mrs Branko liked to wander the shop, encouraging her customers to spend more than they could afford, while her husband remained behind the vast oak counter.

Bogdan Branko often wondered how he had come to marry Natalia Dobinsky. He had forgotten how they had met. He was a small, mild man with a slanting-back sort of face, his receding chin blending into a flat nose, and a wrinkled caved-in forehead that disappeared beneath thin strands of sandy hair. Bogdan had been very surprised when the exotic Natalia had chosen him above all her other suitors. Lately he had begun to wonder if it was because of his appalling memory. If you can't remember how you came to be married, you're inclined to blame yourself rather than your wife. You're also likely to forget all the appalling things she has done.

Beneath Bogdan's counter were boxes containing

everything from size 20 ballroom dresses to fur-lined wellingtons. If a customer asked Mr Branko for anything out of the ordinary, such as a pair of rainbow-striped stilts, Bogdan would delve beneath the counter while Mrs Branko stared at it, from wherever she happened to be in the shop, and the stilts would obligingly materialise within an inch of Mr Branko's desperately delving hands.

Every Saturday morning the Brankos would receive a visit from their benefactor. In other words, the person who had loaned the Brankos enough money to buy their shop, and who would, every now and again, give them a little more money to refurbish the place with fancy lights, brocade seats and extra shelves.

This Saturday, Natalia was even more restless than usual. The benefactor would be coming to inspect the small café that he had suggested the Brankos should open at the back of the shop. 'Just a few chairs and tables,' he said, 'a good coffee machine and some nice herbal teas; I'll leave the choice of food entirely to you, Natalia.' He gave her a knowing wink.

The benefactor also suggested that Mr and Mrs Branko should change the name of their shop. From

'Fine and Fancy' to 'Not the Pets' Café'.

Natalia and the benefactor seemed to find this suggestion absolutely hilarious, although Mr Branko could see nothing at all to laugh about. However, before he forgot the new name, he managed to telephone a signwriter and today the new sign would be going up.

It was now 8.30 a.m. The shop was due to open at 9.00 a.m. Mrs Branko had instructed the twins, Idith and Inez, to tidy the shelves, and they were now sitting on the counter rearranging the tins telekinetically. The twins didn't always get on with each other, and today they were both becoming increasingly angry, as tins that Idith had just arranged on the bottom shelf were sent flying up to the top shelf by her twin.

Mr Branko sat in a corner reading his newspaper while, outside, two men on ladders hammered the new sign into place.

At that very moment Charlie's friend Benjamin Brown was walking down Spectral Street with his dog, Runner Bean. They were heading, in a roundabout way, for the park.

Benjamin lived opposite Charlie in Filbert Street.

They had been friends since they were four years old, but Benjamin wasn't endowed, either magically or in any other way, so he didn't go to Bloor's Academy, for which he was truly thankful.

Benjamin was almost at the end of Spectral Street when he saw two men on ladders fixing a sign above a shop door. He stopped to watch the men, and remembered that the shop had once been called 'Fine and Fancy'. Benjamin read the new sign and his mouth dropped open. He rubbed his eyes, not quite able to believe what he was seeing.

'"Not the Pets' Café"?' he said in a loud and shocked voice. Then he repeated himself in an even louder and even more shocked voice, '"NOT THE PETS' CAFÉ"?'

Runner Bean gave three hearty barks in sympathy.

'What's your problem?' said the man on the left-hand ladder.

'Not . . . not . . . not . . .' Benjamin stuttered as he pointed to the sign.

'Shove off!' said the other man, hammering the last nail into the sign. 'You'll give the place a bad name.'

'It is a bad name,' cried Benjamin, and Runner Bean barked in agreement.

'That dog can read,' said the first man with a nasty laugh. 'Not the Pets' Café! Ha! Ha!'

Both men came down their ladders, folded them up and began to fix them on to their van.

Benjamin stared and stared at the sign, and then he became aware that two girls were glaring at him through the shop window. They had very pale faces and very black hair. One of them stuck her tongue out at Benjamin. This brought on a storm of howling from Runner Bean. A woman appeared in the shop doorway. She looked exactly like the girls, except that she was bigger and a lot older.

'We don't open until nine o'clock,' the woman said coldly. 'If you want to come in you'll have to wait. And get rid of the dog.'

'I don't want to come in!' Benjamin backed away. He pointed at the sign. 'Why does it say "Not the Pets' Café"?'

'That's my business,' the woman replied.

Benjamin suddenly felt compelled to look at the two girls. There was something very odd about them. He could almost feel the intense concentration in their dark eyes. Runner Bean's hair was standing up like a brush. Benjamin shook his head and shivered. The girls

were staring at one of the ladders and the ladder was sliding off the van. It hovered for a moment and then began to move towards Benjamin.

'STOP!' roared the black-haired woman, glaring at the girls in the window. 'Wrong time.'

The ladder gave a shudder and slid back into place.

The two workmen looked at each other in disbelief. 'What was that?' one muttered.

'Wind,' snapped Mrs Branko and strode back into her shop.

Benjamin had seen enough. He tore down the street, with Runner Bean bounding and barking beside him. They didn't stop running until they had reached number nine Filbert Street.

Benjamin leapt up the steps and rang the bell, calling, 'Charlie! Charlie!'

The door was opened by Maisie. 'Good heavens, Benjamin Brown, what's the trouble?' she asked.

'There's another café, Mrs Jones,' Benjamin said breathlessly. 'Only it's Not the Pets' Café.'

Maisie frowned. 'There are lots of other cafés, Benjamin, dear,' she said gently.

'But not Not the Pets' Café cafés.'

Maisie didn't know what to make of this. Benjamin was a nice boy but he sometimes got the wrong end of the stick. 'I think you need to see Charlie,' she said. 'He's gone round to see Mr Onimous.'

'The Pets' Café!' cried Benjamin. 'That's where I should be.' He jumped down to the pavement and tore up the street with his long-legged dog racing in front of him.

Maisie watched them for a moment, shook her head and closed the door.

'Who was that?' a voice called from the sitting room. 'Was it the post? I'm expecting something.'

'It wasn't the post, Grizelda,' said Maisie.

'Who then?' Grandma Bone came into the hall. 'I hate mysteries.'

'It's not a mystery,' Maisie told her. 'It was just Benjamin Brown. He was rambling on about a café that wasn't for pets.'

To Maisie's surprise Grandma Bone began to laugh. 'Ha, ha, ha!' she cackled. 'That'll teach them.'

It always worried Maisie when Grandma Bone's laughter turned spiteful. Perhaps Benjamin wasn't so deluded after all.

Benjamin and Runner Bean were now racing, side by side, along the High Street. It was still early and there were only a few shoppers about. They turned the corner into Frog Street and came upon a dreadful scene. The Silks' old van was parked halfway down the narrow alley, and Charlie, Gabriel and Mr Silk were piling boxes and furniture into it. The small yard in front of the café was crammed with chairs, cupboards, tables, boxes and a large iron bedstead. Two woebegone figures sat on the bed: Mr and Mrs Onimous. Mrs Onimous was weeping copiously, while her husband held one of her hands and stared stonily ahead.

'What's happened?' cried Benjamin.

'Bailiffs,' shouted Charlie as he and Gabriel lifted a roll of carpet into the van.

'Bailiffs? But I thought . . .' Benjamin looked at the Onimouses.

'Yes, Ben,' Mr Onimous said bitterly. 'The bailiffs turn you out if you haven't paid your rent. But we own the Pets' Café and we've paid our rates. We've done nothing to deserve this. Nothing.'

'So why?' Benjamin approached Charlie and Gabriel.

'The council,' said Charlie. 'They said the café wasn't safe for the public. And the Onimouses can't live here any more because the wall at the back is crumbling.'

'It isn't crumbling,' muttered Mr Silk, throwing an angry glance at the bailiff, a sickly-looking creature with thin, sepia-coloured hair. He was throwing bags from the doorway on to the muddy cobblestones. One of the bags burst open and a pile of socks and stockings rolled out.

Mr Onimous jumped up from the bed and ran across to the bailiff, shouting, 'Have a care, you cur! Those are our belongings.'

The bailiff sniggered and backed into the darkness of the empty café.

'He doesn't look like a bailiff, does he?' Benjamin remarked.

Charlie had to agree. He had never seen a bailiff before, but he was sure that men who spent their lives moving other people's furniture should be a bit more robust than the skinny individual who was flinging bags into the alley. His assistant, however, was built like a heavyweight boxer. He wore only a string vest and

camouflage trousers and his shoulders were as wide as the table he was now manoeuvring through the door.

'I've got something awful to tell you,' Benjamin said to Charlie.

'*This* is awful,' said Charlie.

Mr Silk closed the doors at the back of the van and said, 'I'm sorry, Orvil, we can't get any more in. I'll run this lot up to the Heights and come back for the rest.'

'Oh, let me come.' Mrs Onimous slid from the bed and ran over to the van. 'Please, Cyrus. I want to make sure there's a place for everything in your barn. Are you sure we won't be an inconvenience?'

'Not at all, Onoria. Hop in!' Mr Silk opened the passenger door. 'And you too, Orvil. There's room for three at the front. The boys'll watch your stuff, won't you, boys?'

'Course!' said the boys.

'It's very good of you, Cyrus,' cried Mr Onimous, skipping over to the van. 'I don't know how we'll ever –'

'Only too glad, Orvil.' Mr Silk got into the driving seat and slammed the door while Mr Onimous climbed in beside his wife.

All at once, the little man jumped out again and ran over to Charlie. 'Keep this for me,' he said, pressing a small gold key into Charlie's palm. 'You know what it's for.' He winked at Charlie and ran back to the car. Mr Silk hooted once and the van rattled down the alley and into the High Street.

'What was that all about?' said Gabriel as Charlie tucked the key into his pocket.

'It's for the door into the castle tunnel,' Charlie said quietly.

Gabriel and Benjamin looked at him as though they expected him to say more.

'It might come in handy,' Charlie said with a shrug.

'Are the Onimouses coming to live with you?' Benjamin asked Gabriel.

Gabriel nodded. 'It's going to be a bit of a squash, and my sisters aren't too happy about it, because they've all got to sleep together. But where else can the poor Onimouses go? We've got a nice dry barn for their stuff, and some of it can go in my gerbil house, at a pinch. But we couldn't take the café chairs and tables. They've already been taken away.'

'I wish I could have the Onimouses living with me,'

Benjamin said wistfully. 'Mrs Onimous makes lovely pet food.'

Just then the bailiff and his assistant walked out of the café, slamming the door behind them. The bailiff produced a bunch of keys and, carefully selecting one, locked the door. He rubbed his hands together and declared, 'All done!'

As the two men passed the boys, the one in the string vest said, 'Looks like rain, boys. Hope this stuff doesn't get wet!' He jerked a thumb at the bed. 'Could be ruined.'

The boys glared at him and then, as the men walked down the alley, Charlie muttered, 'Thinks he's so macho in his vest, but I can see goose pimples.'

The vest-man came to a halt and looked back with a snarl on his face. Runner Bean gave one of his famous throaty growls and the man hurried after his companion.

'This is an awful, awful day,' moaned Benjamin as soon as the men were out of sight.

'You can say that again,' agreed Charlie.

'I mean worse than awful,' cried Benjamin, and he told them about the Not the Pets' Café, the peculiar

twins and the floating ladder.

'The Brankos!' Charlie exclaimed. 'So that's where they live!'

'Brankos?' Benjamin looked puzzled.

'They're telekinetic,' Charlie explained. 'I'm sure I've told you about them. They're forever moving stuff when we're trying to do homework: books, pencils and things. They knocked a wall down once, and nearly buried me. They're Manfred's slaves.'

Benjamin was even more glad that he didn't have to go to Charlie's school.

'I bet Manfred put those Brankos up to it,' Gabriel grunted. 'I mean, it's like a slap in the face, isn't it, calling it Not the Pets' Café when he knows the Pets' Café was our favourite place?'

'Look!' Charlie suddenly pointed to the sloping roof of the café. Three bright cats had appeared at the very top; Leo, the orange cat, stood on the apex, the other two perched either side of him.

'They've lost their home,' Gabriel said sadly.

'No, they're wanderers,' Charlie told him. 'Their home is everywhere and nowhere. I think they're guarding the place.'

'There's nothing left to guard,' said Gabriel.

'There's the secret tunnel that leads under the wall to the castle,' Charlie reminded him. 'And I bet those bailiffs are going to come back later and look for it. The Bloors have always wanted to find it, and now's their chance. My dad hid something very, very precious, that old Ezekiel wants, and now I'm wondering if Dad hid it at the end of that tunnel.'

Gabriel and Benjamin were now regarding Charlie with very puzzled frowns and Charlie realised he would have to tell them a bit more. 'There's a box,' he went on. 'My uncle told me about it. He thinks there's a will in it, a will that proves Billy Raven should have inherited Bloor's Academy and all the money the Bloors have stashed away.'

'Wow!' Benjamin collapsed on to the iron bedstead, causing a great rattling of springs.

Gabriel, however, continued to stare at Charlie with a frown that grew deeper every second.

'What?' said Charlie. 'Don't you believe me?'

'Why did your father hide it in the first place,' Gabriel asked in a slow, deliberate voice, 'if he knew there was something so important in it?'

'He *didn't* know,' Charlie said patiently. 'The box couldn't be opened. The key was lost. Before Billy's father died he asked my dad to look after the box. He didn't tell him what was in it because *he* didn't know. And then my dad was hypnotised, as you very well know, and . . .' Charlie grimaced; it was hard for him to admit that his father had not completely recovered from his long ordeal, and that his memory had not been entirely restored. It meant that Lyell Bone would never again be the brave young man who had once defied the Bloors. Charlie found that difficult to accept.

'And what?' Benjamin gently prodded.

'And he hasn't remembered everything that happened before,' said Charlie. 'But he will,' he added confidently, 'when he comes back from his holiday.'

'Course he will,' said Benjamin.

'But the Bloors don't want him to remember,' Gabriel said thoughtfully. 'Do they, Charlie?'

'No,' Charlie admitted.

It took Mr Silk another two journeys to get all the Onimouses' possessions up to the Heights. Gabriel joined his father on the last trip, and Benjamin and Charlie were left in the deserted alley. They gazed sadly

at the silent café, and then walked into the High
Street, both hoping desperately that it wouldn't be long
before the Pets' Café would once again be full of
joyfully lapping, munching, chewing, pecking creatures
and their equally happy owners.

Benjamin's parents were private detectives and were
often working on a Saturday. But today they were at
home and Mrs Brown had promised Benjamin he
would have lamp chops and mint sauce for lunch. As
soon as they reached Filbert Street, Benjamin ran
eagerly towards number twelve, while Runner Bean,
who sensed that good bones were soon to be had, raced
beside his master.

Charlie had carrot soup and cheese for lunch.
Grandma Bone was spending the day with her three
sisters, and Uncle Paton had left on yet another
mysterious journey.

'Gathering information, that's what your uncle said,'
Maisie told Charlie. 'Are you going over to Benjamin's
after lunch?'

'Yes,' Charlie lied, although, at the time, it wasn't
really a lie because he *might* have gone over to
Benjamin's. It was just that the more he thought about

it, the more inclined he became to return to the Pets' Café.

When he had helped Maisie to wash up, Charlie went to his room and did his homework. At half past three, with a shout of, 'See you later, Maisie,' he left the house and made his way back to the empty café. Pressing his face close to the window, he looked for a light that might be showing in the kitchen. But the place was dark and silent. Nothing moved. Charlie now had a burning desire to get into the café, but he had no key and he had seen the bailiff lock the door. He tried it, just in case. The handle turned but the door wouldn't budge. Charlie told himself that he was being foolish; if anyone intended to search the place, they would probably wait until nightfall. And then he heard footsteps in the alley.

Charlie darted round the side of the café and pressed himself into the corner, where the café wall met the great stone edifice of the old city wall. He heard the clink of keys. The door opened and was closed. Charlie waited breathlessly, and then tiptoed round to the front of the building. He looked through the window, but could see nothing. As quietly as he could, he turned

the door handle and pushed. The door opened. Charlie was in.

Footsteps creaked above him. Whoever had entered the café, they were beginning their search upstairs. There was a chance that Charlie could reach the place he wanted before anyone saw him. He crept through the kitchen and into a long passage. The further he went the more dark and narrow it became. Soon the stone floor gave way to an earthen path. Now the brick ceiling was so low that Charlie could touch it with his fingers. Eventually he reached a small circular cavern where Mr Onimous stored food for the café. Crates of apples, along with sacks and tea chests were still piled against the walls. Perhaps this place would never be found, thought Charlie. And yet he didn't hold out much hope of that. Whoever the Bloors had chosen to search the Pets' Café, they wouldn't give up until they had explored every room and every passage. They would move the sacks and crates and eventually they would find the door that Charlie was about to open.

Grunting with the effort, Charlie began to push two heavy tea chests away from the wall until he revealed an ancient door, little more than a metre high.

Squeezing himself behind the tea chests, Charlie fitted Mr Onimous's key into the lock. It turned with a light click and the door creaked open. Behind it lay a darkness so intense Charlie hesitated. He had been in the tunnel twice before, but never alone. It was time for the gift from his Welsh ancestor.

Charlie had inherited two strains of magic. His picture-travelling came from the Red King; his wand from Mathonwy, a Welsh magician. The wand was now a white moth; a moth with such bright wings, she could illuminate the deepest darkness.

'Claerwen!' Charlie said softly.

Answering to her name, the white moth crawled from beneath Charlie's collar, where she had been sleeping. In English the name meant 'brilliant white'. She was nine hundred years old.

The white moth fluttered into the tunnel and Charlie followed, bending his head as he stepped through the low doorway. Before he went any further, he closed the door, hoping that it would not be seen behind the two tea chests. If he had locked the door, things might have turned out differently. But he forgot.

The tunnel was damp and airless. Several times,

Charlie slipped on the wet ground. Claerwen's light gave the damp walls a misty shine. The tunnel began to curve and twist and Charlie had to put one hand on the wall to keep his balance. Halfway down the tunnel a long fissure appeared in the wall. Charlie squeezed through it and into another tunnel, this one so narrow he had to shuffle sideways. The little moth swinging above gave him courage, and after five long shuffling minutes, Charlie emerged into an astonishing room.

Outside, the sky was a dull grey, but here everything was bathed in sunlight. The ground was paved with tiny squares of colour: yellow, red and orange; a mosaic of a burning sun. The walls showed golden domes, silver clouds and leafy arbours, where tall robed figures strolled together, or rested on long marble seats. And in the vaulted roof a painted sun appeared again, but in the very centre a perfect circle opened to the sky.

Charlie walked round the perimeter of the circular floor, touching the pillars set at intervals between the painted walls. What had he expected to find? A wooden box placed neatly behind a pillar, or tucked into a small cavity in the wall? For this room was very special. It had once been the Red King's chamber, hidden from the

world. Even now only a very few people knew of it, and Charlie was certain that the Bloors were not among them. It was a perfect hiding place.

Charlie felt the smooth painted walls; he knelt and scrutinised the paved floor, running his hands over the coloured squares. He squinted up at the vaulted ceiling and prodded the bricks at the base of each pillar. But there was no sign of a box. Perhaps his father had hidden it in the castle? It was too late to search the vast ruin. Charlie decided to give up for now, but as he gazed round the bright room he felt a great surge of hope. He was convinced that he would find the box. Perhaps not today, but sometime very soon. And Billy would have his inheritance – if he could be rescued from Badlock.

Charlie edged back along the narrow gap and stepped into the tunnel. He would have to return the way he came. If he went on, into the ruined castle, he would be trapped in the school grounds.

With Claerwen's light to guide him, Charlie began to walk back to the small door, hoping that no one else had found it. Turning a bend in the tunnel, he suddenly found himself caught in the light of a leaping flame.

'Aha!' said a mocking voice. 'What have we here? A boy with a box, no doubt.'

Charlie stood frozen to the spot. 'I haven't got a box,' he said, his voice husky with fear.

'Oh no? I think you have!' The leaping flame drew nearer, and Charlie could see the bailiff's sneering features in the flaring light of a long tarred stick.

'What . . . what's that you're holding?' Charlie asked in a faint voice.

'Fire! That's what it is,' cackled the bailiff. 'Amos Byrne has come to warm you up, Charlie Bone.'

Charlie escapes

Charlie realised that there was no chance of his returning the way he had come. Leaping away from the flames, he ran towards the castle entrance. Too bad if he was caught in the Academy grounds; at least he wouldn't be burnt to a cinder. He had no doubt that Amos Byrne was in deadly earnest.

Charlie wished he had told someone where he was going. He could feel the heat of the flames on his back. The bailiff was gaining ground. He held the torch at arm's length and Charlie inhaled an acrid bitterness. His head felt as though it was on fire and, bringing his hand to the back of his neck, he found that his hair had been scorched by flying embers.

Yelping with fear, Charlie rushed towards the distant light at the end of the tunnel. But a sudden ray of hope was immediately dashed when he realised that a ruined castle would be no protection from a villain with a fiery torch.

Where can I go? Charlie's eyes were open but his mind was closed to his surroundings, for he was desperately seeking a way of escape. He was never sure when the knight appeared. Perhaps he had been there at the end of the tunnel all the time, sitting astride the white mare, his armour glimmering faintly in the dusk.

Charlie almost stopped dead in his tracks. But he didn't. He found, to his surprise, that he was still running. Faster and faster. As he drew closer to the horse and its rider, the Red Knight suddenly lifted his sword and, again, Charlie was choked with fear and almost stopped. But a voice reached into his head, quiet and commanding.

'Run, boy. Run!'

And Charlie ran. Losing his terror of the sword, he put on a burst of speed he didn't dream that he had. But the bailiff was not deterred by the sight of a gleaming sword. He had great confidence in the fire he carried. It

was what he lived by and it had never let him down. He kept up his pace and rushed at the horse, hoping to terrify the creature into throwing its rider.

Charlie bounded past the mare and tore into the trees that grew inside the ruin. Flinging himself behind a broken wall, he lay, gasping for breath, while a stream of oaths filled the air.

The white mare gave a high-pitched snort of fear, then came a scream that curdled Charlie's blood. There was a moment of utter silence, before hoof-beats could be heard receding slowly into the distance.

It was several minutes before Charlie felt brave enough to raise his head above the wall. Darkness was falling fast, but he could just make out a dark figure lying close to the tree whose branches hung above the tunnel entrance.

Amos Byrne lay motionless, one outstretched hand reaching for the long torch that lay just beyond him, its flame extinguished. Charlie was caught between a sigh of relief and a shudder of horror. Now he must find a way out of the ruin, and then out of the Academy grounds. All at once, he felt very weary. The next few minutes were going to be very tricky.

Charlie had often explored the ancient castle. He knew that if he continued along the hedged walkway behind him, he would eventually come to the glade where he had once seen the Red King, or rather, the enchanted tree that the Red King had become. But then where could he go? He had never approached the glade from the Academy grounds. It was a secret place, impossible to find except by going through the tunnel.

'Claerwen!' Charlie called.

The white moth crawled out of his sleeve and sat on his hand. Charlie was glad to see her. For a moment he had wondered if she had flown into the flames, as moths are inclined to do. 'But you're too clever for that, aren't you, Claerwen?' Charlie said cheerfully. 'The thing is, how are we going to get out of here?'

Claerwen had no answer for him. She fluttered on to a branch and closed her wings until they became a tiny triangle of light.

Something brushed against Charlie's legs. First one side, then the other. He looked down and saw that he was surrounded by cats. Three of them. With both hands Charlie stroked their heads; first Leo's, then the other two. They all began to purr.

Charlie's laugh was both happy and nervous. 'You're going to get me out of here, aren't you?' he said.

The cats gazed at him with their bright golden eyes, and then they were off. They moved fast, jumping over broken walls and slipping easily through the undergrowth, and if ever Charlie fell too far behind one of them would wait until he caught up with them again.

They came, at last, to the wide expanse of grass that lay between the school and the woods that surrounded the castle. The cats became more cautious here. They sniffed the air and moved carefully through the bare trees, turning now and again to look back at Charlie. He was heavier than the cats – twigs snapped beneath his feet and the undergrowth rustled as he brushed it aside.

The Bloors are too far away to hear me, he thought. But suddenly several lights came on in the school, and a distant voice called, 'Is anyone there? Show yourself, you miserable, creeping thing.'

Charlie recognised Weedon's voice. *He can't possibly have seen me*, thought Charlie. The surly porter was surely not clairvoyant. But someone else could be. Mrs Tilpin? Who knew what witches could do. And then he

began to wonder if the bailiff had recovered and returned to tell the Bloors that Charlie had run into the school grounds. Standing still wasn't going to get him anywhere, Charlie reasoned. The cats were growling now, anxious to get him on the move again. He began to follow them, keeping an eye on the school building. It was as well that he did. For he saw the door open and two figures step out; they stood beneath the lamp that hung over the door, and stared across the grounds. Charlie could see them clearly. One was Lord Grimwald, the other the swordsman from the past, Ashkelan Kapaldi. They began to stride across the grass. Lord Grimwald held a tall lantern that swayed violently as he lurched over the ground. Ashkelan's sword danced in the air beside its master.

The cats' growling turned to a soft hissing, and they flew away through the woods. This time Charlie kept up with them. As he ran he couldn't help thinking about the wall they were approaching; it was ten feet high and stood between the grounds of Bloor's Academy and the outside world. How would he ever scale it? He wasn't a cat.

The ancient wall was covered in ivy and it was

difficult to make out in the gloom. Charlie first became aware of it when he saw Leo's bright form climbing quickly to the top. Aries followed, but Sagittarius waited. At dusk he was the brightest of the three, his coat gleaming like a star. He seemed to be waiting for Charlie to climb.

Charlie squinted up at the mass of dark ivy; he saw a thick stem protruding from the wall a foot above him and reached for it. With both hands he pulled himself up, bringing his feet behind him. The leaves were slippery and it took him some time to get a foothold. Leo and Aries looked down and, following their gaze, Charlie saw another stem. It appeared to be out of his reach until Sagittarius, climbing swiftly beside him, clawed at the leaves, revealing a strong loop lower down. Charlie pulled himself up another foot. It was freezing cold, but he could feel the sweat running down his forehead.

Voices rang out from the direction of the ruin. Lord Grimwald and Ashkelan must have found the bailiff. They hadn't yet realised that Charlie was on the wall. He gave a sigh of relief and, letting go of the ivy for a moment, wiped his forehead – and lost his grip. He tumbled to the ground with a groan.

'Sorry!' Charlie whispered to the cats. They regarded him with impatience, disappointment showing in the downturned tails and whiskers.

At least Charlie remembered where his footholds were, and he swiftly climbed to the place from where he had fallen. With the cats' help he pulled himself up the next few feet. He was very near the top when he heard the voices again. His two pursuers were crashing through the trees close to the wall.

With a superhuman effort Charlie heaved himself up, crouched a moment on the bumpy stones at the top of the wall and, following the cats' example, let himself drop to the ground. He lay on the rough grass beside the wall winded, shaken and bruised, while the Flames howled and mewed in his ear.

'Give me a moment,' groaned Charlie. 'I'm safe now.'

But he didn't have a moment. Glancing sideways, he saw a shining blade standing upright in the road. Ashkelan's sword had flown over the wall.

'No!' yelled Charlie. In a second he was on his feet again and running.

The sword pranced behind him, now slicing the air, now clanging on the hard tarmac. The Flames darted

round it, hissing and spitting, furious with the rod of steel that seemed to have a life of its own.

Ashkelan must have lost control of the dreadful weapon at last. Perhaps it could only move in close proximity to its owner. But when Charlie got to the High Street, the sword was no longer behind him. Charlie slowed his pace. He had a stitch in his side and his legs felt like jelly, but at least he was alive. The Flames accompanied him to number nine and then they left him, melting into the dusk without a sound.

Charlie wearily climbed the steps up to his front door. When he walked inside, the first thing he noticed was the dark interior of the kitchen. Maisie was always in the kitchen at this time of day. Where was she? Charlie heard voices coming from the other side of the hall. Could she be in the sitting room? He popped his head round the door.

Grandma Bone and her three sisters were sitting round the fire, eating crumpets. There was a plate of toasted teacakes on the coffee table.

'Oh!' said Charlie, quickly withdrawing his head.

'Come in, Charlie!' called Grandma Bone.

'No, it's all right.' Charlie tiptoed across to the dark kitchen.

'It's NOT all right!' shouted Great Aunt Lucretia. 'Come here, this minute!'

Charlie ground his teeth. 'Now what?' he muttered. He went back to the sitting room and looked in. 'I just wondered where Maisie was,' he said.

'Gone shopping!' Grandma Bone told him.

'But it's late.' Charlie looked at his watch. It was only half past five. He felt that a whole day and a night had passed since he left the house.

Grandma Bone sniggered. 'She's probably dropped in to see the kettle woman.'

'Oh!' Charlie wondered what he could have for tea. He eyed the pile of teacakes.

'Maisie's left something for you in the fridge,' said Grandma Bone.

Charlie's heart sank. He would have liked something hot to eat.

'Where've you been?' asked Great Aunt Eustacia. 'You smell of smoke.'

Eustacia's power was obviously not at its best today, thought Charlie. And then it occurred to him

that she was taunting him. She knew very well where he had been. But did she know about the bailiff with the fiery torch?

'I think I'll go and have some tea,' said Charlie, beginning to back out.

'Eustacia asked you where you had been,' said Grandma Bone.

Charlie hesitated. If they already knew where he'd been, what would be the point of lying about it? 'If you must know,' he said, 'I've been to the Pets' Café. But, as you also know, it's been closed for good. But someone was in there, searching for a box. So I went in too. But I didn't find anything; neither did he.'

All four women stared at him, their thin mouths grim, their black eyes hooded. They seemed to be temporarily struck dumb. And, with a sudden shock, Charlie knew that he'd said too much. He wasn't supposed to know about the box.

Now the hunt would really be on. The Bloors would have to find the box before Charlie's father came home. The search had become a deadly game, and Billy Raven's future hung in the balance; so did Lyell Bone's life.

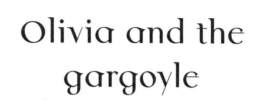

Olivia and the gargoyle

The silence lasted only a few seconds, but in that time so many thoughts swept through Charlie's head he began to feel dizzy. In his mind's eye he saw Billy wandering endlessly through the enchanter's forest; and he saw a wooden box, inlaid with mother-of-pearl; a box that held a secret which could change the lives of everyone he knew.

Grandma Bone's voice reached Charlie as from a great distance. 'What's wrong with you, boy? Pull yourself together.'

'I am, I am,' murmured Charlie, just managing to focus on the pale face that loomed above him.

'What's in your mind?' asked Grandma Bone.

'Nothing,' said Charlie.

'Well, Eustacia?' Grandma Bone turned to her sister.

'He was thinking of Billy,' said Eustacia, 'and the box.'

Charlie was rattled. Eustacia was on top form today. 'I've never seen the box,' he cried. 'Well, not the box you mean,' he ended lamely.

'Charlie, where's your father?' asked Eustacia, coming to stand beside her sister.

'I don't know, do I? I don't know any more than you do. He's whale-watching.'

'But when you think about him, what do you see?' Eustacia leaned very close to Charlie, and he flinched at her stale breath.

'Nothing,' he said.

'We know you have a gift, Charlie.' His grandmother snorted angrily. 'We know you can see your father in your mind's eye when you think hard enough. Stop dissembling.'

'I don't know what you mean,' said Charlie. They must never know about the boat, he thought. And he filled his mind with pictures of his friends: Benjamin and Runner Bean, Fidelio, Olivia and Lysander . . .

'Well?' Grandma Bone looked at Eustacia.

'Rubbish,' said Eustacia. 'His mind is filled with rubbish.'

Grandma Bone grabbed Charlie's arm and drew him into the kitchen, where she sat him down and made him drink a cup of cold milk. A plate of cheese and crackers was put before him and Grandma Bone said, 'Get it down you. We're all going out.'

'But –' Charlie began.

'No buts,' she snapped.

Grandma Bone's three sisters crowded into the kitchen. They paced around the table, looking at Charlie. Great Aunt Eustacia never took her eyes off him. Perhaps she was still trying to read his mind. He must keep the name of the boat from her; the name on the side of a boat that rode the dangerous sea. For if the name reached Lord Grimwald, there was no knowing what he might do.

'Maisie's not back,' Charlie said, through a mouthful of dry crackers. 'If I go out again, she'll wonder where I am.'

'We'll leave a note,' said his grandmother.

'Uncle Paton's not here,' cried Charlie desperately. 'My parents said that he was in charge.'

'They were wrong,' said Great Aunt Lucretia coldly.
'We're your guardians now.'

'That's not true!' retorted Charlie.

'You're coming to Darkly Wynd with us, and there's
an end to it.' Great Aunt Venetia whisked away the
plate of half-eaten crackers. 'And we have to go now.
My little boy needs me.'

Venetia's stepson, spiteful little Eric, had never
needed anyone as far as Charlie knew. He spent his
time animating stone figures, a dangerous talent, often
ending in disaster for his unsuspecting victims.

'I don't understand why I have to go to Darkly
Wynd.' Charlie twisted nervously in his chair as
Grandma Bone snatched his cup and poured the rest of
his milk down the drain.

'We want to ask you some questions,' said Great
Aunt Eustacia.

'Can't you ask your questions here?' Charlie knew
the answer as soon as he saw the cold, closed-in look on
Grandma Bone's hard face. They couldn't risk being
interrupted by Maisie or Uncle Paton. And that meant
they were going to give him a real grilling.

Charlie knew it would be useless to resist. He could

kick and scream but they would get him to Darkly
Wynd in the end, and he would have wasted precious
energy. He needed all his strength to fight Great Aunt
Eustacia's clairvoyance. And now he thought about it,
he almost looked forward to the challenge.

The four sisters frog-marched Charlie out of the
house and down the steps. He was bundled into the
back of Great Aunt Eustacia's car, where he sat
squeezed uncomfortably between the bony thighs of
Lucretia and Venetia.

Eustacia drove very badly. She was forever bumping
on to the kerb and lurching recklessly round corners.
After driving much too fast down a narrow alley, she
braked, with a screech, in a long cobbled yard. They
had reached Darkly Wynd.

Three tall houses stood in a row at the far end of the
yard. They had steep turrets and wrought-iron
balconies, and their narrow arched windows were
framed by carved stone creatures: gnomes, gargoyles
and unlikely beasts. All three houses were numbered
thirteen.

The smaller houses on either side of the courtyard
appeared to be deserted; their windows were boarded

up, their steps covered in moss. Some grim force had driven the occupants away; a force that was evidently not strong enough to dislodge the Yewbeam sisters, unless it was they themselves who had caused the exodus.

Venetia's house, on the right, looked in better condition than the other two. Since the fire in her house a year ago, the slates on the steep, sloping roof had been renewed, and her front door had been freshly painted.

At the top of the steps stood a squat stone troll. Charlie kept an eye on it as he passed. Eric liked to animate the thing, and Charlie didn't want to be knocked flat before his interrogation began.

Venetia unlocked the door and led the way into a dark hall. It had a pungent, bitter smell. A huge gold-framed mirror, hanging on one side, reflected the long coat-rack on the other. The rack was filled with garments of every size and description, and Charlie didn't need reminding that Venetia could bewitch her victims with clothing. The collars and cuffs, buttons and belts of these exotic-looking outfits were, in all probability, impregnated with poison. Charlie gave a

shudder and kept as far away from them as possible.

They walked in single file down a long corridor beside the staircase. Venetia led the way, followed by Charlie, who was prodded in the back by Grandma Bone's sharp nails every time he hesitated.

Charlie had never been inside any of the three number thirteens. He had looked through their windows and, secretly, crept into their back gardens, but none of his great-aunts had ever asked him into their home. And Charlie had certainly never wanted an invitation.

'Here we are!' Venetia opened a door on the left of the corridor and Grandma Bone pushed Charlie into a large, gloomy room. An oval table stood in the centre, and huge glass-fronted cabinets filled the entire wall opposite the door. Charlie gave an involuntary gasp when he saw the figure standing in the bay window.

Manfred Bloor wore an expression of malicious amusement. 'Didn't expect this, did you, Charlie?' he said.

So that's why they brought me here, thought Charlie. They needed Manfred's help. And he wondered how often Manfred visited the Yewbeams.

Grandma Bone was prodding him again. His back probably resembled a Dalmatian's by now, with all those black bruises. In spite of his precarious situation, Charlie couldn't help grinning.

'What are you smiling at?' Manfred asked coldly.

'It's not a smile, actually,' said Charlie. 'It's a wince.'

Having prodded her grandson into a chair at the table, Grandma Bone and her sisters began arguing over the seating arrangements. Eustacia was going to be working, therefore her needs were a priority. So Charlie found himself sitting opposite Manfred and beside Eustacia, who was at the head of the table with her back to the window. Grandma Bone sat on Charlie's other side, with Venetia directly opposite. Lucretia didn't sit, because she hadn't got the chair she wanted. She stood by the glass cabinet, regarding the shelves of labelled bottles and talking to herself.

'Where's Eric?' said Charlie, hoping to delay the proceedings.

A forlorn hope.

'He's outside,' snapped Venetia.

Charlie craned sideways, tipping his chair, and looked down into the lamplit garden. What he saw

there gave him another shock.

Lumbering between bushes of bright winter berries were stone figures, pale as ghosts: hideous beings carrying stone clubs, knights in armour, horses, goblins, trolls and massive dogs, all moving in slow deliberate steps. And there was Eric, sitting on a stone head; a small, skinny boy with a sickly colour. His head twisted this way and that, and his right hand swung back and forth across his body, as though he were orchestrating the movements of an army.

'Sit up!' Eustacia ordered, and Charlie lurched back, almost tipping his chair too far in the other direction.

'Impressive, eh?' said Manfred with a smile. 'Our little Eric's coming on a treat.'

Charlie didn't bother to reply. Manfred's black eyes held a chilling gleam, and Charlie knew that all the will his mind possessed must be used in the next few minutes. He lifted his gaze to the top shelf of the cabinet and started counting bottles.

'Look at me,' Manfred demanded.

Charlie kept his eyes on the row of dark bottles; green, red, brown and blue. How many fatal potions did Venetia keep? One, two, three . . .

'Look at me.' Manfred's voice had taken on a fatal silkiness. Try as he might, Charlie couldn't resist it. He found his gaze drifting down to Manfred again, and he remembered the first time that Manfred had tried to hypnotise him. Charlie had fought him then. He had looked into the treacherous black eyes and then into the mind behind them.

Charlie met Manfred's gaze. He looked at him steadily and tried to read his thoughts.

'Stop that!' said Manfred.

'What?' said Charlie.

'You're trying to block me. Well, you won't get away with it this time.' Manfred leant across the table. His face came closer and closer. So close that Charlie could see the deadly glitter at the centre of those dark eyes. He felt as though he were falling into them. All he wanted was to escape, to close his eyes, to sleep. Desperately, he tried to avoid the images that crowded into his head. I mustn't, I mustn't, he thought. But it was no use. He saw the boat *Greywing*. He saw the heaving foamy sea and a night sky crammed with stars.

'What does he see?' Grandma Bone's voice was very faint.

Eustacia's answer was even fainter. 'A boat called *Greywing* . . . sunrise . . . whales calling . . . a night sky, but . . . aha . . . the constellations are upside down.'

The voice droned on and on, and Charlie was powerless. He could neither move nor open his eyes. They were asking him another question now. A question he couldn't answer.

'Who is the Red Knight, Charlie?'

'I don't know.'

'We think you do.'

'No.'

'Who is he?'

'The Red King.'

'Not true. Concentrate, Charlie.'

Charlie's head drooped. He tried to lift it, but it was too heavy. He found himself thinking of the stranger that came to Gabriel's moonlit yard; the stranger in a duffel coat who carried the Red King's cloak away. Did Charlie know anyone who wore a duffel coat? No. No one, except . . . except . . . Manfred's grandfather Bartholomew Bloor. He was utterly different from the other Bloors. He had even helped Charlie to find his father. Before Charlie

could prevent it, an image came into his mind. The last time he had seen Bartholomew Bloor he had been wearing a dark blue duffel coat.

Eustacia's muffled voice said, 'Aha!'

A loud bark broke into Charlie's thoughts. He raised his head. The dog must have been at the front of the house, but its bark came ringing down the hall. Charlie didn't know that Benjamin had lifted the flap on the letter box and Runner Bean was barking right through it.

Charlie's eyes flew open. Manfred had straightened up but Eustacia sat in a confused silence, gazing at the table.

'Snap out of it, 'Stace!' Grandma Bone clicked her fingers close to Eustacia's nose, and Eustacia frowned up at her. 'Well done, we got what we wanted.'

'There's more,' mumbled Eustacia.

'And there's a ruddy dog at the door,' shouted Venetia. 'We'll have to deal with it.' She rushed out, followed by Lucretia and Grandma Bone.

'I think Eric's already dealing with it,' Manfred said easily.

Charlie leapt up and ran blindly towards the front

door. He had to blink several times before he could focus properly, but when the hypnotic haze had lifted he saw that Eric was standing in the open doorway with Venetia at his side.

There was a loud thump, and then another. Someone screamed and a dog howled. When Charlie had pushed his way past Venetia, he saw Benjamin, Runner Bean and Olivia, trying to dodge the stone gargoyles that came flying at them from the wall. Eric was enjoying himself. He gave a little jump for joy every time a gargoyle came loose and crashed on to the pavement.

'That's enough, Eric,' said Venetia. 'You'll ruin the house.'

'Charlie, get out of there!' cried Olivia.

Charlie was already leaping down the steps. 'Run, Liv! I'm right behind you!' he shouted.

A stone gargoyle came flying after him and caught his heel. Runner Bean bounced round him, barking furiously.

'Eric, enough!' Venetia commanded.

'Let's get out of here!' yelled Benjamin. 'Runner! Here, boy! Quick!'

The three children raced away from the number thirteens. If they had all kept on running they would have escaped with a few bruises, but then something happened. And for one of them, nothing would ever be quite the same again.

Olivia suddenly turned round. She picked up the headless body of a broken gargoyle and was about to throw it back at Eric when, horribly, it stretched out a puny arm and grabbed her wrist. Olivia let out a shriek that brought the boys to a skidding halt. They ran to help her, tugging at the squirming stone body, pulling its legs and trying to prise the rigid fingers away from Olivia's wrist. Eric began to laugh.

All four sisters had now crowded on to the top step behind Eric. Venetia was laughing. Eustacia and Lucretia joined her and then, in spite of herself, Grandma Bone gave in to a bout of loud, undignified giggling.

Olivia glared up at Eric and the four women. She wondered what would frighten them. What would wipe the silly grins off their faces and stop their spiteful giggling? She imagined a tall skeleton in a black hat and cloak, wielding a long sabre.

And there he was! Standing in front of the steps, his sabre lifted to strike.

Laughter turned to screams of horror. Eric and the sisters disappeared, slamming the door behind them.

'Oh, Liv! Why did you do that?' asked Charlie.

'I couldn't help it,' Olivia replied as the headless gargoyle relaxed its grip and dropped to the ground. 'Anyway, it did the trick. Eric obviously loses concentration when he's scared.'

'It was pretty impressive, that thing!' Benjamin was disappointed to see the skeleton slowly fading. He gave Runner Bean a reassuring pat, as the dog's legs were still trembling. 'It was only an illusion, Runner.'

They hurried out of Darkly Wynd, Charlie throwing worried looks in Olivia's direction. She had betrayed herself. The Bloors had no idea that she was endowed, but as soon as the Yewbeam sisters had recovered from their shock, they would know. And they would certainly pass on the news.

Olivia ignored Charlie for a while. She deliberately refused to meet his eye, but at last she cried, 'Stop looking at me like that, Charlie. We rescued you!'

'But you betrayed yourself, Liv!' said Charlie. 'My

grandma and her sisters will know you conjured up that skeleton and they'll tell everyone. And then what?'

'Then what?' Olivia mimicked Charlie. 'We'll see, won't we?' She rubbed her wrist where the gargoyle had left ugly marks on her skin.

'Sorry,' said Charlie, feeling guilty. 'And thank you for rescuing me. How did that happen, anyway?'

Benjamin explained that he had gone to number nine and found Maisie in a 'bit of a state', as he put it. She'd found the note from Grandma Bone, but she didn't like to think of Charlie in one of the Darkly Wynd houses. So Benjamin had offered to come and find Charlie. 'With Runner Bean, of course,' Benjamin added. 'I wouldn't have come without him. And then I met Olivia on her way to the bookshop, and she said she'd come too. Safety in numbers kind of thing.'

'Thanks,' said Charlie. 'Sorry I barked at you, Liv.'

'I should think so!' She tossed her bleached hair and grinned.

'Manfred was there,' Charlie said quietly. 'He hypnotised me.'

Olivia and Benjamin stopped. They stared at Charlie until he felt quite uncomfortable.

'The trouble is, I don't know if I told them anything I shouldn't have. I tried not to, but I can't remember.' He stroked Runner Bean's shaggy head. 'Runner Bean woke me up.'

They had reached the top of Filbert Street and Charlie was relieved to see Uncle Paton's camper van parked outside number nine.

Olivia, Benjamin and Runner Bean followed Charlie into the house, where they found Maisie and Uncle Paton enjoying a candlelit meal of salmon pie and chips. There was plenty for all, and while everyone tucked in, Charlie recounted his day, reliving his escape from Amos Byrne with such dramatic gestures he twice sent the pepper pot flying off the table.

'Good grief!' cried Maisie. 'Your hair's all singed, Charlie. I thought I could smell burning. You mustn't run off without telling me where you're going. You could have been . . . oh, I can't bear to think of it.'

Uncle Paton nodded. Although his expression was very grave, and although he made all the right exclamations of horror and concern, Charlie sensed that something else was troubling his uncle. He did not seem to be wholly engaged with the conversation

round the table. His gaze kept drifting away from them.

'Uncle Paton, where have you been?' asked Charlie.

His uncle regarded him thoughtfully. It was as though he'd had to drag his mind back from somewhere far away. 'Where I have been doesn't matter for now,' he said. 'But tell me, did my sisters question you about the Red Knight?'

Charlie's mind had cleared a little. The troubling hypnotic haze was lifting. 'Yes, they did ask about the knight, and although I didn't put it into words, I remember thinking that he might be Bartholomew Bloor.'

'Bartholomew?' Uncle Paton looked incredulous.

'Wow! That's interesting.' Olivia cupped her chin in her hands. She wore a pair of mittens threaded with gold and silver ribbons. 'I hope you didn't tell them about Tancred,' she said.

Charlie shook his head. 'Don't think so. No. They didn't get round to asking about Tancred.'

'Phew! That's good.' Olivia raised her head and clasped her mittened hands together. 'He's still safe, then.'

'Yes. But you're not, Liv,' said Charlie.

The Sea Globe

The huge Sea Globe now stood in the centre of the ballroom. The white cladding had been removed but the globe was enclosed in a large glass box. Behind the glass, blue-green water could be seen, rippling over the surface of a glowing sphere: the World, mapped out in oceans and continents. The land appeared a dull brown colour, while the water glowed with countless shades of blue and green, grey and silver.

The ballroom lights were out, but the chandelier above the globe reflected the sea-green radiance of the waves, and beams of brilliant light spilled out into the room.

All that could be heard was the faint

swish of waves and the low murmur of the World's vast oceans.

Lord Grimwald stood before his treasure, and his stern features softened as his gaze swept over the oceans: north to the Arctic, two feet above him, then down through the Atlantic to Antarctica and up again through the Pacific.

'So much sea,' he murmured and the smile that crept into his face made him appear almost amiable. If Lord Grimwald had a heart then it was held in the glowing sphere before him. He loved it above everything else. Alone on his rocky island, with only the globe for company, he was happy. Sometimes the memory of his wife's gentle singing caused him to look down into the waves, where she had drowned in a net, crushed by a ton of fish. And then he would think of the gold charms she had made for their son, so that he should survive the curse that lay upon their family.

It was regrettable, Lord Grimwald reflected, that if he was to live on, he must destroy his only son, now that he was twelve years old. Dagbert had proved to be a talented drowner, and would no doubt become a powerful Lord of the Oceans, if he survived.

The reason for the Grimwald family curse had been lost through time. But it was as strong as it had ever been. When Lord Grimwald was twelve he had caused his own father's death, and for his father it had been the same. But, occasionally, a father had survived a son, and the present Lord of the Oceans didn't intend to die for a long time yet.

He'll hide those charms, that son of mine, but I will find them. Lord Grimwald laughed out loud. He had a plan that involved Mrs Tilpin's son, Joshua. The Magnet. He hoped the boy was up to the task.

The Lord of the Oceans put a scaly hand against the glass and a white plume of water rose beneath his fingers. When it fell back, bright circles rippled away from it across the ocean, like the ripples in a pond. Only these foamy circles would appear on the real ocean as a mountain of water. Lord Grimwald was so entranced by his work, he didn't hear Manfred come into the ballroom.

'So this is the Sea Globe!' said Manfred in an awe-struck voice. 'It is,' he stretched out his hand, 'so vast!'

Lord Grimwald turned, almost guiltily, as though caught in the act of admiring himself in a mirror. 'The

Sea Globe, yes. I'm pleased that it has travelled so well, despite its size. Not a wave, not an ocean out of place.'

Manfred leant close to the glass. 'It defies gravity,' he said with a frown. 'Why does the water not tumble to the ground? How, how can it possibly rise like that? The waves . . .' he leant even closer, 'some of them are rolling upwards.'

Lord Grimwald smiled with satisfaction. 'It is what it is. And has always been so. I know nothing of its history. My father told me once that an ancestor in the distant past was endowed with magnetism. He attracted water, if you like. He gathered it into his arms, out of the North Sea, and lo and behold, a sphere of water grew out of his gatherings, dotted about with parcels of land.'

'And it's with this globe that your family has been able to control the oceans?' Manfred's tone was tinged with doubt.

'For eight hundred years,' Lord Grimwald replied. 'It was encased in glass in the nineteenth century, to protect it from pollution, you understand.'

Manfred nodded. 'Naturally.'

'Did you get anything out of the boy?' Lord Grimwald asked.

'Oh, a great deal,' Manfred replied with a smile. 'The boat was on his mind, and it has a name, *Greywing*. Eustacia saw it all – the sea, the night sky and constellations upside down.'

'Upside down?' The Lord of the Oceans rubbed his chin. 'So they are in the southern hemisphere.' He put his finger against the glass and the waves beneath it sparkled with silver foam. 'There are whales aplenty on the coasts of Australia. I'll wager our quarry is in this vicinity.' He slid his finger up the eastern coast of Australia, and a line of white foam followed the course he took.

Manfred watched the long, fish-like finger with a slight frown of distaste. 'You've caused a few shipwrecks there, I imagine,' he said.

'Mustn't let it run away with me.' Lord Grimwald turned to Manfred. 'So, what else did this clairvoyant have to tell you?'

'The Red Knight's identity. We believe he must be my grandfather, Bartholomew Bloor, black sheep of the family.'

'Why do you believe this?' Lord Grimwald asked curtly.

'Because he turned his back on us, went abroad. Became an explorer, wouldn't have anything to do with the family.'

Lord Grimwald sighed impatiently. 'No. Why do you believe the Red Knight is this Bartholomew person?'

'Oh, he was in Charlie's mind.'

'Proves nothing. The boy doesn't know. He's guessing.'

'Well, it's a start,' said Manfred indignantly. 'Eustacia's on top form lately. I bet she could tell me what was in your mind.'

'I doubt it,' muttered Lord Grimwald. 'What about this unknown endowed child that's on the loose?'

Manfred grimaced. 'Charlie got away before we could ask. His friend's ruddy dog came barking through the letter box. It broke our concentration.'

'Tch!' Lord Grimwald thrust his hands into his pockets. 'Not that I'm bothered, but Kapaldi wants to know. He's always in such a state, it's unsettling.'

'We did find out about one of the other kids,' Manfred said, a touch smugly. 'One of the girls; Olivia Vertigo. Turns out she's an illusionist, quite a good one. We had no idea. So it's a bit of a coup.'

'Indeed,' agreed Lord Grimwald. 'Get her under

control and she could be useful.'

One of the great ballroom doors was suddenly pushed open and Mrs Tilpin shuffled in, dragging Joshua behind her.

'Weedon said you wanted us,' she grumbled. 'I was taking a nap. Can't get a wink of sleep at night. Place is haunted.'

'What's that?' cried Joshua, pointing at the Sea Globe.

Lord Grimwald stared at the puny boy disdainfully. Joshua's thin hair was covered in bits of paper, crumbs and pencil-shaving clung to his sweater and his shoes were coated with dead leaves and mud.

'I can see that you're magnetic,' Lord Grimwald observed.

'But what is *that*?' Joshua demanded, his eyes never leaving the Sea Globe.

Lord Grimwald wrinkled his nose. 'I suppose you'll do,' he murmured.

'If you want him to do something for you, you'd better be a bit nicer,' said Mrs Tilpin, hobbling towards the globe. 'Tell him what it is.'

'That is a Sea Globe.' Lord Grimwald tossed the

words out as though the Tilpins hardly deserved an answer.

'WOW!' Joshua ran to the globe, his arms outstretched.

'DON'T TOUCH!' shouted the globe's owner.

Joshua halted within inches of the glass. 'It's all wrong,' he declared, staring up at the gigantic sphere. 'It's impossible. The waves are going up. How does the water do that? And how can the earth stand on water?' He pointed at the base of the globe. 'Why doesn't it all fall down?'

'Because it doesn't,' Lord Grimwald said crisply.

Joshua fell silent. He gazed up at the water tumbling far above him in the Arctic Ocean. His pale face was bathed in the shifting blue-green light of the great sphere and his paper-covered hair was dappled with rainbow colours from the crystals in the chandelier. He looked at his mother and decided she was almost beautiful in sea light. It certainly improved Manfred's appearance.

At last Joshua turned his head and stared up at Lord Grimwald. 'Who are you?' he asked.

The man beside him looked down as from a great

height, and Joshua noted the crinkled, almost green hair, the chilly arctic eyes and the greyish glimmering skin. 'You look like a fish,' he said.

His mother dug him in the ribs. 'Behave yourself, Josh,' she said. 'This man controls the sea; he's like Dagbert, only cleverer.' She glanced at the Lord of the Oceans. 'He wants you to do something for him.'

'What?' Joshua stared at the stern features.

Lord Grimwald dug his hands into his pockets. 'You are acquainted with Dagbert Endless?'

'He's a year above me, but I know him,' said Joshua. 'He's almost my best friend.'

'Ah. Is he? Well, Joshua, Dagbert is my son and, you may not believe this, but he has stolen something from me.'

'I believe you. Dagbert and me often steal things.' Joshua gave the man a crooked smile. 'What's he stolen from you?'

'Seven golden charms, Joshua: a fish, five crabs and a sea urchin.'

Joshua wrinkled his brow. 'But they're his charms, Mr Grimwald –'

'Lord Grimwald,' Manfred hastily corrected him.

'Lord Grimwald,' said Joshua. 'Dagbert said his mother made the charms for him, so he'd be protected.'

'From *me*,' said the Lord of the Oceans. 'I know his story. All lies, Joshua.'

Joshua kicked the floor with the toe of his boot, and Manfred scowled at the dried mud falling on to the polished floorboards.

Lord Grimwald sighed heavily and paced around the globe, saying, 'I suppose you want a reward for your services, Joshua?'

Joshua looked at his mother, who said, 'Of course he does.'

'Very well.' Lord Grimwald, having circled the globe, stopped beside Mrs Tilpin and sighed again. 'Your accommodation here is not up to much, I imagine.' Manfred's scowl deepened. 'Damp probably,' Lord Grimwald continued. 'I can see you've got a touch of arthritis. I can offer you a small castle in the North. A servant. Heated rooms and . . .'

Mrs Tilpin began to sway with pleasure. She had to steady herself on Manfred's arm, which he didn't much like. 'And?' she prompted.

Lord Grimwald turned to Joshua. 'What is your

favourite food, Joshua?'

The boy gave a broad grin and, without hesitating, said, 'Chocolate, sausages, Battenberg cake, lemon sherbets, strawberry jelly, chips and beans.'

'Fish?' asked the Lord of the Oceans.

'I hate fish,' said Joshua.

Lord Grimwald's cheeks turned a greenish pink and for a second a look of hatred passed across his face but, pulling himself together, he waved a hand and said, 'You'll get all those things, but –'

'Yippee!' Joshua gave a little jump for joy.

'But only when you've done what I ask.'

'Spit it out,' said Mrs Tilpin, momentarily forgetting to be grateful. 'I'm tired.' She shuffled over to one of the gold-painted ballroom chairs and sank down on it.

Lord Grimwald became very businesslike. 'I know that Dagbert will hide the charms. You will find them, Joshua. Wherever they are. You are magnetic. The charms will be drawn to you, they will cling to you, even if you are four metres away from them.'

'I've never done gold before,' said Joshua doubtfully.

'Believe me, you will attract gold if you think about it. If you truly want it. I know a little about magnetism

and the mind plays a great part in it. Why are you covered in paper, mud and crumbs, for instance? Do you *want* to look a mess? Think them away,' Lord Grimwald flipped a hand at the mess on Joshua's sweater, 'and you'll feel much better.'

Joshua frowned at the crumbs, but nothing happened.

'I think we are done here,' said the Lord of the Oceans. 'You may go now. Bring me the charms as soon as you can.'

'Yes, sir.' Joshua turned to his mother, who shuffled forward and grabbed his hand.

'I'll come and see you later, Titania,' said Manfred. 'I want your opinion on a new development. Olivia Vertigo is endowed.'

This news brought a twisted smile from Mrs Tilpin. 'Indeed?' she murmured. 'I can have some fun at last, a little shape-shifting,' and her blackberry eyes glittered with excitement.

As the Tilpins walked out, a few bits of paper floated off Joshua's head and, squeezing his arm tightly, his mother whispered, 'You're going to make our fortune, Josh.'

Manfred waited until the Tilpins had gone before asking, 'When will you find Lyell Bone's boat then? I'd like to watch the drowning.'

'Patience,' said Lord Grimwald. 'I want those charms. If I don't get them, I might not survive long enough to help you.'

Manfred found it difficult to believe that the powerful man standing beside him could be overcome by a twelve-year-old boy. But a curse was a curse, he told himself, and there was no getting round it. 'I haven't told Great-Grandpa the latest news,' he said, striding to the door. 'I'd better go up to his attic right now. He always likes to be the first to know things.'

Lord Grimwald followed Manfred into the passage. 'Must be suppertime,' he said. 'Can your cook make fishcakes?'

'No idea.' Manfred closed the ballroom doors, slid a bolt across and locked them. 'Don't want anyone tampering with your globe,' he said.

The two men made their way down the gloomy passage, opened the low door at the end and stepped into the hall. As soon as the door had been closed, a small person emerged from the shadows at the other

end of the passage. Cook had been listening through a crack in the ballroom door, and had heard almost every word of the conversations that had taken place. Certainly enough to know that she must tell someone about the Sea Globe. She had even caught a glimpse of the awful thing.

Cook and Lord Grimwald had a history. Not once, but twice, he had asked her to marry him. She had refused both times, and for this he had swept away her house and drowned her family. Tears stung her eyes when she thought of the dreadful day she had returned to her island home to find nothing but a few planks of wood bobbing beside a rock.

'He won't get away with it again,' she muttered as she tiptoed hastily down the passage. 'Better the boy than the man. Whatever Dagbert has done, it can't be worse than what that slimeball has in mind.'

Cook opened the door into the hall. Looking quickly about her, she ran across the hall and down the corridor of portraits, to the blue canteen. Once there, she nipped into the kitchen and over to a broom cupboard. Her assistants were all offduty at the weekend, and so she was able to use the access to her

secret apartment without fear of being observed.

At the back of the broom cupboard, covered by aprons and towels, a small door opened on to a softly lit corridor. Cook hurried along, muttering under her breath, 'Mustn't let him. Must stop him,' until she came to a flight of steps leading down to yet another cupboard. This one opened into a cosy room, where bright coals flickered in an old black stove. The walls were hung with paintings, and an ancient dresser was filled with gold patterned china. There was a comfy sofa and an old armchair beside the stove. In the armchair sat a large man with a lot of white hair and a lined but handsome face.

Dr Saltweather, Head of Music, was Cook's friend and ally. It was only recently that she had begun to trust him enough to let him into her secret room. And how he loved it. What a contrast it was to the cold, gloomy room he had been allotted in the Academy.

When he saw Cook's anxious face, Dr Saltweather flung down his newspaper and exclaimed, 'What is it, Treasure?' This was not an endearment, although the doctor was very fond of Cook. Treasure was actually her name.

'Oh, Arthur. It's dreadful!' cried Cook, and she related everything she had heard – and caught a glimpse of. 'I've got to warn them,' she said, putting on her tweed coat and woolly hat. 'Charlie and his uncle have got to know. We've got to stop that wicked, murdering, drowning monster.'

'Let me go,' said Dr Saltweather, springing up.

'No, no. You're too . . . er . . . distinctive.' She blushed slightly. 'You'd be noticed. I'll go to the bookshop, rather than risk being seen by the Bone grandmother. Mr Yewbeam is bound to be with Miss Ingledew today.'

'If you're sure, my dear. But do take care.' Dr Saltweather anxiously watched Cook dart about, putting things into her bag. And then, with a little wave, she was off again.

Dr Saltweather sank back into the armchair and patted the old dog at his feet.

'I don't like it, Blessed,' he said. 'I don't like it one bit.'

The false godmother

Cook remembered that she was on duty tonight. She would be expected to produce a meal for the Bloors and their unwholesome guests. Fishcakes had been mentioned.

'Nothing for it; Mrs Weedon will have to take over,' Cook said to herself as she ran through the blue canteen. 'Better warn her.'

Cook hurried down to the green canteen, where Mrs Weedon could usually be found, dozing beside the kitchen range or reading thrillers. But today she was nowhere to be seen. Cook found her, at last, in the yard outside the kitchen, feeding an evil-looking dog.

'Bertha, what on earth are you doing?'

147

cried Cook as the animal bared its teeth and lunged at her.

'Poor thing, it's hungry,' said Mrs Weedon. 'It's a stray. I'm very fond of it. And so much food goes to waste in this place.'

Cook had given up wondering why Bertha Weedon always looked so sour. She decided that the poor woman probably couldn't help it. After all, being married to Mr Weedon could be no picnic.

'Why are you all dressed up? You're on duty,' said Mrs Weedon, looking at Cook's woolly hat.

'I'm hardly dressed up,' said Cook, 'but as you rightly point out, I am supposed to be on duty, but I'm going out, so you'll have to do supper tonight.'

Mrs Weedon put her hands on her wide hips and stamped her foot. 'Why should I? Where are you going?'

'I'm visiting a sick friend. She's very ill. No one else to look after her. So, toodle-oo!' Cook stepped nervously round the dog that now had its nose in a bowl of cold stew, and ran up the flight of stone steps that led to the road. Ignoring Mrs Weedon's indignant shouts she hurried down to the High Street and then on into the old part of the city. She was quite puffed by

the time she reached Cathedral Close, and thinking of a nice cup of tea, but as she approached the bookshop, something happened that put the cup of tea completely out of her mind.

Two figures stepped out of the bookshop, slamming the door behind them, so that the bell rang frantically and the glass pane at the top of the door rattled alarmingly. The strangers did not look at all like Miss Ingledew's usual customers. One wore a string vest and camouflage trousers, and the other was dressed in a hooded black tracksuit. They were both laughing in a rather unpleasant way.

Cook shrank against the wall as the men jogged past her, chatting in low voices. She couldn't hear what they were saying, and hoped they wouldn't notice her but, unfortunately, the string-vest man caught sight of her bright red hat. 'What're you looking at, Grandma?' he shouted in a mocking voice.

Cook was tempted to reply that she was too young to be a grandmother and who was he to cast aspersions when he was wearing a silly string vest on a freezing March night. But she thought better of it and kept her mouth shut.

The two men ran on, laughing, and eventually turned into Piminy Street. 'Might have known it,' muttered Cook as she hurried towards the bookshop, and she thought of her friend, Mrs Kettle, the only trustworthy person in Piminy Street; all alone now, in a street of thugs and tricksters and probably worse.

When Cook reached the bookshop she found that the 'Closed' sign had been removed and, looking through the window, was horrified to behold a scene of utter devastation. Piles of precious books lay strewn across the floor. Two shelves had collapsed, the ladder that was used to reach the highest shelves was broken and the till had been turned on its side. Miss Ingledew stood leaning against the counter, her hands covering her face, while her niece, Emma, knelt on the floor, smoothing the pages of a large, leather-bound book.

Cook rang the bell and then knocked frantically. 'Julia!' she called. 'Julia, let me in.'

Miss Ingledew lowered her hands, revealing a tear-stained face, and wearily climbed the steps to the door, unlocking it with trembling fingers.

'My dear!' cried Cook, entering the shop. 'Whatever has been happening here?'

'I hardly know where to start,' said Miss Ingledew. She locked and bolted the door, then followed Cook down into the shop.

At that moment, Olivia Vertigo appeared through the curtains behind the counter. She was carrying a tray containing three large mugs and a plate of biscuits. 'Hello, Cook,' she said cheerfully. 'D'you want some cocoa? It won't take a sec.'

'That would be nice, dear,' said Cook, gazing round the shop, her horror growing every second.

Olivia put the tray on the counter and retreated behind the curtain, saying, 'Okey-doke.'

'What can I do to help?' asked Cook. 'Oh, dear, dear me. Those wonderful books. Have you rung the police, Julia?'

'I did,' said Emma. 'They told me they had a lot to deal with tonight, and if we hadn't actually been burgled, which we haven't, then we weren't a priority.'

'But they've done so much damage,' cried Miss Ingledew. 'My books are priceless.'

'Tell me everything.' Cook took Miss Ingledew's arm and drew her into the little room behind the shop. Here there was yet more chaos. Books lay open, their

pages torn and crumpled, all over the floor.

Miss Ingledew sat on the edge of the sofa, with Cook beside her, and in a tremulous voice began to describe the events that had followed the arrival of the two threatening-looking strangers.

'I had some very important customers, and they didn't leave until half past six,' Miss Ingledew explained, abstractedly lifting her mug of cocoa to her lips. 'I was just about to put the "Closed" sign up and lock the door, when these two villains pushed their way in, nearly knocking me over.'

'I saw them!' Olivia came in with another mug of cocoa and handed it to Cook, saying, 'I'd just come from supper at Charlie's place – boy, what a lot he's been through, I can tell you – anyway, when I came into the bookshop, I saw these men hauling books on to the floor. It was pretty scary. They said they were looking for a box, and if I knew anything I'd better come clean. Well, we all know what box they meant, don't we? But I wasn't going to say anything.'

'They seemed to think it might be hidden in one of my larger tomes,' said Miss Ingledew, 'but they just hauled the whole lot out and shook them, as if they

were . . . as if they were so much . . . rubbish. They rummaged under my counter, turned over the till, and then started in here. Olivia came and shouted at them, but they just laughed. One even threw a book at her.' Miss Ingledew's shoulders heaved. 'And then they went upstairs.'

Cook put an arm round her. 'There, there, my dear. It's all over now. I don't know – all this fuss over a box that *might* contain a will. And even if it does, and Billy Raven proves to be the heir, what's the point of this trouble if Billy is lost to us?'

'He isn't,' Olivia said confidently. 'Charlie will get him back.' She skipped across the room and through the curtains, back into the shop.

'Well, it's good to see that *someone* is optimistic,' said Cook.

'She's a treasure,' Miss Ingledew declared. 'She's always cheerful, and such a help. I know people think she's a bit odd, in those rather flamboyant clothes of hers. But then her mother is a famous film star, so what can you expect? She often stays with us when her parents are on location, and Emma loves her company.' Miss Ingledew wiped her nose and actually smiled.

Cook decided that her own news could wait until the bookshop had been put to rights, and with the four of them working together, they managed to tidy all the books away in both rooms in under an hour.

'I'll have to get the ladder mended,' Miss Ingledew said ruefully. 'But I'm almost ready for business again.' She beamed round at them. 'Thank you all so much.'

'And we've still got Sunday,' said Emma. 'I'm sure Mr Yewbeam will mend the ladder for you.'

'No, he won't,' said Miss Ingledew in a slightly bitter tone. 'He'll have better things to do. I tried to ring him when those ruffians came in, but he didn't pick up, and so far he hasn't even bothered to return my call . . . a distress call at that.'

There was an uncomfortable silence, and then Olivia suggested that Paton was in a place where his mobile couldn't get a signal. 'He did look a bit preoccupied when I saw him earlier,' she said.

'He told me he was coming round after supper this evening,' Miss Ingledew said coldly. 'So where is he?'

'Detained?' Cook suggested helpfully. 'In times like these anything can happen. Now I want you all to sit down and listen to what I have to tell you. Something

quite . . .' she raised her hands, '. . . quite dreadful is going on at Bloor's. And if I hadn't suffered personally at the hands of a certain person, I wouldn't have believed such a thing could happen.'

Their eyes wide with apprehension, the two girls sank on to the sofa, while Cook and Miss Ingledew took chairs on either side of the dying fire. And Cook told them of Lord Grimwald's great Sea Globe, describing in graphic detail the gravity-defying waves, the eerie sea light and the way the water responded to the Lord of the Ocean's scaly hands. 'Only his son can stop him,' she said. 'But if you ask me, Dagbert Endless doesn't stand a chance against a father like that. Someone must get a message to Lyell Bone,' she went on earnestly. 'Surely Paton Yewbeam knows where he is. Wireless messages can be received. There are numerous ways of contacting people at sea. Lyell must put to shore at once; I know only too well the consequences of being on the ocean when the Lord of the Oceans has decided to eliminate you.'

'I feel I should go there tonight.' Miss Ingledew twisted her hands together. 'But we would only be waylaid by Charlie's grandmother. She seems to bear a

grudge against her own son. And it would be the same with the telephone. If only Paton would answer his mobile – but he won't.'

'Try again, Auntie,' urged Emma.

Miss Ingledew took her mobile out of a pocket, dialled a number and waited. 'Nothing,' she said flatly.

'In that case I suggest we all have a good night's sleep and contact Charlie first thing in the morning.' Cook stood up and pulled on her woolly hat. 'I've heard that Grandma Bone is usually in bed till noon on a Sunday morning. So you shouldn't have any trouble. As for me, I'd be missed at the Academy. They're demanding big breakfasts these days, especially that wretch with the sword.'

'Treasure, take care!' Miss Ingledew suddenly stood up, her voice harsh with misgiving. 'It is not just a matter of a will and a box; it is not just a problem of a Sea Globe and a storm. There is much more at work here.'

Everyone looked at her expectantly.

'Have none of you noticed it? The creaks, the whispers and murmurs from another world. The wickedness beneath the city is waking, slowly, called by

a distant voice.' She turned her gaze from the flickering embers in the grate to a shadowy corner shelf. 'What I have managed to glean from the Latin texts in those ancient books tells me that if the enchanter of Badlock cannot rule this city, as he once tried to do, then he will encircle it with his loathsome army, and take it into another world. His world.'

'Badlock?' said Emma, in a frightened voice.

Miss Ingledew nodded. 'If that's what it's called.'

'He could do that?' Olivia said angrily.

'Oh, yes.'

Cook looked extremely indignant. 'What? And do we have no say in the matter?'

Cook's down-to-earth manner caused Miss Ingledew to smile, in spite of herself. 'From what I can understand,' she glanced at the books again, 'we have a chance if one of the Red King's descendants is brave enough to face the enchanter's army.'

'Alone?' said Olivia. 'Surely he'll have other people to help him?'

'Of course,' said Miss Ingledew. She gave them a grave smile. 'If he can find any.'

'There's us,' said Emma in a small voice.

Cook gave a little shiver. 'There are plenty of people who would fight for the Red King's city,' she said confidently. 'I'm off now, my dears. Don't forget to lock the door after me.'

Olivia and Emma were already yawning, and when Cook had gone they took themselves off to bed. Miss Ingledew, however, put another log on the fire, and sat watching the flames for a while. But her gaze kept drifting towards the far bookcase where her oldest books stood, their gold tooling glittering faintly in the low firelight, their leather spines appearing as soft as velvet. And Miss Ingledew felt compelled to go to them, knowing the comfort their touch would bring. She chose the largest, and carried it back to the armchair, where she sat and laid it on her lap, opening it at a page she had studied many times. But as she ran her hand over the thick vellum, a soft whine echoed down the chimney, and the wind outside carried the sound of distant, menacing voices.

Olivia woke up before dawn. She blamed the chimes from the cathedral clock. It was dark and she tried to go to sleep again. On Sundays she and Emma usually stayed in bed until after ten o'clock. But try as she

might, Olivia could not sleep. She screwed her eyes tight shut, pulled the covers over her head and counted sheep. But she only succeeded in making herself feel more and more awake.

A thin light began to creep through the curtains, and Olivia remembered that her parents were coming home today. They'd been on location in Morocco, and were bound to have found something special for her. A necklace, perhaps; an embroidered waistcoat or some silk trousers.

It was no use just lying in bed and thinking, Olivia decided. She would go home and start to cook something special for her parents' lunch. They had told her that they would be in the city by midday.

Olivia sprang out of bed and began to put on her clothes. Her bag was filled with an assortment of tops, jackets, hats and scarves. Today she chose a scarlet dress to wear over her tight black jeans, a white scarf with a glittering fringe, a fur-lined denim jacket and a black felt hat. Her red gloves exactly matched her boots.

She made quite a noise throwing on her clothes, but Emma didn't wake up.

Olivia wrote her a brief note and left it on the dressing table. In the bathroom she splashed her face with water, brushed her teeth and, reckoning that her tangled hair looked distinctly cool, she carried her bag downstairs and left the shop.

It was a grey, misty day, but that didn't take the spring out of Olivia's step. She swung along, humming lightly to herself. There was no one about, and the voice that suddenly called out took her by surprise.

'Olivia!'

Recognising the voice, Olivia hurried on. There came a second call, which she ignored.

'Olivia, hold on!'

'Bother him,' Olivia said to herself. She swung round and faced Manfred Bloor. He was strolling towards her, his hands deep in the pockets of a long green coat with a small cape attached to it.

'What d'you want?' Olivia demanded.

'You're out early, Miss Vertigo.'

'So are you,' she retorted. 'What do you want? I'm in a hurry.'

'Are you?' Manfred came right up to Olivia and stared into her face, his dark eyes glinting. 'This is so

opportune,' he said. 'I was coming to visit you at the bookshop.'

Olivia frowned. 'Why?'

'Why do you think? I want to discuss your wonderful endowment with you.'

'There's nothing to discuss.' Olivia turned away and began to run towards the High Street, where she could see an elderly couple walking their dog.

'Off to see your godmother?' Manfred called. 'Alice the Angel.'

Olivia stopped in her tracks. Without turning round, she said, 'My godmother isn't here.'

'Oh, but she is.' Manfred's voice was silky smooth. 'I'm surprised she hasn't been in touch with you.'

Against her will Olivia found herself moving, very slowly, to face Manfred. She could see the thin green figure, swathed in mist, his dark hair shining with dew, his eyes like black coals. 'What . . .' she croaked. Her voice seemed to have disappeared.

Manfred waved a hand at her. 'Don't let me keep you. We can have our chat another time.'

'Yes . . . a chat.' Olivia took a few steps backwards and then turned and walked on towards the High

Street. She passed a man with a newspaper under his arm. The man smiled pleasantly and said, 'Morning.'

Olivia frowned, as if she hadn't heard him, which made the man shake his head and murmur, 'These young things! Anyone would think I was the man in the moon.'

A boy and a large yellow dog came running up the road. No one could fail to recognise Runner Bean.

'Hi, Olivia!' called Benjamin Brown. 'Are you going to see Charlie? He's not up yet.'

Olivia didn't stop when Benjamin reached her. She didn't even smile, but kept on walking.

'*Good morning*, Olivia!' Benjamin shouted after her. 'Nice of you to stop.'

'Goodbye,' she called over her shoulder.

Benjamin looked at his dog and shrugged. 'She's in a funny mood,' he said, and Runner Bean barked in agreement.

As Olivia drew closer to her home, she began to think about her godmother, Alice Angel. Alice kept a flower shop in a place called Steppingstones. It was Alice who had helped Olivia to discover her endowment. Alice knew things instinctively. She always knew when Olivia

needed her. Alice was a white witch and Olivia recalled her warning, 'Where there is a white witch there is always another, of a darker nature.' And so it had proved, when Mrs Tilpin had revealed her true identity.

And now Olivia found herself passing the turn to her own street and walking on towards the park. She turned the corner into Park Road, murmuring, 'Number fifteen.' The houses in this street were half-hidden behind tall hedges and overgrown shrubs. The gate of number fifteen had come off its hinges and stood propped against the fence. The path was overgrown with moss and the white paint on the door had all but peeled away. Ivy covered the walls and had even made its way across the windows.

Alice Angel had lived here once. Had she returned, as Manfred said? The house looked deserted. Olivia walked up the mossy path and pulled a rusty chain that hung beside the door. A soft chime could be heard within the house.

Olivia waited. A lace curtain twitched in the window that overlooked the garden, and a voice came whispering out of the house. Was it a voice, or the rustle of evergreens?

Come in, my dear!

Olivia tried the door handle. It turned smoothly and the door creaked open. She stepped inside a chilly hall. Was Alice living here? The house felt as though it had been empty for a very long time. At the end of the hall a door opened into Alice's sitting room. The ivy covering the windows made the room so dark Olivia could barely make out the furniture. It was so cold her breath condensed into tiny clouds.

Olivia blew on to her hands. Even in gloves her fingers were freezing.

'Alice?' she said tentatively.

Here, my dear!

The voice made Olivia jump. She peered into the corner where the voice had come from. A woman sat in an armchair. Her hair was smooth and white, just like Alice's. Her face was pale and her eyes had a greenish tinge. It must be Alice, and yet . . . The face wavered and almost disappeared. One moment the features were clear and then they became vague and incomplete.

'Alice, is it really you?' asked Olivia, her throat contracting in the cold air.

'Of course it is, my dear.' Alice's voice was little

more than a whisper. 'I haven't been too well. Come and kiss me.'

Olivia hesitated.

'What is it? You're not afraid, are you?' Alice's voice was stronger now, and yet . . . was it her voice?

Olivia walked over to the armchair. She looked down at the woman resting against a faded blue cushion. It was Alice and yet, how thin she had become.

'Oh, Alice, I've missed you!' Olivia bent and kissed the cold cheek. Immediately her heart flooded with love for this frail woman, the godmother who had watched over her from far away.

'I've got a present for you.' Thin fingers pushed at Olivia's arms. 'It's on the table over there. Try it on, dear.'

Olivia saw a white package on the table; tissue paper wrapped around something soft and sparkling. She peeled back the paper and drew out a black velvet waistcoat covered in tiny circles of mirror-like silver.

'Oh, it's beautiful!'

'Try it on.'

Olivia slipped out of her denim jacket and put on the glittering garment. The silver was so bright she could hardly look at it and, for some reason, the

feather-like fabric pressed heavily on her shoulders, as though it were weighted with stones. And yet she could not bear to take it off.

Three hundred miles away, Alice Angel was arranging flowers at the back of her shop. She liked to do this very early on a Sunday morning, when the shop was closed. As soon as she had made up a dozen or so small bouquets, she would display them on a stand outside, where she would wait beneath a white canopy for people visiting relatives or friends in hospital.

Alice sold only white flowers. She was surrounded by tall vases of blooms whose pale petals ranged from deepest cream to bluest white. It was cool in the shop but Alice kept warm, moving through her flowers, snipping, twisting, wrapping and binding. The sweet fragrance made her sing.

A petal fell on to her arm, and then another. Alice looked up from her work, surprised that her fresh flowers were shedding petals already. A white rose dropped from its stalk, and then another and another. Petals began to fall like snow. They became a white

storm, showering Alice with the scent of dying flowers. She dropped the bouquet she had been holding and pressed her hands to her face.

'Olivia!' she cried. 'What has happened to you?'

Tigerfield Steps

Charlie sat in the kitchen eating porridge. He felt as though he'd run a marathon. He ached all over and could hardly keep his eyes open. On the other side of the table Emma was drinking tea. She had just told Charlie about her aunt's unwelcome visitors and now, in a rush, she repeated Cook's description of the Sea Globe.

Charlie's eyes widened, just a fraction. 'So that's how he does it,' he mumbled, through a yawn.

'You don't seem very surprised.' Emma looked disappointed.

'After yesterday nothing surprises me,' said Charlie. 'I've been prodded and interrogated, hit by gargoyles, singed by a

mad person, fallen off a ten-foot wall and been chased by a sword.'

Maisie paused in her ironing and gave a huge sigh. 'We've got to leave this city,' she declared. 'It's not a normal place. It's too dangerous. As soon as your parents come back, Charlie, we should pack up and leave.'

'You can't,' said Emma. 'Not until it's all sorted out. And *we've* got to do that.'

'We?' Maisie banged down her iron on a hapless shirt sleeve. 'I suppose you mean you Children of the Red King. Well, it seems to me that half you lot are causing all this trouble.'

'Only half,' Emma pointed out. 'That's why the other half must stop them.'

'Hmm.' Maisie continued ironing, banging down her iron with more force than was absolutely necessary.

Emma watched her for a moment, then turned her gaze on Charlie who was now leaning his head against his hand and yawning again. 'Anyway,' she said sharply, 'we've got to do something today, before it's too late. We'll be back at school tomorrow and things will get more and more difficult. I don't know how

we're going to tackle Lord Grimwald. I've just had to put that at the back of my mind until we've sorted this box problem out.'

Charlie reflected that Emma had been off school for a whole week. No wonder she was so perky. 'Have you seen Tancred?' he asked.

Emma blushed. 'What's that got to do with anything?'

Charlie shrugged but couldn't stop himself from grinning. 'I only asked.'

Emma's blush spread to the roots of her hair, but she carried on, rather fiercely, 'Well, are you coming to see Mr Bittermouse with me?'

'What?' Charlie said slowly. 'Why?'

Emma leant across the table, looking more animated than Charlie had ever seen her. 'I had this idea, you see. Mr Bittermouse is a lawyer, and he knew your dad, so maybe your dad gave him this box, with the will in it. I mean,' she spread her hands, 'what could be more obvious? Auntie Julia agrees with me.'

'Don't you think *they* will have thought of that?'

For a moment Emma's determined look wavered, and then she said, 'Maybe. But it's worth a try.'

Charlie sighed and licked his spoon. He could have done with another bowl of porridge, but he contented himself with a large spoonful of honey, which he sucked very slowly while Emma reeled off the names of all the people she'd phoned before coming to him. Olivia was spending the day with her parents, Fidelio was playing the violin at a concert, and Gabriel was 'doing something important' with Lysander and Tancred up at Lysander's grand house on The Heights.

'So there's only us,' Emma finished breathlessly.

'OK.' Reluctantly, Charlie stood up. 'I'll get my coat.'

'You will not, Charlie Bone. And it is not OK.' Maisie plonked down her iron and walked over to stand in front of the kitchen door. 'I forbid you to leave this house today. Your parents would never forgive me if something happened to you.'

'But Mrs Jones . . .' Emma began.

'Don't you Mrs Jones me, Emma Tolly,' said Maisie. 'I'm surprised at you, forcing our Charlie into dangerous streets after all that he's been through.'

This embarrassed Charlie. 'Maisie,' he cried, 'I'm not a child!'

'Yes, you are,' Maisie retorted.

Charlie didn't like arguing with Maisie, but he hated being made to look a sissy, and a nasty scene might have followed, if Uncle Paton's camper van hadn't arrived outside the house.

Charlie's uncle looked tired when he came in. Maisie asked him where he had been but he merely shook his head and told her it was a long story, and not a very satisfactory one. 'I shall have to go to Ireland,' he muttered, before gulping down a large cup of black coffee.

Charlie noticed that his uncle had a familiar 'don't-ask-me-any-more-questions' look on his face, so he sat beside him at the table and related everything that had happened on the previous day. And then, at last, he got a reaction from his uncle, who quickly helped himself to another cup of coffee, exclaiming, 'I shouldn't have left, I see that now. They're getting too bold, those villains, and yet,' he scratched his unshaven chin, 'I must find out more about that will.'

'I've got an idea,' said Emma. But before mentioning Mr Bittermouse she repeated Cook's description of the Sea Globe and Lord Grimwald's terrible power.

'I never imagined that was how he did it,' Paton

murmured, and an anguished look passed across his face. 'I can't reach Lyell. Every contact I had seems to have gone dead. There was a harbour master, but he left his post, and the captain of the ship that carried your parents' mail hasn't been seen for a month. But there is a ray of hope. The sailor who was with them on one of their journeys says he's received word from Lyell very recently, and will try and contact him again.'

'I had a card from them,' said Charlie. 'Just a week ago. Another whale. The date on it was smudged.'

'But don't you see?' said Emma, wringing her hands fretfully. 'If we find the box, then there'll be no need for Lord Grimwald to drown anyone.'

'Unless he just likes doing it,' said Charlie.

'We've got to try.' Emma groaned with impatience. 'Please, Mr Yewbeam, please, please will you come with us to see Mr Bittermouse? He's a lawyer. He knew Charlie's dad. Lawyers deal with wills, don't they?'

'It's a long shot, Emma.' Paton gave her a rueful smile. 'But I was going to the bookshop this morning, so we could pop in to see Mr Bittermouse on the way.'

'Thank –' Emma began.

'But,' Paton held up his hand, 'not before I've had my breakfast and a shower.'

'Thank you.' Emma sat down, exhausted by her efforts. 'So now can Charlie come?' she asked Maisie.

'We'll see.' Maisie set about cooking Paton's breakfast while he went upstairs. He came down looking very clean and dressed in his blue velvet jacket and a new red tie.

Emma and Charlie waited patiently while Uncle Paton ate a large plate of bacon, tomatoes, asparagus, mushrooms, egg and beans. After two slices of toast and marmalade, a croissant and a third cup of coffee, Paton rose from the table saying, 'Bless you, Maisie,' and made for the hall, where he wound a grey scarf round his neck and put on his black fedora and long woollen coat.

Light snowflakes were drifting through the air, and frost still lingered on the grass and hedgerows. Charlie huddled into the thick scarf that Maisie had bought him for Christmas. He would have preferred to stay at home, but how could he possibly ignore any attempt to save his parents. And again he was beset by worrying, unpleasant thoughts. Why was his father so far away when the city was in trouble? Had he been in a trance

for so long that now he was too weak to face any danger? No. For the ocean was a dangerous place.

Charlie had been so lost in thought, he was surprised to find they were already approaching the street where Mr Bittermouse lived. A large removal van was parked outside the lawyer's house, the wheels on one side resting on the pavement and blocking their way. The cobbled street was so narrow they had to squeeze by the van on the other side of the road.

'I'm sure this is illegally parked,' puffed Uncle Paton as he shuffled sideways, trying to avoid the mud spattering the side of the van.

When they had all got through, they discovered that the van was not parked outside Mr Bittermouse's house, but standing in front of the house next door to his. Here there was much activity. The doors at the back of the van were wide open and several removal men, in brown overalls, were pushing furniture up a ramp and into the van.

'Is someone moving?' Charlie realised that this was a silly question because someone was very obviously moving.

'We are.' A young woman with a baby in her arms

stood in the doorway. 'And not a moment too soon for my liking.'

Uncle Paton touched his hat. 'Paton Yewbeam,' he said. 'What's been going on?'

'What hasn't?' said the young woman. She nodded at the turn to Piminy Street, almost opposite. 'Those ruffians in Piminy Street have made our lives a misery. I just can't take it any longer. Stone creatures banging on the door at night, unearthly singing, laughter like I've never heard. Bats in the chimney. Glowing eyes at the window. It's . . . it's . . .'

'A nightmare,' said Emma.

The woman winced. 'Yes, a nightmare.'

'I'm so sorry.' Uncle Paton looked very concerned. 'If there's anything . . .? But, of course, you'll soon be away from all this.'

'Yes.' The young woman smiled at last. She stood aside as a baby's cot was manoeuvred through the door. 'I'm Lucy Palmer and this is Grace.' She held up the baby's hand. 'We've found a nice little place a hundred miles away from here, and we won't ever come back.'

A cheerful-looking young man came through with a rocking-chair. 'It's all done, Luce,' he said. 'We can be

off soon. 'Oh, hello!' He grinned at Uncle Paton and the children.

After introductions were made all round, Uncle Paton explained that they were intending to visit Mr Hector Bittermouse who lived next door.

'Not any more,' said the young man, whose name was Darren. 'He moved a week ago, along with half the neighbours. Who'd want to live in a place with *them* on the doorstep?' He, too, nodded at the turn to Piminy Street.

This was bad news, especially for Emma. She'd had such high hopes. But all was not lost because Charlie remembered that Hector Bittermouse had a brother, a Mr Barnaby Bittermouse, who lived at number ten Tigerfield Street.

'Charlie, what an excellent memory you have,' Uncle Paton remarked, in surprise.

'It's not the sort of thing you can forget,' muttered Charlie.

Darren thought he knew a Tigerfield Street. He pointed to the cathedral square, telling them it could be one of the small alleys leading off the road at the back. 'I can't be sure,' he said. 'I thought it had another

name, like Tigerfield Way, or Steps, or something.'

They said goodbye to Lucy, Darren and Grace and wished them good luck in their new home. Then they made their way up to Cathedral Close. They had to pass the bookshop on the way, and Uncle Paton was about to stop and look in on Miss Ingledew, when Emma grabbed his arm and said, 'Not now, Mr Yewbeam. Let's find the other Mr Bittermouse first.'

Uncle Paton frowned. Emma's tone seemed to suggest that something was amiss. 'Is your aunt all right?' he asked.

'Yes, but . . .' Emma hesitated. 'She's been sort of burgled.'

'What?' Paton stood stock-still. 'How could you forget to tell me? I must go to her at once.' He began to stride towards the bookshop.

'NO!' cried Emma, so loudly that Uncle Paton was halted in his tracks. 'Auntie doesn't want . . . doesn't need you right now. She wasn't really burgled, she was just . . .'

'What?' Paton demanded. 'Burgled or not burgled?'

'Not,' said Emma lamely. 'Just visited by ruffians. But she's OK. *Please* can we go on to Tigerfield Street?'

Charlie swung from foot to foot, rubbing his hands together. 'It's so cold, Uncle Paton. Can we move on?' He began to walk across the wide square in front of the cathedral, with Emma hurrying beside him. Uncle Paton followed them reluctantly. Glancing back, Charlie saw that his uncle looked troubled, and wondered if it was because Emma had implied that her aunt didn't want to see him.

A small wrought-iron gate led out of Cathedral Close and into a road called Hangman's Way. Charlie remembered that Billy Raven had once been kept in one of the dark alleys leading off Hangman's Way. Emma remembered too. She shivered at the thought of poor Billy, held fast behind the force-field of a sinister man called Mr de Grey.

'There it is!' Uncle Paton announced. He pointed to the sign on a wall that curved into a dark gap, little more than a metre wide.

'Tigerfield Steps,' said Charlie.

'The old boy probably got the name wrong,' said Paton. 'It must be the place.'

They crossed the road and stood at the entrance to Tigerfield Steps.

'It's hardly a street.' Emma stared doubtfully at the flight of stone steps that led up into the darkness. The tops of the buildings leaned so dangerously they appeared almost to touch each other.

'Come on.' Charlie began to mount the steps. They climbed in single file, their footsteps echoing in the confined space, the only sound for miles, it seemed. Charlie counted the numbers on the thick oak doors. Some were missing altogether. There was a sixteen, then nothing until twelve was reached, with an eleven opposite.

'Here,' cried Charlie. 'Number ten.'

The bronze numbers hadn't been cleaned for years and were now green with mildew. Beneath them was a large bronze door-knocker in the shape of a tiger's head. Charlie lifted the head and knocked.

There wasn't a sound within the house. Charlie knocked again. And again. After the third knock something curious happened. The door creaked open, just a fraction.

'It's not even latched,' Uncle Paton observed, pushing the door until it swung right back, revealing a small marble-tiled hall. 'Hello there!' he called. 'Anyone in?'

There was no answer.

A tingle of foreboding ran down Charlie's spine. Something had happened in this house. Was there a ghost in the place, or was it worse than that?

Uncle Paton stepped inside and the others followed. They opened a door at the side of the hall and looked into a small kitchen, where pots and pans were heaped on the draining board. A brown teapot was warm to the touch, and there was steam on the window, but no sign of the person who had recently made a cup of tea.

On the other side of the hall there was a cosy sitting room where a scuffed leather sofa and an armchair clustered round the fireplace. The embers of a recent fire could be seen glowing in the grate.

'Perhaps Mr Bittermouse just popped out for a newspaper, and forgot to lock the door,' Emma suggested.

'Perhaps,' said Uncle Paton.

At the end of the hall an uncarpeted wooden staircase led to the rooms above.

'A lawyer usually has a desk,' said Uncle Paton thoughtfully. 'Mr Bittermouse's study could be up there.'

'And he could have fallen asleep over his books,' said Emma, 'being so old. Old people often fall asleep like that.'

Uncle Paton gave her a look that said, 'You don't have to be old to do that.'

'Let's go up.' Emma's foot was already on the first step. 'Hello!' she called. 'Anyone up there?'

The treads creaked woefully as they mounted the staircase. Charlie came last. His throat felt tight, his ears buzzed and the icy foreboding that clutched at his stomach got worse and worse.

There were three doors leading off the landing, and then the stairs continued up to another floor.

Emma knocked on the door in the centre. There was no answer. She opened the door and looked into a bedroom. The bed was neatly made and a suit of clothes hung on the outside of the wardrobe. She shrugged and closed the door. Beside the bedroom there was a chilly bathroom, with no hint of a woman's touch. No bottles or jars or tubes; just a bar of soap, a razor on the windowsill and a toothbrush in a glass.

'Third time lucky,' said Uncle Paton, marching towards the third door, and Charlie's stomach gave a

lurch. He found that he wanted to cry out, to stop the door being opened, to make them all go downstairs again, without knowing what was in that third room. But Uncle Paton was already opening the door. He stopped abruptly on the threshold, uttering a strangled cry and then a string of oaths – the sort of oaths that Charlie had rarely heard, and certainly never coming from his uncle.

And so Charlie had to look into the room. Peering round his uncle's rigid form, he saw a study that had been utterly ransacked. Bookcases lay at an angle, a desk had rolled on to its side. The floor was littered with books and papers, and in the centre of it all lay a very old man. He had a shock of white hair and fine, if wrinkled, features. He was lying on his back; his tweed jacket had fallen open and on his white shirt, just where the heart might be, was a large red stain.

'Dead?' Emma whispered.

'Looks like it. I'll ring for an ambulance,' said Uncle Paton. 'Who could have done such a ghastly thing?'

It was then that Charlie noticed a mark on the floorboards: a long thin scratch, as though a knife

had been drawn across the floor – or the tip of a sword. And he felt that he knew who had murdered Mr Barnaby Bittermouse. But who on earth would believe him?

Angel in the snow

A police car arrived soon after the ambulance. They were both too late to save poor Barnaby Bittermouse. He was definitely dead, though the detective constable wasn't able to confirm what kind of weapon had actually killed him. There was no question that he'd been the victim of a robbery. But what had been taken? His wallet was still in his pocket, his gold watch was on his wrist and there was ten pounds in change lying in a drawer.

Charlie could see that Uncle Paton was trying to decide whether he should mention the box. If he said too much he would be taken to the police station for questioning. He would have to sit beneath a light, several

lights most probably, and every one of them would explode, to Paton's utter humiliation and embarrassment.

'We should like to leave now,' Paton said in a low voice to PC Singh, whom he recognised from various other encounters. 'Would this be convenient?'

'Yes, sir. But we need your address and phone number.' The policeman peered at Paton suspiciously. There was something odd about the tall man in his black hat. Hadn't he caused some trouble a few months ago? Lights – that was it. Exploding lights. 'Don't leave the city, sir. We might need to talk to you again.'

'Oh, but I want . . .' Paton hesitated. He looked anxious. 'Very well. I'll let you know if I'm thinking of making a journey.'

'You do that, sir.' PC Singh took out his notebook. 'Now, address and phone number, please.'

Uncle Paton gave them, a little reluctantly.

The constable consulted his notes. 'And you didn't know the late gentleman, but were just visiting to enquire about making a will, even though it was Sunday.' He raised his eyebrow a fraction, but continued in the same tone. 'And you found the front door open.'

'Yes,' said Uncle Paton firmly. 'I'm a very busy man and Sunday is the only day I can do these . . . er, things.'

Charlie added, 'The door opened when I knocked on it.'

PC Singh ignored this. They had gone through it all before. But not to be left out, Emma said, 'And I was the one who went upstairs first.'

'You can go now,' said PC Singh, giving a sort of flourish with his pen on the notepad.

They walked down Tigerfield Steps in single file. The ambulance and two police cars were parked in Hangman's Way. Uncle Paton strode across the road without even glancing at them. Charlie and Emma ran to catch up with him and when they reached the gate into Cathedral Close, Charlie burst out, 'It was Ashkelan Kapaldi. He murdered that poor old man.'

'Whatever gives you that idea?' Uncle Paton marched across the cobblestones, his face set in an angry frown.

'Because of the scratch on the floorboards. The sword can do that. It scraped along the road when it was chasing me.'

Uncle Paton slowed down, then he stopped

altogether and looked at Charlie. 'You have a point,' he said.

'I saw the police staring at the scratch,' said Charlie. 'They must have been wondering what had made it.'

'Then why didn't you tell them about the sword?' asked Emma.

Charlie gave her a disappointed look. 'How could I, Em? How could I say, "Excuse me, but there's this man at our school, who came out of a painting, and he's got this sword that works on its own"?'

Emma pouted. 'You could have,' she argued. 'They might have gone and questioned him.'

'I doubt it, Emma,' said Uncle Paton. 'The police don't like delving into the paranormal.'

Emma shrugged. 'I'm going home,' she said.

They watched her run across the square and disappear into the bookshop, and this time Uncle Paton made no attempt to follow her.

'They were looking for the box, weren't they?' said Charlie. 'Whoever murdered Mr Bittermouse was working for the Bloors.'

'Could have been. But did they find it? And why kill the poor old man?' Uncle Paton cast a lingering look at

the bookshop and then resumed his loping stride towards the High Street.

As soon as they were home Uncle Paton rang Mr Silk and told him the news. Charlie could hear the excitement in the room where Mr Silk had taken the call. It was lunchtime and knives and forks were clattering on plates, Mr Onimous was exclaiming very loudly, and then Gabriel's voice sang out, 'Is Charlie all right, Dad? Who's been murdered?'

When Uncle Paton had said all he needed to, Charlie took the receiver and spoke to Gabriel. He wanted to know what the important meeting had been about.

'Not much, really,' said Gabriel. 'We just thought we should work out some kind of strategy for dealing with the swordsman. Emma told us pretty much everything that happened to you, so we reckoned you'd be spending the morning in bed.'

'No such luck,' said Charlie. 'Em dragged me round to see this old lawyer. She thought he might have the box that everyone is looking for. That's when we found him – murdered.' Charlie lowered his voice. 'It was the swordsman, Gabe, I know it. There was a

scratch on the –' He was cut short by someone opening the front door.

Grandma Bone walked in. 'What are you doing?' she demanded, glaring at Charlie.

'Sorry. Got to go, Gabe. Grandma's here.' Charlie put down the receiver.

'I hear you've been involved in a murder.' Grandma Bone stared at Charlie accusingly.

'How d'you know?' asked Charlie. 'It's only just happened.'

'I want to know what you were doing in Tigerfield Steps.'

Charlie didn't answer. He watched his grandmother pull off her black gloves and put them in her pocket. Next, she took off her hat with the purple feathers sticking up at the back, unwound a lavender-coloured scarf from her neck and shuffled out of her black fur coat. When she had hung all these garments on the coat-rack, she said, 'Well?'

Charlie walked into the kitchen where Uncle Paton, having heard everything his sister had said, was making himself yet another cup of black coffee. 'It's amazing how word gets round so quickly in your nefarious

underground, Grizelda,' he said, dropping a lump of sugar into his coffee. 'There is a network of spies in this city that I find truly repellent.'

'What are you talking about? Where's lunch? I'm hungry,' she said, all in one breath.

'We are all aware that you are part of a scandalous conspiracy to defraud Billy Raven of his rightful inheritance.' Uncle Paton's dark eyes never left his sister's face as he slowly stirred the spoon round and round in his cup. 'Even if it means drowning your own son. The question I have often asked myself is why, Grizelda, why? Now, I believe I know.'

Grandma Bone stared at her brother with a mixture of contempt and hatred. 'You have no idea what you're up against this time, Paton Yewbeam,' she snarled, and left the room.

Charlie pulled out a chair and sat beside his uncle. 'What did you mean, Uncle P?' he asked. 'Have you really found out why Grandma Bone's the way she is?'

Uncle Paton was silent for a while. He continued to stir his coffee, almost as if he were unaware of his actions. Charlie began to smell the leg of lamb that Maisie was roasting in the oven. He thought of the

crisp roast potatoes that she always cooked with lamb, and the rich, brown gravy. And because he was still so tired the thought of the wonderful meal ahead filled his mind like a dream, and he forgot that he'd asked a question until his uncle began to speak.

Charlie had heard the story of Uncle Paton's mother slipping on the steps of Yewbeam castle and cracking her head on the flagstones. He knew that Paton's four sisters had remained in the castle after their mother's death, while Paton and their father had left. The castle belonged to an aunt: Yolanda, the notorious shape-shifter. It was she who had turned the girls against their father and their brother. All this Charlie knew, but it didn't explain why Grizelda, the oldest, had taken against her only son.

'It has to do with love, Charlie.' Uncle Paton stared at the window. Snowflakes were tapping gently against the pane and the room was filled with a soft opalescent light. 'Grandma Bone's husband, Monty, fell out of love with her. Who wouldn't have the way she behaved – jealous, domineering, humourless, greedy . . . ? Monty would never have married her, but he was trapped,

spellbound if you like, probably by Venetia with one of her magic garments. She was good at that, even as a child. Poor Monty didn't stand a chance. Grizelda had always wanted to marry a pilot, and she got one. But not for long.'

'What happened?' Charlie stared at his uncle's angular profile, expecting to hear why Monty's plane had crashed. He had often asked how it had happened, but no one seemed to know. Charlie was hoping his uncle had found out at last and he was disappointed when Paton said nothing about the crash, but began to describe a meeting he'd had with a woman called Homily Brown, who lived in the far south-west.

Homily Brown had been a great friend of Monty's. They'd been at school together. It was James, Uncle Paton's father, who had remembered that Monty had been born in a little hamlet called Neverfinding. And that's where Uncle Paton had been on one of his recent trips, as he tried to piece together the troubled history of the Yewbeams and the Bones.

'Monty returned to his old home a week before he died.' Uncle Paton's tone was almost melancholy. 'He went to make a will. Homily found a lawyer for him and

she and a friend were witnesses. He left everything to his only son, Lyell. But that wasn't all. He wrote a letter: a sad, tragic message to be given to Lyell on his eighteenth birthday. He told his only son never to trust the Yewbeams, never to let them rule his life and . . .' Paton paused and drew a deep breath, 'Homily read this letter, but Lyell has never spoken of it and, I have to admit, I found the last part rather shocking.'

'What did it say?' asked Charlie, bracing himself for a dreadful revelation.

Uncle Paton glanced at him and, for a moment, Charlie thought that his uncle could not bring himself to repeat the last part of Monty Bone's letter, and then out it came, on a long sigh. 'Monty told Lyell to put an end to the Yewbeams, before they destroyed him.'

It was Charlie's turn to stare at the snowflakes falling past the window. So many questions filled his head, but before he could even utter them, Maisie came bustling into the kitchen, talking about snow and overcooked potatoes and uncooked carrots, and Grandma Bone sulking in her bedroom.

Before they knew it, lunch was on the table, and Uncle Paton was carving the lamb. But the rich smells

and a yearning, empty stomach couldn't dislodge the thought of Monty Bone's letter from Charlie's mind. He was told to take a tray of food up to Grandma Bone and, as he carried it carefully across to the table in her room, he couldn't stop himself from thinking, She knew about that letter and she doesn't want Dad to come home, ever.

'You've spilled the water,' the old woman grumbled as Charlie left the bedroom.

'Sorry.' Charlie closed the door while his grandmother was complaining about dry potatoes and not enough gravy.

'Are you going off again?' Maisie was asking Paton when Charlie returned to the kitchen.

'Not until Monday night,' said Uncle Paton. 'I'll have to inform the police, of course.'

'But . . .' Charlie stared hard at his uncle. 'Haven't you found out enough?'

'No, Charlie. I'm on the trail of something else. It's all connected, I suppose, but we need to know the whereabouts of that pearl-inlaid box.'

'Maybe they found it in Mr Bittermouse's study,' said Charlie.

Uncle Paton shook his head. 'In that case, why kill him?'

'The sword did it. It acts on its own, you know.'

Maisie's knife and fork clattered on to her plate. 'Please,' she begged, 'you're putting me off my lunch. Can't we talk about something pleasant for a change?'

'The weather?' said Charlie, grinning at the snow. 'Maybe the school will be closed and we can go tobogganing on the Heights.'

'And I'll slip over, fall on my bottom and drop the shopping,' Maisie said with a laugh.

The snow continued to fall.

After lunch Charlie went up to his room. Claerwen was fluttering over the windowpanes as though she were trying to become part of the snow. Charlie took her on to his hand and she walked up to his shoulder where she sat, her wings folded, and watched him writing an essay for English. 'Holidays'.

Charlie didn't have holidays. There was a break from school but he had never experienced a journey to a sunny place with yellow beaches, blue skies and pink and white houses. Now and again, Uncle Paton would

take him to see his great-grandfather who lived beside the sea: a fierce grey sea, where seagulls gathered and wild waves lashed the black rocks. But these visits had to be kept secret, because if Grandma Bone had known her father's whereabouts she would have sought him out and harried him to his grave. There was another reason. Great-Grandfather's brother lived there, a boy called Henry who had never grown up, caught in time by the Twister, a marble of astonishing beauty that Ezekiel had used to try and banish Henry to the Ice Age.

Charlie smiled when he thought of Henry, safe in his own brother's cottage by the sea.

After a few minutes of deep thinking, Charlie imagined a holiday spent on a Caribbean island. And then he realised that he didn't have to imagine it – if he could find a photograph of someone actually sitting on a Caribbean beach, he could travel there. But Charlie had become wary of picture-travelling. It was never quite as much fun as he hoped. He could never take a friend, and the journey home often left him feeling a little unsteady. He must now conserve his energy for the dangerous journey into Badlock, to rescue Billy Raven.

His essay completed, Charlie felt he deserved a biscuit, maybe two. The house was very quiet. His grandmothers were both sleeping, no doubt, and Uncle Paton would be writing up his notes for the next chapter of his book, *A History of the Yewbeams*.

It was not yet evening, but the sky was dark with snow to come, and snow was still falling. Charlie could hardly see his way to the back of the kitchen. Details in the room were vague and incomplete, as though covered by a thin, grey veil. Charlie found a tin of biscuits and took it to the table. He sat down and began to eat them while he watched the snow gently falling.

The doorbell rang.

If the sound had woken the grandmothers they apparently didn't feel obliged to go to the door. Nor did Uncle Paton.

The bell rang again.

Charlie had seen no one pass the window. Filbert Street appeared to be deserted; snow lay on the parked cars, three inches deep.

The third time the bell rang it was hardly a sound at all. Charlie had the impression that it was only inside his head. But he felt compelled to go to the door. He

opened it tentatively and a cloud of snowflakes floated into the hall.

A woman stood on the doorstep. Her hair was as white as the snow. She wore a thick white coat and a soft yellow–gold shawl lay on her shoulders.

Charlie gasped. His hand flew to his mouth. For a moment he thought a snow-angel had landed at their door. And then he recognised the woman. 'Alice Angel,' he whispered.

Alice smiled. 'Hello, Charlie. May I come in?'

He stood aside and she walked into the hall. A delicious smell drifted past Charlie and he remembered Alice's shop, 'Angel Flowers', where tall white blooms perfumed the air with their heavenly scent.

'Where have you been?' he asked.

'I've been in my other shop,' she said, putting a small leather case on the floor. 'It's a long, long way from here.'

Charlie took Alice's soft white coat and hung it on a peg. 'Why have you come back?' he asked.

'Olivia,' she said.

'Olivia?' Charlie took Alice into the kitchen and put on the kettle. The room seemed suddenly brighter,

especially where Alice stood, in her white dress and long silver-grey boots. 'It's funny you should come here now,' he said, 'because Olivia may be in trouble.'

'I know,' said Alice, with a frown of concern.

'She betrayed herself.'

'Tell me how.' Alice sat at the table while Charlie made her a cup of tea. She hadn't asked for one, but was very happy to drink it as Charlie told her about the stone gargoyle and the skeleton Olivia had conjured up to scare Eric-the-animator.

Alice Angel's solemn face broke into a smile. 'How very appropriate: a skeleton. Olivia certainly has a wild imagination. But she shouldn't have let her endowment be known. Now I've lost her.'

There were footsteps on the stairs and Charlie and Alice looked at the door. Charlie hoped it wasn't Grandma Bone. But Uncle Paton looked into the room, and immediately recognised Alice Angel.

'Dear Alice, what brings you here?' he asked. 'In a snowstorm, too. It must be urgent.'

'It is,' she said earnestly. 'I may live three hundred miles away, but I always know when Olivia needs me. It's an instinct I have; I can't explain it. As soon as I got

to the city I went round to Olivia's house.' Her face clouded and she sipped her tea nervously. 'They wouldn't let me see her.'

'Wouldn't . . .?' Uncle Paton sat down abruptly. 'Why on earth?'

'Olivia's father came to the door,' Alice continued. 'He said that Olivia wasn't quite herself. I begged him to tell her that I had arrived, that I wanted to see my dearest goddaughter, so he went up to her room while I waited in the hall.' Tears glittered in the corners of Alice's large hazel-green eyes. 'When Mr Vertigo came down he said . . . he said . . .' She stopped and dabbed her eyes with a white handkerchief.

Paton laid a hand on her arm. 'What did Mr Vertigo say?'

Alice straightened her back and tucked her handkerchief into her sleeve. 'He said that Olivia didn't want to see me, and would I please leave the house immediately.'

Charlie couldn't believe his ears. Olivia loved her godmother. What had happened to turn her against Alice Angel? Unless . . .

'I'm afraid *they* have got to her already.' Alice's voice

was firmer now. 'But I am not going to give up, and I am certainly not going to leave this city. I shall stay here until Olivia is herself again. The trouble is,' she hesitated, 'I'm not sure where I can stay. The house I used to live in is still empty, but it's very, very cold.'

'You must stay here,' said Uncle Paton, springing up. 'I insist.'

Maisie came into the room, just as Paton was about to run and fetch her. She listened to Alice's story with the resigned expression that she frequently wore these days. And yet, Charlie could see her warming to Olivia's godmother, and it wasn't long before she was offering her cake and 'maybe a glass of wine?' and then shooting upstairs to make up a bed in the room where Charlie's mother had slept.

In all this time there was no sign of Grandma Bone. She didn't even put in an appearance at supper. Charlie knocked on her door, but there was no reply. Had she gone out? Or was she still sleeping?

'She's asleep,' said Maisie, tiptoeing out of Grandma Bone's room at nine o'clock. 'Can't you hear the snoring?'

Charlie took himself off to bed. It was school tomorrow. Would Olivia be there? he wondered. And

what would she do? Whose friend would she become?

In spite of the questions filling his mind, Charlie found himself drifting easily into sleep. He thought of Alice Angel, in the room above him. It was comforting to know that she was in the house, even if she was someone else's guardian angel.

We're borrowing her, Charlie said to himself, just for a while, until Olivia wants her. And then his thoughts turned to Billy Raven, pulled nine hundred years through time, to the enchanter's palace. No wonder Billy didn't want to come home. His companion was the most beautiful girl in the world – a girl with dark curls and a gentle smile; a girl called Matilda whom Charlie would give anything to see again.

Billy wasn't having such a good time as Charlie imagined. He was being punished, and he blamed Rembrandt. Rembrandt was Billy's rat; he was sleek and black with shining eyes and long, impressive whiskers. He happened to be in Billy's pocket when Billy was whisked into the painting of Badlock thanks to a nasty spell of the enchanter's (or Count Harken of Badlock to give him his full title).

Life in Badlock had been very good to Billy. He had fine clothes to wear, delicious food to eat and a jungle of animal enchantments to visit every day. There was also Matilda, Count Harken's granddaughter, the kindest friend Billy had ever known. But Rembrandt wanted to go home. He nagged and complained and chewed Billy's new shoes and generally made himself a terrible nuisance. Billy could communicate with animals. He understood every squeak, whine, purr, twitter – and a lot more.

One day Rembrandt went too far. It was during supper, the worst time he could have chosen. Supper in the enchanter's palace was a very important affair. It was served in a vast black marble hall. False stars shone down from the vaulted ceiling and the walls were hung with glittering weapons.

The glass-topped table was seven metres long and the count and his wife, sitting at opposite ends, had to converse in shouts that made Billy's head ache.

Billy and Matilda sat next to each other, facing Edgar, Matilda's brother, a hard-faced boy who liked to frighten Billy by appearing suddenly through a wall or a door. The diners only had to utter the name of the

food they wanted, and it would instantly be conjured up. Billy usually chose whatever Matilda was having. This was often Cordioni soup, although sometimes she recommended Sofabunda Pie or Milliflorum Mundi. Billy tried to feed Rembrandt as much as he could without Edgar catching sight of him. Edgar loathed the rat; he called Rembrandt an abomination, not fit to walk the earth, let alone live in a palace.

So when Rembrandt, tired of the usual titbits, leapt on to the table and made a dash for Edgar's plate, Edgar jumped up with a yell, seized a knife from the wall and flung it at the rat. Luckily it missed Rembrandt and slid across the table, but Billy was already on his feet, screaming at Edgar.

'You vile, mean, horrible boy!' Billy cried. 'You nearly killed my rat!'

'It's a pity he didn't,' the countess remarked.

The dreadful coldness in her voice stunned Billy. Rembrandt jumped into his arms, and he sat down abruptly.

'The creature must be killed,' the countess continued. 'Don't you agree, Harken?'

Billy stared at the countess's long face. Her small black

eyes rested on the rat he was clutching to his chest.

'Well, Harken? Say something!' the countess demanded, raising her voice.

Billy turned to look at the enchanter who, until that moment, had been ignoring the drama and carrying on with his meal, as though nothing out of the ordinary had happened. Taking a sip of wine from a golden goblet, he regarded Billy with a thoughtful expression and stood up.

Billy cowered under the enchanter's chilly gaze. His green robe glittered with diamonds and emeralds and his abundant hair shone with a dusting of powdered gold. Sometimes Billy was so overawed by his host's magnificence he could barely look at him. He waited, fearfully, for the count's pronouncement. At last it came.

'We shall not bother with the rat,' said the enchanter.

Billy's heart gave a flutter of relief. His hopes were dashed, however, by the enchanter's next words. 'The creature can keep the boy company in the dungeons.'

'Sir, you can't do that!' cried Matilda. 'Billy is our guest.'

'I am tired of guests!' the count roared at her. 'Guards, take the boy away.'

Before Billy could think what might be coming next, two guards stepped forward and grabbed his arms. Rembrandt dropped to the floor and scuttled at Billy's heels as he was marched out of the hall. He could hear Matilda's protesting cries receding into the distance as he was taken further and further down the long dark passages that led to the dungeons.

The sea-gold charms

When Charlie went down to breakfast next morning he found Alice in the kitchen. A pot of tea had been made, porridge was cooking on the stove and slices of golden-brown toast filled the toast rack on the table.

'Good morning, Charlie,' Alice said brightly. 'Watch the porridge for me, I'm going to take Maisie a cup of tea.' She spoke as if she had lived at number nine for much longer than a night.

'Morning, Alice.' Charlie took up a wooden spoon and began to stir the porridge, while Alice slipped out, carrying a cup of tea with two biscuits on the saucer. Her footsteps were so light, they could hardly be heard on the stairs.

By the time Alice came back, Charlie had eaten his porridge. The gritters had been working through the night and the roads were clear, although the pavements were still covered in snow. The sky was bright blue and the sun made roofs, walls, trees and hedges blaze with light. Alice opened the window and breathed in deeply. 'I love the smell of snow,' she said.

Charlie sniffed the cold air and agreed with her. The world smelled deliciously fresh. He ran upstairs to fetch his school bag. As he pulled on his blue school cape, he found that he was glad of its warmth. Sometimes other children in the street would tease him for attending Bloor's Academy and wearing a fancy cape. And Charlie would stuff the embarrassing garment in his bag, trying not to draw attention to himself. But today he felt warm and confident.

The house was still very quiet, almost as if it were buried in snow. There wasn't a sound from Grandma Bone's room.

Alice came to the kitchen door just as Charlie was leaving. 'Watch Olivia for me, Charlie,' she said. 'Don't let anything . . . anyone . . . I hardly know what I'm saying because it's obvious that she's become one of

them now. But I'd like to know how it happened, so that I can deal with it.'

'I'll do my best,' Charlie promised. He still couldn't believe that the Olivia he knew would allow herself to be *taken over*.

On the other side of the road, Benjamin was throwing snowballs for Runner Bean to fetch. 'No school for me today,' he called happily. 'School's closed, 'cos of the snow.'

'Lucky thing,' Charlie shouted back. He knew the blue bus would be waiting for him at the top of the road. Only an avalanche would close Bloor's Academy.

Charlie hardly saw Olivia during the day. Sometimes he'd catch a glimpse of a bleached blonde head above a purple cape, but then she'd be gone, swallowed in a sea of purple. Drama students surrounded her like bees round a honeypot. It wasn't until the homework hours began that Charlie discovered what he was really up against.

After supper, Charlie climbed the back stairs up to the King's Room, where the endowed children had to do their homework. He was halfway up when a voice behind him whispered, 'Charlie.' He turned round and

saw Emma's pale, distraught face. Her eyes were red from crying.

'What's up, Em?' Charlie asked.

The Branco twins came up behind them and tried to push past. Idith (or was it Inez?) hissed, 'You're in the way, morons.'

Charlie's fist itched. He would have liked to land a punch on Idith's doll-like face, but reluctantly he stepped aside and let them pass. When the twins were out of earshot, Emma said, 'Something's wrong with Liv. She hasn't spoken to me all day.'

'*They've* got her,' Charlie whispered.

'What?' Emma's blue eyes widened in disbelief. 'They can't have.'

'She betrayed herself, Em. Once they knew, they were bound to try and change her.'

'No.' Emma shook her head vigorously. 'They couldn't. Not Liv. I won't believe it.'

Dorcas Loom trudged past them, breathing heavily. 'What's wrong with you two?' she mumbled, without looking back.

Charlie and Emma didn't bother to reply.

'It's true,' Charlie said in a low voice as Dorcas

disappeared round a bend in the stairs. 'Alice Angel has come back. Olivia wouldn't see her.'

Emma's mouth fell open.

'We'd better go, Em,' said Charlie. 'We're late.'

They began to hurry up the stairs, but hearing slow footsteps at the foot of the staircase, Charlie glanced back. Dagbert Endless stood brushing the shoulders of his blue cape. His hair was like wet seaweed and the bottoms of his trousers were wet with snow. Feeling Charlie's eyes on him, Dagbert looked up.

Charlie couldn't stop himself from asking, 'Have you hidden your charms?'

Dagbert gave a silent nod.

'Good.' Charlie didn't want to know where they were. But he was glad they were out of Lord Grimwald's reach. He ran up the stairs with Dagbert plodding after him.

The King's Room was almost circular. Its curved walls were lined with books and in the centre stood a large, round table. The endowed children sat at the table to do their homework, watched over by the Talents Master.

When Charlie walked into the room that night he

was surprised to see that Olivia had already made herself at home. She had never worked in the King's Room before, but here she was, sitting between Dorcas and one of the twins, with her books laid out neatly before her. She had been accepted as one of the endowed and quickly taken her place among them.

There were always two distinct groups at the table. Manfred sat with Dorcas, Joshua and the twins, while on the other side of the table, Lysander, Gabriel, Emma and Charlie sat close together. Dagbert was always alone in the gap between the groups; never on one side or the other.

Lysander and Gabriel were already immersed in their work. Charlie took a chair beside Gabriel, with Emma on his other side. When Charlie put his books on the table, Gabriel looked up and rolled his eyes, inclining his head towards Olivia. Charlie grimaced and shrugged. Gabriel frowned. Charlie grinned.

'Stop making faces, you two,' said Manfred. 'If you want to welcome our new member, do it sensibly.'

Gabriel and Charlie stared at him. Neither said a word.

Manfred sighed. 'For your benefit and everybody

else's, I might as well formally announce that Olivia Vertigo has joined our elite company. Olivia is an illusionist, something that she has been keeping to herself for quite a while, but now that her endowment is out in the open, we expect her to use it only when Bloor's Academy requires her to.'

Everyone stared at Olivia, who took absolutely no notice. She was bent over her exercise book, writing feverishly.

'Do you think,' said Joshua, in his eager whine, 'that Olivia could show us, just once, what an illusionist can do?'

Manfred pondered this before replying, 'I don't see why not.' He turned to Olivia. 'Olivia, show them.'

Olivia's head came up. She looked slightly confused.

'An illusion please, Olivia,' said Manfred, enunciating every word as though Olivia were deaf.

Olivia blinked, and then looked up at the ceiling. When she brought her gaze back to the table, all at once a miniature safari park appeared. Sand covered the table's polished surface, while scrub and acacia trees bloomed from books and pencil cases. Charlie had seen Olivia's larger-than-life illusions before, but today she

had chosen to captivate rather than terrify. Among the trees, tiny animals could be seen: elephants, giraffes, lions, zebras and many others. Faint howls, growls and shrieks were heard as lions chased their prey and minute birds fluttered out of the branches.

Everyone gazed at the scene in silent wonder. And yet Charlie could not feel enthralled for there was a coldness in Olivia's blank face, a chilling emptiness. He could see something sparkling in the opening of her purple cape. Olivia often wore sequinned scarves or waistcoats, but this was different somehow. Now and again she would twitch her shoulders, as though her clothes were too heavy for her.

'That's enough,' Manfred commanded.

The marvellous scene disappeared and Dorcas and the twins stared at Olivia in admiration.

Joshua said, 'Well done!'

'Get on with your work,' said Manfred.

Books were opened and heads bent over them. Pens and pencils set to work, but Charlie couldn't concentrate. He found himself staring at the gilt-framed painting on the wall. It was an ancient portrait of the Red King, cracked and darkened with age. The

king's features were blurred but his red cloak was still bright and a slim gold crown was just visible in his black hair.

So often Charlie had tried to travel into the past to meet his ancestor, but every attempt had been blocked by the shadow that stood behind the king. Count Harken was an enchanter whose shadow had found its way even into a painting. And it was the shadow that Charlie focused on today. It was the shadow that held Billy Raven captive in Badlock.

'How many times have I told you to stop staring at that portrait?' Manfred's cold voice broke into Charlie's thoughts.

'I haven't counted,' said Charlie.

Before Manfred could make another withering remark, Lysander said, 'Why is the portrait there, if we're not supposed to look at it?'

Taken off-guard, Manfred glared speechlessly at Lysander. The African, seizing his advantage, went on, 'We are sitting in the Red King's room; he is our ancestor; without the king we would not be here. Does it not strike you as ridiculous, sir, that we should be commanded never to gaze on his portrait?'

What a joy it was to see Manfred's angry, incredulous face. Of all the endowed children, it was only Lysander whom Manfred feared. Lysander could conjure up his spirit ancestors; no mere illusions, but ghostly warriors who could throw a spear straight at your heart.

Everyone waited to see what Manfred would do. Eventually the Talents Master made a contemptible remark. 'I hope you don't find yourself in the same predicament as your friend,' he said, glancing at Dagbert-the-drowner.

It was obvious that Manfred was referring to Tancred, but Dagbert didn't appear to have heard him. His eyes had a glazed look, and Charlie guessed that he was thinking of his sea-gold charms.

Frowning at Dagbert, Manfred told everyone to get on with their work.

The minutes ticked by. After almost two silent hours the endowed children packed up their homework and made their way to bed.

In the girls' dormitory, Olivia took off her purple cape, revealing a velvet waistcoat covered with shimmering mirrored circles.

'That's very beautiful,' Emma remarked.

Olivia gave her a half-smile and sauntered off to the bathroom. Emma threw on her dressing gown and began to follow her. Dorcas Loom was sitting on her bed just inside the door. She was wearing a frilly pink nightdress and trying to straighten her crimpy fair hair. When Emma passed her bed, Dorcas said quietly, 'Something wrong with your friend?'

Emma stopped and looked at Dorcas, who said, 'What's eating you?' And suddenly Emma knew that Olivia had been bewitched by that sparkling waistcoat. Because that's what Dorcas could do; it was also what Charlie's great-aunt Venetia prided herself on. Both could make bewitching garments.

Emma ran to the bathroom. Olivia was brushing her hair in the mirror. She had taken off the waistcoat to put on her pyjamas, and now the sparkling waistcoat lay on a chair. Seizing her chance, Emma made a grab for it.

'DON'T TOUCH IT!' Olivia's long nails dug into the back of Emma's hand. For a moment Emma resisted. She clung to the waistcoat, but Olivia, raising her hairbrush, brought it down, crack, across Emma's knuckles.

Emma let go with a cry and Olivia pulled the

221

waistcoat on over her pyjamas. 'Don't ever do that again,' she said.

Emma followed Olivia back into the dormitory. She watched her friend get into bed, still wearing the waistcoat. It scratched and tinkled against the covers and Emma shuddered. ''Night, Liv!' she murmured. Without replying, Olivia turned over and closed her eyes.

After 'Lights Out', Charlie and Fidelio went to the bathroom, where they could talk in peace. Fidelio might not have been endowed, but he was Charlie's loyal friend and always would be. Sitting crossed-legged beside Charlie on the bathroom floor, he listened, with mounting horror, to the account of his best friend's grim weekend.

'I haven't heard about anyone being murdered,' whispered Fidelio. 'Poor old Mr Bittermouse.'

'It was probably in all the papers this morning,' said Charlie. 'But the swordsman will be back in his portrait before anyone can catch him.'

'Do you think . . .' began Fidelio.

The bathroom door opened and Dagbert Endless looked in. Charlie noticed that he was shaking and

wondered if they would soon be engulfed in one of Dagbert's underwater illusions.

Dagbert stepped into the bathroom, closed the door softly behind him and came to sit beside Charlie. There was a long silence while Charlie and Fidelio tried to think what to say. The whiff of fish that usually hung about Dagbert had been replaced by the tang of seaweed; it was a raw, melancholy scent.

After several silent seconds had elapsed, Dagbert said, 'I'm sorry.'

Charlie turned to look at him. In the faint light from the window, Dagbert appeared to be a bluish-green.

'Are you saying that you're sorry about Tancred?' asked Fidelio.

Dagbert nodded. 'About Tancred and about the things my father is going to do. He's brought his Sea Globe here and means to drown your parents with it, Charlie.'

Charlie said, 'I know.'

'You do?' Dagbert seemed surprised. 'I . . . I'm sorry. If I could stop him I would, but I'm not strong enough yet. And if I tried without the sea-gold charms, the globe would swallow me. My father's often warned me that would happen.'

'And if you had the charms?' asked Fidelio. 'Could you destroy the Sea Globe then?'

Dagbert shrugged, and then he said, 'I'm not like *them*, you know. I'm not with Manfred and Joshua and the Bloors.'

'I didn't think you were,' said Charlie quietly.

'Sometimes I can't help . . . doing what I do,' Dagbert continued in a desperate voice. 'I just find myself getting angry or – or scared, and the world turns to water all around me.'

'Look, Dagbert,' Charlie said. 'I happen to know that Joshua is going to try and find your sea-gold charms, wherever you've hidden them. I'll do everything I can to stop him but – I might not be able to.'

'They're –' Dagbert began.

'Don't tell me,' said Charlie sharply. 'Manfred might try and get it out of me.'

'OK.'

Fidelio suggested that they should go to bed before they froze to death. The bathrooms in Bloor's Academy were the coldest rooms in the building.

Charlie woke up feeling that it was going to be a rather

difficult day. One look at Dagbert's troubled face reminded him that he would have to watch Joshua Tilpin's every move. It wouldn't be easy. Joshua was in the first year, Charlie in the second. Joshua took art, not music. He ate in a different canteen, changed his shoes in a different cloakroom and had Assembly with another group. Charlie could only hope that Dagbert had hidden the charms outside.

Dagbert had done just that. Joshua made his move during the first break. He had been practising with some of his mother's jewellery, and was now fairly confident that he could attract gold. But where to start? He had to have some hint of where the sea-gold charms might be.

In the end it was Dagbert who gave the game away. He was lost without the charms, and so anxious about their safety he began to gravitate towards them.

Snow lying on the field had been turned to a muddy slush by three hundred pairs of feet. But there were still some children who could not give up a last attempt at making snowballs. Joshua and the Branko twins were among them. But while he collected handfuls of slopping ice, Joshua was watching Dagbert out of the corner of his eye.

Charlie was kicking a football about with Emma and Fidelio. Emma looked depressed. Olivia was nowhere to be seen. Charlie made a half-turn to see if Joshua was still with the Branko twins, and found that he wasn't. So where was he?

'Where's Joshua?' Charlie shouted.

Fidelio pointed to a small figure walking stealthily up to the castle.

'OK. I'm off,' said Charlie.

'I'll come with you,' Fidelio offered.

Charlie shook his head. 'Better not. It'll look too obvious.'

'What's going on?' Emma asked irritably.

Fidelio mouthed, 'Tell you in a minute.'

Trying to look casual, but putting on speed whenever he thought no one was looking, Charlie hurried after Joshua. He saw him disappear under the great red arch, waited a few seconds and then dashed after him. Joshua had vanished again. Charlie found himself staring at the five small arches set into a stone wall, all of them leading into the ruin. Charlie had tried each one before. He knew that the central arch led straight into the castle, while beyond the others

four long tunnels twisted their way into the more obscure parts of the ruin. But which route had Dagbert and Joshua taken?

A scream came echoing up the tunnel on the far left. Charlie groaned. Dagbert had chosen the most difficult way in. There was nothing for it but to follow him. As Charlie plunged into the tunnel there was another scream, this one more terrible than the last. It was a scream of terror and despair.

Slipping and sliding down the wet, musty tunnel, Charlie groped desperately for the wall to steady himself, but the bricks were slimy with mildew and he slithered on, now falling to his knees, now on all fours. He emerged, at last, on to a snow-covered bank. Tall trees either side of him sighed in a wind that had suddenly blown up, filled with the scent of the sea.

Below Charlie, in a patch of muddy snow, Dagbert and Joshua were fighting round a large black rock. Lying on its smooth surface were the seven sea-gold charms. Dagbert must have hidden them beneath the rock, Charlie realised, but Joshua had drawn them out of their hiding place.

Charlie slid down the bank. As he reached the

bottom, Joshua suddenly gave Dagbert a shove and he fell back into the snow.

'Mine!' cried Joshua, holding up his hand, and the golden charms floated over to him. He closed his fist over them and began to run up the bank.

'No you don't!' Charlie shouted, grabbing Joshua's ankle.

Down he came, with a yell of pain.

'Drop those charms, Joshua Tilpin,' said Charlie, clinging to Joshua. 'They're not yours.'

'And they're not yours either,' screamed Joshua. 'Get off me, Charlie Bone.' He kicked out with his other foot, catching Charlie on the nose. Blood poured into Charlie's mouth, and he let go of Joshua's ankle.

Dagbert rushed at Joshua and seized his hands. He tore at the puny fingers and prised them open, but the charms stuck to Joshua's palms like limpets.

'Give them to me!' cried Dagbert, peeling the fish off Joshua's skin, while the small boy writhed like an eel.

Charlie straightened up and wiped his nose on his sleeve. Blood was now dripping on to his sweater. Dagbert tore a crab from Joshua's open palm, but the fish-boy was beginning to shake like a leaf.

'I'll get the rest,' Charlie told Dagbert. 'Take a break!'

Dagbert rolled on to his back, clutching the two charms. Joshua began to crawl up the bank again, and Charlie was about to grab him when the air seemed to shiver and a flash of light streamed over their heads, striking the earth with an ear-splitting twang.

A long sword rocked to and fro, its tip stuck fast in the earth, an inch from Charlie's hand.

'Get thee gone, wretched boys,' said a voice. 'Or suffer the wrath of my sword.'

Charlie turned his head, very slowly, afraid of what he would see. And there was Ashkelan Kapaldi, standing on the black rock, his hands on his hips and on his face the mocking smile of his portrait.

'Give me thy charms, Dagbert Endless,' said Ashkelan, holding out a gloved hand.

Dagbert shook his head and clutched the two charms to his chest.

Ashkelan lost his smile. ''Tis a pity,' he sighed. 'Sword, do thy work.'

'Dagbert!' cried Charlie as the sword flipped out of the earth and came at Dagbert, its deadly tip pointing at his heart. Dagbert jumped back, but the sword

followed him. Charlie couldn't bear to look. He was about to close his eyes when, in a blaze of light, a white horse leapt out of the trees and another sword, held by a knight in shining armour, caught the lethal weapon and tossed it sideways.

'Vile, cursed, hateful knight!' screamed Ashkelan. 'Thou shalt not have it thy way.'

Ashkelan's sword swung in an arc and sliced the air with whining, hissing strokes. It came at the knight's arm, but the white mare flew sideways.

The three boys sat on the bank, petrified and entranced, while the knight, his red plume flying and his cloak filling like a scarlet cloud, struck and parried the enchanted sword. Ashkelan stood on the rock, uttering a stream of incomprehensible commands, but suddenly he fell silent, waiting for his sword to find a position from where it could strike a fatal blow.

The white mare paced between Ashkelan and the bank, while the enchanted sword hovered at the edge of the trees, above the boys. Joshua was so frightened he loosened his grip and the five remaining charms trickled out of his hand.

'The charms,' Charlie whispered.

Dagbert grabbed them.

Joshua yelled and caught Dagbert's hand.

As the Red Knight turned to look at them, Ashkelan shrieked a command and the sword came flying at the knight's throat. With a warning scream, the horse reared up, tilting the knight out of harm's way. The sword swept past her thrashing hoofs and entered Ashkelan's chest, just above the leather belt that held his scabbard. The swordsman fell back with a moan, the sword buried deep in his heart.

The knight removed his gauntlet and laid a bare hand on the white mare's neck, calming her instantly. He turned his head and Charlie found himself staring at the dark holes in the blank, featureless helmet. Whose eyes were looking out at him? he wondered. Was the face behind the steel mask known to him?

The knight sheathed his sword and lifted his hand, briefly, in farewell. The horse whinnied and they left the scene, trotting quickly into the dense wood that filled the ruin.

For a moment the three boys were too stunned to speak, and then Charlie cried, 'Run, Dagbert, run!'

The roaring wave

Dagbert ran. No one knew where. He wasn't seen for the rest of the day.

Charlie left Joshua sitting on the snowy bank, cradling his hand and whimpering, 'Mum, Mum, Mum.'

As Charlie made his way back to the school, he began to wonder who would be blamed for the death of Ashkelan Kapaldi. But he's dead already, Charlie told himself, and he wondered how they would get Ashkelan back into his portrait.

Only Joshua saw what really happened to the swordsman's body. He was rubbing his eyes with a muddy fist and at first he couldn't quite believe what he was seeing. A snowy mist began to seep into the glade,

covering the broken walls, burying the trees and seeping round the black rock. The mist was filled with the sounds of battle: steel on steel, leather creaking, hoofs thundering, men screaming and cannons booming.

Joshua put his hands over his ears and watched in disbelief as the sword lifted itself out of Ashkelan's chest and lay down beside him. And then his body was raised from the rock – and vanished.

Joshua stopped whimpering. His mouth fell open and his eyes widened. 'Gone!' he murmured. 'How?'

Joshua didn't know that, by a strange coincidence, Ashkelan Kapaldi met his second death in exactly the same way that he had met his first. He had, in fact, been killed by his own sword during the Battle of Edgehill in 1642. The sword didn't mean to kill its master, of course. It was just unfortunate that Ashkelan happened to be in its way both times.

When he got back to the school Charlie tried to clean himself up in the blue cloakroom. He remembered that bloodstains could be removed with cold water, but he didn't make a very good job of it. Luckily, his cape covered most of his sweater, and his

nose had stopped bleeding by the time he reached Madame Tessier's classroom.

'What happened?' whispered Fidelio as Charlie took the desk beside him.

'Tell you later,' said Charlie.

'Ssssssh!' commanded Madame Tessier. 'Regardez vos livres!'

Charlie didn't get another chance to talk to Fidelio until lunchtime. Gabriel carried his bowl of soup over to their table, just as Charlie was describing the battle in the ruin. When he had finished, Gabriel looked very excited.

'I knew it!' he exclaimed.

Several children looked in their direction and Fidelio said, 'Keep your voice down, Gabe.'

Lowering his voice, Gabriel said, 'I took a good look at Ashkelan's portrait when I passed it, and do you know, I could swear I saw a kind of light in his eyes that wasn't there while he was "out".'

'He's back where he belongs now,' said Charlie grimly.

Fidelio looked round the canteen. 'Where's Dagbert?' he said. 'He should have been in French.'

Charlie frowned. 'I'm sure he's got all his charms. But he's at risk now. Mrs Tilpin's going to be furious. I hope he's somewhere safe.'

'That sounds a bit odd, coming from you,' Gabriel remarked.

Charlie stared into his bowl of soup. 'He needs our help,' he said.

The storm began when Mr Pope was halfway through a History test. The teacher's heavy-jowled face was always an angry shade of red. Even when he wasn't furious, he was cross. The windows in his classroom fitted very badly and on windy days their constant rattle drove Mr Pope into a frenzy. He would thump his desk and roar out his questions, confusing his class and even himself.

The wind had blown up from nowhere. One minute the air was calm, the next, hail was beating on the windowpanes, thunderclaps reverberated through the building and the draught from the ill-fitting windows whipped spitefully round everyone's legs.

'How am I supposed to teach in a storm like this?' screeched Mr Pope. 'I'm going to stop this test and go home if it continues.'

Realising that he'd said something silly because, of course, no one would have minded if he went home, Mr Pope muttered, 'I suppose you've all heard about the storms at sea? No, I suppose you haven't.' (Televisions and radios were only allowed in the sixth form.) 'Well, I shall enlighten you.' There was another deafening clap of thunder, and Mr Pope looked up to heaven. When the thunder had rumbled away, he said, 'Severe weather in the southern hemisphere has caused havoc on the coasts. Many drowned. Ships wrecked. Boats lost.' His last words were shouted above another violent rumble.

Charlie put up his hand.

'What is it, Charlie Bone?' Mr Pope asked irritably.

'Did you say boats, sir?' asked Charlie.

'Yes, *boats*! Are you deaf?' Mr Pope bellowed. 'The storms have been appalling. Waves a hundred feet high. Wouldn't fancy being in a boat. They don't stand a chance.' He nodded at the rattling window. 'Mind you, this is just a breeze compared with the tempests out at sea. But that's no consolation when you've GOT TO TEACH HISTORY TO A GROUP OF NITWITS!' And with that Mr Pope gathered up his

books and strode out of the classroom, banging the door behind him.

As soon as the teacher had gone, Simon Hawke leapt up from his desk, yawned, stretched and said, 'We've got twenty minutes before the next lesson. Let's do some push-ups.'

Boys groaned and girls made scornful remarks. Undeterred, cheerful Simon spread himself on the floor and began to do his exercises.

Fidelio leant over to Charlie saying, 'Let's go.'

They left the classroom together. Their next lesson was music. Fidelio had violin with Mr O'Connor. Charlie was due to see Señor Alvaro. With twenty minutes to spare they decided to go and visit Cook. They hurried across the hall and along the corridor of portraits, but Charlie slowed down and then stopped altogether beside the portrait of Ashkelan Kapaldi. He leaned closer, staring at the eyes. 'I can't see that it's changed,' he said.

Fidelio grabbed the back of his cape. 'You'll be in there with him if you don't look out,' he said. 'Don't forget, Gabe's kind of clairvoyant. Come on, we've only got fifteen minutes now.'

They had almost reached the blue canteen when Dr Saltweather came striding out and asked them what they were doing. Fidelio explained that Mr Pope couldn't teach in a storm. The music master smiled. 'If he thinks this is bad, he should try a bit of sea-fishing,' he said, and then he glanced at Charlie.

'Is it really that bad?' asked Charlie.

Dr Saltweather nodded. 'I'm afraid it is, Charlie.'

Charlie swallowed. He could taste the tomato soup he'd had for lunch, and hoped he wasn't going to be sick. 'My parents are whale-watching, sir.'

'I know, Charlie,' said the music master.

'D'you think –'

Fidelio broke in, saying, 'Do you know about the Sea Globe, sir?'

Charlie stared at Fidelio, surprised that he had mentioned the Sea Globe to a master. Dr Saltweather frowned for a moment, then he said, 'I have heard that it is here.'

'And do you believe that Lord Grimwald can control the oceans with it?' Charlie blurted out.

Dr Saltweather took a deep breath before saying, 'How could I not believe, Charlie? Cook is my friend,'

and he marched off down the corridor, his hands clasped behind his back and his big head bent.

'Can you help, sir?' Charlie called after him. 'Can you stop him?'

Dr Saltweather murmured softly in reply, and then turned into the hall.

Charlie clutched Fidelio's arm. 'What did he say? Did you hear?'

Fidelio's musical ear had picked up the music master's rueful answer. 'I think he said, "Only the son can do that."'

'He means Dagbert,' said Charlie, 'and Dagbert will do it.'

'What makes you think that?'

Charlie shrugged. 'We have to find him, Fido.'

But where to look?

Charlie had an idea, but he had to wait until lessons were over before he could find out if he was right. Fidelio had orchestra practice, but he offered to give it up to help his friend. Charlie insisted that it was only a hunch and one pair of eyes was enough to find someone.

'So where are you going?' asked Fidelio.

'The Music Tower,' Charlie told him.

It was called the Music Tower because once Charlie's father had taught piano in the room at the very top. To reach it, Charlie had to go down the same dark passage that led to the ballroom. The Music Tower was out of bounds now, and Charlie had to choose the right moment to make a dash for the small door into the passage. He waited in the blue cloakroom while shoes were changed, hands washed, toilets flushed and wet capes shaken out.

'You OK, Charlie?' Gabriel asked.

Charlie nodded. 'I'm going to look for Dagbert,' he whispered.

'Want any help?'

'Not yet.'

'OK.' Gabriel left the cloakroom murmuring to himself, 'But I'm going to make sure you're not alone.'

Gabriel was the last person to leave the cloakroom. When he had gone Charlie peeped into the hall. It appeared to be deserted so he made a dash for the tower door. Twisting the heavy bronze handle, he pulled open the door and slipped into the passage. At that very moment Dorcas Loom left the green cloakroom. She

screwed up her eyes and stared at the closing door. If she was not mistaken she had just seen Charlie Bone going into the Music Tower. Someone would have to be informed.

Unaware that he'd been spotted, Charlie hurried down the passage. When he came to the ballroom doors he stopped and noted that the heavy bolt at the top had been drawn back. He put his ear to the door. A faint sound reached him: the swish and splash of water, the boom of giant waves rising and falling. And then another sound. A curious humming. Lord Grimwald was humming to the tune of his own drowning seas. Charlie stepped away from the door as though he'd been stung. He clenched his fists, powerless to stop the awful events that Lord Grimwald had set in motion. As he turned to run up the passage, a figure appeared in the small circular room at the end.

'Dagbert.' Charlie spoke in a hoarse whisper. 'Where have you been?'

'Thinking,' Dagbert replied. 'I've got to stop him.' He came towards Charlie, holding the sea-gold charms in both hands, as though he was afraid that he might drop them.

'How will you do it?' asked Charlie. 'The curse, Dagbert – your father will try and overwhelm you.'

'Yes,' Dagbert agreed. 'But I have to make an attempt. No one else can stop him, and your parents will drown, Charlie.'

'They may have drowned already,' said Charlie. He was surprised to find that he wanted to give Dagbert a chance to avoid the confrontation with Lord Grimwald.

But Dagbert was determined. 'You saved my sea-gold charms, and they will stop him. My mother would have wanted it.'

The boys stood side by side, facing the ballroom doors.

'I'm coming with you,' said Charlie as Dagbert pushed open one of the tall doors.

Charlie had expected to see a sphere of rolling water, but the sight of the huge globe took his breath away. The glass panels had been removed and the unbridled waves now swept out in gigantic arcs that splashed against the high ceiling.

Lord Grimwald was standing with his back to the boys, but turned as soon as they entered. He seemed to be expecting them. 'Dagbert,' he said. 'Welcome. I see you have brought a friend.'

Dagbert remained silent. He approached the globe, the charms still held firmly in both hands. Charlie followed, wondering what Dagbert would do.

Lord Grimwald stared at his son's hands and his eyes narrowed. 'Give me the charms,' he commanded. His voice was soft but his face was as hard as stone.

Dagbert clasped the charms more tightly. He stepped towards the globe and Charlie followed. Sea spray flew in their faces and soaked their hair.

'Give them to me!' Lord Grimwald's mouth was clenched in a terrible smile. He held out his hand.

Dagbert shook his head.

'Don't come any closer,' his father warned him. 'If you harm the globe it will destroy you.'

All at once Charlie knew what Dagbert intended to do. He would throw the golden charms into the sea. Would this calm the giant waves all over the world? Without his mother's protection, Dagbert would die.

'Give them to me,' Lord Grimwald demanded, seizing his son's clasped hands.

'No!' cried Dagbert. He fell to his knees, his body hunched over the precious charms.

Snarling with fury, the Lord of the Oceans raised his

arm and a wall of water curled out from the globe. With an angry roar it rose to the ceiling and then began to fall. Charlie found himself enclosed in a tunnel of thundering black water. He fell to his knees beside Dagbert and waited for the roaring wave to crush them. Just before it smothered them, the sound of drums broke through the boom of water. And then Charlie was beaten down by the weight of the wave. He couldn't breathe, his lungs were bursting. He closed his eyes, his head full of shrieking sounds.

And then the weight of water was gone and he opened his eyes. He was lying in a pool of water with Dagbert's blue fist only inches from his face. A golden fish floated through Dagbert's fingers and Charlie grabbed it before it could be washed away. Black boots splashed towards him. One came down hard on Charlie's hand.

'Aaaah!' Charlie heard his muffled scream through the thunder of drums. The boot lifted from his fingers and Charlie rolled on to his back, still clutching the fish. Dagbert lay beside him; his eyes were closed, his face blue and lifeless. His hands were empty.

'Dagbert!' Charlie screamed, shaking the limp arm.

Dagbert didn't move.

The drumbeats grew louder. Faster. Deeper. They filled the air with their threatening rhythm. Charlie sat up and rubbed his eyes. Lord Grimwald stood less than two metres in front of him. His back was towards Charlie, his arms spread wide.

The blue sea-light had been replaced by the red and gold of leaping flames. Charlie rose shakily to his feet. Now he could see them: Lysander's spirit ancestors. Tall, dark figures lined the walls. There was not a hand's width between them. Gold adorned their necks and arms, their robes were white, their belts coloured like rainbows. Each man held a spear in one hand, a flaming torch in the other.

The drumming came from figures on the stage. Standing two rows deep they beat their drums with feverish intensity, making the chandelier crystals chime like a thousand tiny bells.

Lysander moved so fast about the great room that Charlie could only catch a glimpse of his dark face and flashing eyes. The graceful whirl of his arms caused his cape to move through the air like a spinning green circle.

Charlie stepped away from the Sea Globe. Now he

could see Lord Grimwald's face. It was grey with fury and terror. He lurched from side to side, his arms outstretched protectively as he backed towards his precious globe.

The lines of warriors began to advance. Closer and closer to the globe. Charlie could feel the heat of their torches. Clouds of steam rose from the globe and the spirits moved closer still. For a moment Charlie panicked. He didn't know where to go. They were almost upon him, their dark, impassive faces only inches away. And then they were flowing either side of him, and he could taste the fire, and smell the pungent scent of their robes.

They encircled the globe. Closer and closer. Their ranks were four men deep now, as the circle became small. And still Lysander whirled, and still the drums beat.

Charlie could no longer see Lord Grimwald. He was trapped in the circle of warriors. They were so densely packed their torches had become a ring of fire. There was a sudden, awful scream as the Lord of the Oceans was forced into the very seas that he had used to drown so many.

The scream became a gurgle, the gurgle a desperate

thrashing, as the Sea Globe churned and boiled and swallowed its master.

Above the rows of spears and torches, Charlie could see the top of the globe. The blue water had turned a dull grey; it was now more steam than water. The patches of brown land were cracking and shrinking. Slowly the globe began to sink. Charlie dropped to his knees, desperate to see what became of it. Through the lines of white robes he glimpsed steaming oceans and scorching land. The Sea Globe was dwindling, sinking and boiling away.

Minutes after Lord Grimwald's scream, the spirit ancestors still held their lines, and then, slowly, they began to move back. Once more Charlie felt them drift past him. The flames of their long torches were dying now, their white robes fading into clouds of steam. Charlie couldn't say when the drums stopped, or when the warriors vanished, because he was staring at the Sea Globe, or rather at the space it had occupied. There was nothing there – except . . .

A small glass sphere, slightly larger than a tennis ball, rocked gently to and fro in a pool of water. Dagbert lay beside it.

Charlie felt a hand on his shoulder, and he looked up into Lysander's grave face.

'You finished it,' Charlie said, hardly able to believe what he had seen.

'There was no other way,' said Lysander. He nodded at Dagbert. 'But perhaps it was too late for him.'

Charlie got up and ran over to Dagbert. His face looked utterly lifeless. And then, suddenly, his eyelids fluttered and his strange arctic eyes stared up at Charlie. 'Am I alive?' he croaked.

'*You* are,' Charlie said, helping Dagbert to his feet. He pressed the golden fish into his palm and then, seeing the crabs and the sea urchin floating at the edge of the pool, he scooped them up and gave them to Dagbert, saying, 'You're safe now.'

Dagbert thrust them into his pocket and then stood swaying slightly as he gazed around the ballroom. 'Where is it?' he said, turning a full circle and looking down at the water round his feet. 'Where's the Sea Globe?'

Lysander picked up the small blue–green sphere. He shook it free of water and handed it to Dagbert. 'I think you'll find that this is it,' he said.

Dagbert looked utterly bemused. He stared at the tiny globe and then at Lysander. 'How did it . . .?' he breathed, and then, 'Where's my father?'

'The globe swallowed him,' said Charlie in a matter-of-fact voice. There didn't seem to be any other way to tell a boy that he was holding his father in his hand.

Dagbert grimaced. 'Then he's . . .?' He looked at the globe.

'In there,' said Charlie.

Dagbert shook the globe and turned it upside down, as though he half expected a tiny version of his father to drop into the puddle. Sparkling sea-spray trickled slowly from the top to the bottom, but nothing fell out of the sphere.

'It's quite pretty,' Charlie remarked. 'Like one of those snowstorms in a glass snow globe.'

'A sea-storm,' Dagbert murmured.

Lysander took Dagbert by the shoulder and nudged him towards the doors. 'You can't stay here, Dagbert,' he warned him. 'The Bloors will be furious that Lord Grimwald and his globe have gone. We'll get you out, but then it's up to you.'

'Where will I go?' Dagbert asked desperately. 'I don't

know anyone in the city. I have no family.'

Where could Dagbert go? Lysander and Charlie realised that he wouldn't be safe in the fish shop where he stayed at weekends. The Pets' Café was closed and he couldn't go to Charlie's house while Grandma Bone was there.

'I know!' cried Charlie. 'The Kettle Shop. It's only a few doors up from the fish shop where you've been staying.'

Lysander looked doubtful. 'It's in Piminy Street, Charlie. A nest of vipers if I may say so.'

'I know, I know, but Mrs Kettle is very strong,' Charlie argued. 'She's withstood them all so far. And I can't think of anywhere else right now.'

For a moment Lysander looked thoughtful. He stroked his chin in a manner reminiscent of his father, Judge Sage, when he was passing judgement. But whatever objection had passed through Lysander's mind, he quickly banished it and agreed with Charlie. 'Tell her you've come from us,' he said. 'Show her the globe.'

'Tell her,' Charlie hesitated. 'Say "Matilda" and she'll know you're with us now.'

Lysander gave Charlie a questioning look and

Dagbert said, 'Who's Matilda?'

'Never mind,' said Charlie, going pink. 'Just say it.'

'OK.'

They took Dagbert down the passage and across the hall to the garden door. There was no one about and they realised that the bell for supper must have rung. The entire school was in the underground dining hall.

'How shall I get out?' Dagbert looked utterly exhausted. Pale and frightened, he stepped into the garden and looked back at Charlie.

Charlie told him where to climb the wall. He hoped the twisted vines of ivy would still show signs of his own speedy clambering.

'Hurry, Dagbert,' urged Lysander.

They watched Dagbert run towards the trees, and then Lysander closed the door.

As they hastened across the hall, someone came out of the passage leading to the ballroom.

'Very impressive, Lysander Sage,' Manfred said through clenched teeth. His whole frame shook with fury; fury at his own cowardice, for he'd been unable to screw up enough courage to face Lysander's spirit ancestors.

'But you're too late,' Manfred went on, enraged by Lysander's look of disdain. 'Charlie's parents will never come home now.' And he gave Charlie a terrible smile.

A perplexing postcard

Charlie watched Manfred step back into the passage and swiftly close the door.

'It can't be true, Sander. Can it?' said Charlie.

Lysander put an arm round his shoulders. 'You mustn't let yourself believe it, Charlie. There's no proof. Your parents might have been safe on shore when the storm blew up.'

'Yes,' said Charlie desperately. His head was spinning. He wanted to run home to Maisie and Uncle Paton. But would they know the truth?

When Lysander steered him down the corridor of portraits he suddenly remembered the danger they were in. Someone was going to have to pay for the Sea Globe's

destruction, and the end of Lord Grimwald.

Lysander, sensing what Charlie was thinking, said calmly, 'Don't worry. You've done nothing wrong, Charlie. *I* destroyed the globe and the Bloors can't touch me. They're too afraid of my ancestors.'

No one seemed to notice their late arrival in the dining hall. The staff sat at a table on a raised platform at the end of the hall. From here they could keep an eye on the tables below them. But today they were all too keen on their suppers to notice Lysander and Charlie slip stealthily into the hall.

Charlie quickly cast an eye over the three tables running the length of the hall. On the left, blue-caped music students chattered over their stew. No one looked in his direction, until Fidelio gave him a wave. As he made his way over to Fidelio Charlie noticed Olivia, sitting at the centre table, with a Branko twin on either side of her. Lysander went to the Art table where Emma was sitting several places away from Dorcas and Joshua, whose left hand was all bandaged up.

'What happened, Charlie?' Fidelio asked in a low voice, as Charlie squeezed on to the bench beside him.

'Tell you later,' said Charlie, and then whispered into

his friend's ear, 'Lysander destroyed the Sea Globe – and Lord Grimwald!'

'WHAT?' Fidelio stared at Charlie in disbelief.

At that moment, Weedon appeared through one of the doors behind the staff table. He moved quickly to Dr Bloor's side and, bending over his shoulder, said a few words. Dr Bloor leapt up, pushing over his heavy chair, so that it fell to the floor with a loud bang.

The other teachers stared at him and all the children watched the staff table expectantly. Dr Bloor rushed out, followed by Weedon. An excited shouting and chattering broke out. Prefects hushed and shushed in vain. Eventually Dr Saltweather stood up and clapped his hands. The hall fell silent. Dr Saltweather commanded a great deal of respect. 'Calm yourselves!' he bellowed. 'Just because the headmaster has left the room, it doesn't mean that you can squeal like animals. Lower your voices, please.'

There was a moment's hush and then the chatter was resumed on a quieter note.

Gabriel, sitting opposite Charlie, leant over the table and asked, 'Lysander found you then, Charlie? What happened?'

'Thanks for telling Lysander, Gabe. He saved my life and Dagbert's.'

'Dagbert's?' Gabriel frowned.

'Let's talk later,' said Fidelio in a warning voice. Several children were already looking at Charlie.

Gabriel glanced at the inquisitive faces and said, 'OK.'

After supper Charlie headed for the blue cloakroom with Fidelio and Gabriel following close behind. They had five minutes before they would be expected to start their homework. Almost without pausing for breath, Charlie told his friends what had happened in the ballroom.

For a moment they were too stunned to speak, and then Gabriel said slowly, 'When I told Lysander you were going to the Music Tower I never imagined . . . I mean I just knew he was the only one who could help you.'

'Weedon must have told Dr Bloor,' said Fidelio. 'No wonder he rushed out.'

'Manfred saw it all,' Charlie told them.

His friends frowned at him and Fidelio said, 'Didn't he try and stop it?'

'Stop Lysander?' Charlie found that the cold chill of

Manfred's words had suddenly lifted and he felt irrationally cheerful. 'Nothing can stop Lysander.'

Gabriel grinned. 'Course not,' he agreed.

Charlie was reluctant to spoil their positive mood, so didn't mention Manfred's dreadful prediction.

The three boys left the cloakroom, and while Fidelio hurried to his classroom, Charlie and Gabriel made their way up to the King's Room. Just before they went in, Gabriel said, 'Charlie, I forgot to tell you. I saw Cook after lunch. She's got something for you.'

'What?'

Gabriel rubbed his head. 'Postcard I think she said.'

'A postcard? What . . . ?'Charlie felt something sharp poke into the small of his back and he swung round to see Joshua holding a pencil in his bandaged hand.

'Are you going in or not?' asked Joshua sullenly.

Without replying, Charlie opened the door and Joshua pushed past him.

It was a surprise to see Manfred sitting in his usual place, as if nothing had happened. He gave Charlie a cold glance when he came in; otherwise there was nothing in his manner to suggest that he had seen the giant Sea Globe swallow its master, and then

disintegrate. For a moment Charlie wondered if this was because the Bloors had no further use for the globe. If Lyell Bone had really drowned, then the pearl-inlaid box would never be found. But Charlie refused to accept this. He had decided that as long as he kept believing his parents would come home, then nothing could prevent them.

A quiet snuffle beside him made Charlie aware that Emma was dabbing her nose. He hadn't spoken to her all day and felt guilty for leaving her out of things. Nudging her gently he whispered, 'See you in the Art Room later, Em.'

Emma nodded and smiled, and then, while Manfred's head was bent over his book, she whispered back, 'It's the waistcoat,' and she looked straight at Olivia on the other side of the table.

Charlie frowned. He didn't have a chance to ask Emma what she had meant because Manfred was glaring at him again. So was Olivia. She wasn't herself, he could see that. Her skin was dull and dark circles ringed her eyes. As she turned the pages of her book he caught a glimpse of the glittery thing she wore beneath her cape. Of course – a waistcoat!

After homework Charlie made straight for the Art Room. Gabriel and Lysander stayed behind to finish some work and Charlie found that he was being followed by a group of girls. He looked back and saw Dorcas, the twins and Olivia. They stopped at the bottom of the staircase that led up to the girls' dormitories, and when Charlie continued on to the Art Room, he could feel their eyes on him.

The Art Room was at the end of the passage leading to Charlie's dormitory, so he hoped the girls wouldn't guess where he was heading. He quickly glanced over his shoulder and, seeing that the girls had gone, made a dash to the end of the passage and into a large room with long windows overlooking the garden. The place was crammed with easels and canvases and Charlie quickly switched on one of the lights in case he tripped over. It was easy for someone to hide behind one of the tall easels and, for a moment, he wasn't quite sure if he was alone. 'Emma?' he called softly.

There was no reply so Charlie walked round the easels towards the dark windows. He had to pass a trapdoor covering the spiral staircase that led down to the Sculpture Room The room where Dagbert

had tried to drown Tancred. Or had he?

Charlie reached the windows and peered out into the misty garden. Thick cloud obscured the moon and stars and he could see nothing beyond a row of stone statues directly beneath him. Old Ezekiel had a fondness for garden ornaments, and groups of figures, human and animal, had been placed about the grounds. Sometimes you would come upon a single statue in an unexpected place, and the grey form, appearing above shadowy bushes, could give you quite a fright.

'Charlie!' came a whisper.

'Em?' said Charlie.

Emma came tiptoeing towards him. 'Come away from the window,' she said. 'Someone might see you from the garden.'

Charlie hadn't thought of this. He backed behind a group of easels and found Emma crouching on the floor. She was obviously very nervous.

'What's been happening, Charlie?' She sounded aggrieved. 'You were late for supper, your sweater's got blood on it and Dagbert Endless has disappeared.'

Charlie hesitated. Emma looked so scared he

wondered how he could tell her about his dangerous day without making her even more fearful.

'Charlie, please, what's been happening?' she begged.

So Charlie told her. He tried his best to speak calmly when he described the fight with Ashkelan Kapaldi, but he failed to keep the terror out of his voice when he relived the drowning sensation he felt as the roaring wave swept over him, and he could hardly contain his excitement when he recounted the astonishing shrinking of the Sea Globe.

Charlie needn't have worried. By the time he had finished, Emma's spirits had risen considerably. In fact, she looked almost cheerful. 'Oh, Charlie, perhaps we are winning after all,' she said happily. 'I was feeling so gloomy about everything, but now I believe we stand a chance, and if I can get that awful waistcoat away from Olivia, she'll be her old self again.'

'I saw something glittering under her cape,' said Charlie. 'So that's the waistcoat that you reckon has changed her?'

'I'm sure of it. I tried to get it away from her when she was changing in the bathroom, but she nearly tore my hand off.'

'Hmm.' Charlie scratched his wiry hair. 'Take a good look at that waistcoat,' he said. 'Try and memorise every stitch and sequin. Then come round to my place on Friday night. Alice Angel is there.'

'Alice!' Emma clapped her hands delightedly. 'Oh, Alice can save Liv, I know it.'

A voice suddenly cut across the room. 'Charlie, are you there? Matron is on the warpath.'

Charlie and Emma jumped up. Fidelio was standing by the door, his hand on the light switch. 'Come on, quick,' he said, turning off the light.

They ran for the door and as soon as they were through, Fidelio closed it quickly behind them. When the boys reached their dormitory, Emma kept running towards the next staircase.

'Where *is* Matron?' Charlie whispered.

'In the bathroom,' Fidelio told him. 'Rupe Small has lost his toothbrush, and Matron's waiting for him to find it.'

Charlie grinned. But when they got into the dormitory, they found that the toothbrush had been found and Matron, alias Lucretia Yewbeam, was standing at the end of Charlie's bed with her hands on

her hips. 'Where have you been?' she demanded as Charlie walked in.

'Working,' lied Charlie. 'Mr Pope gave me extra homework.'

The lie worked. Charlie's great-aunt gave a nasty smirk and said, 'Serves you right.' He could only hope that she didn't mention the extra homework to Mr Pope.

From the other end of the dormitory, Simon Hawke piped up, 'Dagbert Endless isn't here.'

'No,' the matron said flatly and left the room.

'Odd,' said Simon. 'She doesn't seem bothered about the fish-boy. Does anyone know where he is?'

'Probably gone home,' said Bragger Braine.

'Can't have,' argued Simon. 'We're only halfway through the week.'

'Haven't you noticed?' Bragger plumped up his pillow. 'Lots of kids have left.'

Charlie went to the bathroom. What did Bragger mean? No one ever left Bloor's Academy halfway through the week. It wasn't allowed. He took a long time brushing his teeth and combing his impossible hair. By the time he left the bathroom, the lights were out and some of the boys were already asleep.

Charlie didn't even expect to sleep. Scenes from his extraordinary day kept chasing each other through his head. One moment he felt elated, the next full of doubt. And then he remembered the postcard. How could he possibly sleep when news of his parents might be only a few floors beneath them. Swinging his feet to the floor, he shuffled into his slippers and put on his dressing gown. Everyone brought a torch to school and although the battery in Charlie's was running low, it gave him enough light to see his way down the unlit passage to the landing.

Here was the tricky bit. A small light was always left burning in the hall, and at any moment a member of staff could walk through one of the doors opening on to the hall, and see Charlie. There was nothing for it but to hurry and hope. Taking a deep breath, Charlie tiptoed down the creaking stairs as fast as he could. Without pausing to look back, he flew along the corridor of portraits to the blue canteen. Raised voices could be heard, coming from the direction of the green canteen. Mr and Mrs Weedon arguing again, thought Charlie. He quickly slipped into the blue canteen and then into the kitchen beyond.

It was pitch dark in the kitchen; a strong smell of cooked cabbage filled Charlie's nostrils and he pinched his nose. He hadn't visited Cook's apartment for some time, but shining his torch across the rows of cupboards, he quickly recognised Cook's entrance. He always felt slightly apprehensive when he opened this door, because if anyone discovered Cook's secret she would be banished from the Academy. The Bloors believed she slept in a cold little room in the East Wing, and were completely unaware of the wonderful labyrinth beneath the building.

Charlie stepped into the cupboard and, closing one door behind him, opened the other. Now he was in the softly lit passage that led to the next cupboard, and then into Cook's room.

'My heavens!' cried Cook as Charlie walked out of the cupboard at the end of her room. 'What are you doing here, Charlie Bone?'

'The postcard,' said Charlie. 'Gabriel said you had a postcard for me.'

'So I have,' said Cook. 'But you could have waited until tomorrow.'

'I couldn't,' said Charlie. 'I'm sorry, but I had to know what my parents had written.'

'Ah, you guessed. Yes, Maisie gave me the card when we met at our usual time in the greengrocer's. Luckily your other grandma didn't see it.' Cook reached for the postcard that sat on a shelf above her stove. 'Sit down and read,' she said, 'while I make a cup of cocoa and then, seeing as you're here, we can discuss what's been going on. It hasn't entirely escaped my notice that a few reversals of fortune have taken place today.'

Charlie grabbed the postcard and dropped into an armchair by the stove. There was a low grunt behind him, and Blessed eased himself out from the back of the chair and tumbled on to the floor, landing in an untidy heap.

'Sorry, Blessed. Didn't see you,' Charlie muttered as he quickly scanned the writing on the back of the card. 'It makes no sense,' he complained, after reading the card a second, then a third time.

'Why's that?' asked Cook. 'It makes perfect sense to me. Your parents are safe, Charlie.'

'Are they? Are they really? This card might have

been posted before the storms, by someone on a ship that passed them.'

The card was from Charlie's mother, and it read:

> *'We're on our way home. Not long now. We've missed you so much. But soon, we'll all be together. Your father says you mustn't look for the box.*
> *We love you,*
> *Mum xxxx'*

'So what don't you understand?' asked Cook, handing Charlie a cup of cocoa.

'The box,' said Charlie. 'It's such a puzzle. How did they know I was looking for a box, and why did my dad tell me to stop looking for it?'

'Probably because he knows where it is,' Cook replied.

Charlie sipped his cocoa. 'But how . . .' he began. 'I just don't understand. Has he suddenly remembered where he put it? Or has he always known? And . . . and where is it?'

'Best not to know,' said Cook in her warm, wise voice.

Charlie gazed at the comforting red glow in Cook's stove. 'I don't know why Dad went away when the city got so dangerous,' he murmured. 'And sometimes I've felt angry with him, and kind of disappointed. But he must have had a reason, mustn't he?'

'Of course,' Cook agreed.

'A very, very good reason. And even if I never find out, I'll never believe that he . . . he didn't care about me, or any of this.'

Cook smiled. 'Charlie, you're wise beyond your years.'

No one had ever said that to Charlie. In fact, they usually said the opposite. He felt rather pleased.

'Now, tell me what's been going on,' said Cook, 'although I've already made a few good guesses.'

While he slowly drained his cup of deliciously sweet cocoa, Charlie related everything that had happened. By the time he had finished his eyes were beginning to close, and Cook had to give him a little shake to wake him up. 'Charlie,' she said gently. 'Can you bring Billy back to me? I miss him so much.' She looked at the old dog. 'And Blessed is so depressed. I try to talk to him, but it's not the same. Billy can speak his language.'

Charlie rubbed his eyes. 'I'll try,' he said. 'But first

I've got to find the painting of Badlock. It's my only way in. Actually, I'd really like to see Matilda again.'

Cook shook her head. 'The enchanter's grand-daughter? Forget her, Charlie. She's from another world. I'll see what I can find out about the painting. Now, you'd better get back to bed before you're missed.'

Charlie reluctantly dragged himself away from Cook's warm stove and stepped into the cupboard.

'You take care now, Charlie,' Cook whispered as she closed the door behind him.

As before, the hall was deserted and Charlie slipped up the stairs to his dormitory without being seen. He was unaware that the staff had all decided to keep well away from the west wing that night. In fact, most of them had gone to bed earlier than usual, rather than face any of the people who were, at that moment, insulting each other in the ballroom.

Old Ezekiel couldn't believe what had happened. 'That lovely globe,' he wailed, wheeling himself round and round the ballroom as if his endless rotation might somehow conjure up the Sea Globe. 'Did he drown them, did he, did he?' he demanded.

'I've told you, yes!' shouted Manfred. 'He must

have. You should have seen those waves.'

'So you saw it all and didn't do a thing about the Africans!' Ezekiel shrieked. 'You coward. You lily-livered milksop.'

'I'd like to see you try and stop a hundred spirits with spears and torches and . . . and everything,' Manfred shouted back.

'You didn't have to attack *them*,' argued Ezekiel. 'You could just have given Lysander Sage a bang on the head.'

'Couldn't!' Manfred kicked at the pool of water lying in the centre of the ballroom; all that remained of the Sea Globe, as far as he knew. He hadn't seen the tiny sphere that Dagbert now possessed. An unpleasant fishy smell wafted from the pool of water, and Manfred kicked it again. 'Anyway, Lyell Bone has been drowned, so he won't be coming home to rake up that box.'

'What about me?' screeched Mrs Tilpin, swaying at the edge of the pool. 'My little boy has been injured, my swordsman has been . . . sent back. And Lord Grimwald promised me a castle, servants, money. All gone. Poof! Just like that. I'll strangle someone. I'll do worse. I'll turn them into toads.'

'As if . . .' muttered Manfred.

'Stop it!' Dr Bloor bellowed from a chair at the end of the room. 'There's nothing to be gained by endless bickering. If we are to achieve anything we must pull together.'

The headmaster's commanding voice managed to silence everyone. Mrs Tilpin gazed into the murky pool, Manfred tapped his wet foot quietly at the edge and Ezekiel wheeled himself to a standstill.

'Nothing's changed,' Mrs Tilpin said at last. Her tone was soft and sly and they looked at her uneasily. 'Because *he's* coming. Harken, the shadow, the enchanter. His people are here already, and there'll soon be more. So you can keep your precious school.' She flung out her arms and danced around the pool, her glinting black skirt sweeping through the water, sending little ripples across the surface. 'And then Charlie Bone and Billy Raven, Lysander Sage and his spirit ancestors will all be a distant memory.'

'What about the Red Knight?' asked Manfred.

'Ah, the Red Knight,' said Mrs Tilpin, and she stopped dancing.

Fog!

Billy's bed was a bale of prickly straw, his light a thin candle that always burnt through before nightfall. Not that Billy would have noticed when night began and ended. There were no windows in his chilly cell. At least he had Rembrandt to talk to.

But Rembrandt had found a friend: a small, brown-coated, green-eyed rat he called Gloria. Billy could see the attraction. Gloria was very pretty; she was also helpful. Being two sizes smaller than Rembrandt she could squeeze through a tiny hole in Billy's cell, and she would bring Rembrandt delicious titbits from the kitchen waste-bucket. So Rembrandt didn't need Billy's

black bread and instead of fading away, he grew fatter
and fatter.

Count Harken and his wife were the only people in
Badlock ever to have seen a rat before Rembrandt
arrived. They had brought a pair of rats back from the
Red King's city many years ago. But the rats had
vanished and the count assumed they had been eaten
by a greedy servant (though they all swore they had
never set eyes on them). In fact, the clever pair had
burrowed deep into the mountain and raised a family.
Gloria was their last surviving great-great-grandchild.

Sometimes Rembrandt and Gloria would go off for a
whole day. They would wait until Billy's gaoler was
having his meal in the kitchen and then slip through
the bars of the cell and leap up the steep stone steps
into the palace. Rembrandt would return with stories of
their wonderful adventures and eventually Billy would
fall asleep while his rat's gentle voice squeaked on and
on and on. Without those stories Billy reckoned he
would never have slept at all.

A troll called Oddthumb guarded Billy's cell. He was
a squat, ugly being with a grotesque thumb, as big as his
hand. He hated everyone and everything from Billy's

world, especially Charlie Bone who had once managed to slip in and out of Badlock without being caught. He had also managed to rescue his ancestor, the giant Otus Yewbeam, right under Oddthumb's nose.

Billy had refused to be rescued by Charlie. How he regretted that decision. A week in the dreadful dungeons had broken Billy's spirit. He now longed for home as much as Rembrandt. But he knew there was little hope of Charlie making the dangerous journey a second time.

'Billy! Billy!'

The soft voice couldn't wake Billy, who had fallen into a deep sleep after one of Rembrandt's stories. He lay with his head snuggled against the rat's soft back, his glasses folded neatly on the floor beside his mattress.

'Billy! Billy!'

This time the voice broke through Billy's dreams. He reached for his glasses, pushed them on to his nose and sat up. Candlelight flickered in the room outside his cell. Billy blinked and tried to focus. The candle was raised and he saw a girl's face framed in long black curls.

'Matilda?' Billy whispered.

'I'm going to make you a key,' Matilda said softly.

She showed Billy the big iron key that usually hung round Oddthumb's neck. 'I've given your gaoler one of my grandmother's sleeping potions. I slipped it into his mug of ale before the servant brought it down here. So Oddthumb won't wake before I can get this key back to him.'

'Matilda!' called Billy as she began to mount the steps. 'Why can't you let me out now?'

She looked back, her face in the candlelight shadowed with regret. 'Where would you go, Billy? They'd find you and then things would only get worse. We must wait until Charlie comes.'

Billy clutched the iron bars of his cell. 'Do you think he'll come back, then?'

'I'm doing my best,' she said mysteriously.

When Matilda left the dungeons, she climbed a long, winding stair to a small room at the top of the palace. Here, Billy's faithful attendant, Dorgo, awaited her. Dorgo was one of the beings who had inhabited Badlock long before the enchanter invaded and turned their world into the fearful, barren place it had become. There were many beings like Dorgo in the palace. They were all servants of one sort or another, and they all

looked alike, their bodies short, square and lumpy, their faces without eyebrows, their hair (if they had any) hidden under woollen caps. And they shared one characteristic. Once they had befriended a master, they were loyal unto death.

Dorgo was a blacksmith, of sorts. In the little room that Matilda had found for him, he had set up a modest furnace and, in a wooden tray, moulded enough soft clay to take the imprint of a key. Liquid metal was waiting in a bowl hanging from a beam above the furnace.

'Got it, Dorgo!' said Matilda, as she leapt through the door. 'How long will it take?'

Dorgo never said very much. He took the key from Matilda and, pressing it into the clay, murmured, 'Short!'

It was difficult to guess how many minutes went into 'short'. But Dorgo didn't deal in minutes so it was no use asking him for a precise time. Matilda wasn't too sure about time anyway. The enchanter had a clock, a magical contraption that showed constellations and clouds as well as hours and minutes, and Matilda had learned that there were five hours between each meal.

Her stomach told her that there were probably two hours to go before supper, but she would have to get the key back to Oddthumb sooner than that.

'See you in an hour,' Matilda told Dorgo and, leaving his makeshift smithy, she went down to the room where Count Harken kept his paintings. The enchanter was an excellent artist, but how much was skill and how much enchantment, Matilda couldn't guess. She was only interested in one painting anyway. Among the brightly coloured landscapes and the pictures of incredible animals, there was a painting of Billy's city.

Matilda had spent many hours gazing at this city. Billy had told her where Bloor's Academy stood, close to the ruins of a great castle built by the Red King. The king who was her great-grandfather, and also Billy's ancestor.

Sometimes, when she heard someone coming, Matilda would hide among the big canvases. She had never been forbidden to look into this room, but something made her afraid to be found there. One day, while she was hiding, she had heard a woman's voice coming from the painting of Billy's city. The enchanter

had replied to it. And that was how Matilda had found out about the woman called Titania, who was trying to help Count Harken to get back into the city. Why he found it so difficult, Matilda couldn't imagine.

The painting was beautiful, in its way. It was as if the count had painted it from a cloud, for you could see all the streets and buildings laid out in a great pattern, and yet the angle of the houses was not so steep that you couldn't see walls and doors and windows slanting away from the grey slate roofs.

Matilda would stare at the buildings, trying to guess what was happening behind their dark windows, and often she would hear a snatch of music, a dog barking, someone singing or a hoot from one of the extra-ordinary looking machines that filled the streets – cars Billy called them. But most of all Matilda liked to watch the house with a big tree in front of it, for this was where a boy called Charlie Bone lived; a boy who'd be brave enough to venture into Badlock; a boy who lived nine hundred years away. Could she get to Charlie's world? Matilda wondered. Could she?

Matilda put her hand on the painting. Her fingers touched a high window, just above the tree outside

number nine, Filbert Street. 'Can I? she whispered. 'Can I? Charlie, are you there?'

On Friday Alice Angel decided to tidy the box room on the top floor. Maisie never seemed to have the time. The shelves lining two walls were crammed with suitcases, old clothes, sets of china, books, newspapers and boxes of goodness-knows-what. The floor space was occupied by long rolls of cloth, chairs in need of re-caning, occasional tables, an ancient treadle sewing-machine, and an old rocking chair. Alice pushed the rocker up to the window and sat down. 'Hmm, the window needs a wash,' she observed, running her hand over the grimy pane.

A curious tingle shot through Alice's fingers. If she hadn't been who she was, she might have thought the surface of the glass had been electrified. But being Alice, she thought nothing of the sort. And being Alice, she wasn't too surprised when a distant, yet sweet, clear voice said, 'Charlie, are you there?'

'Charlie's not here right now, my dear,' said Alice, lightly touching the windowpane. 'Try again later.'

'I thank you,' said the voice.

Alice smiled to herself. She wondered how far the voice had travelled. How many years?

'Shall I see him again?'

Alice didn't know how to reply. This time the voice sounded wistful and slightly hesitant. Alice had always found it impossible to lie. She could only tell the truth. 'I don't know, my dear.' She knew the girl had gone as soon as she had spoken.

'I wonder . . .' Alice said to herself. She couldn't sit still any longer, and so she continued to tidy, dusting the books and stacking them neatly on the shelves.

It began to rain. Alice looked at the window, hoping another storm wasn't brewing. The last one had been ferocious. She knew who had brought it about, of course. Alice was well aware that Lord Grimwald was in the city, and she knew that he was trying to drown Lyell Bone. She made it her business to know these things. Intuition told her that Lord Grimwald wasn't around any more. But on rare occasions, intuition had let her down. She couldn't be absolutely sure.

The rain was now falling very heavily. It was extraordinary rain, the drops as large as cupfuls of water. The cupfuls soon became bucketfuls. Whoosh!

Splash! Cars hooted, birds flew for cover.

Looking down into the street, Alice saw a solitary pedestrian in a brown raincoat and a wide-brimmed waterproof hat. He was striding along, swinging an old-fashioned doctor's bag, and didn't seem at all concerned about the rain. He stopped at number nine and rang the bell.

The front door was opened and, from the hall far below, a little scream echoed up the stairwell. Alice dropped the book she had been dusting and ran down the two flights of stairs. When she got to the kitchen, she found the person in the waterproof hat sitting at the table with the bag in front of him. The hat dripped, the raincoat dripped and the man's large brown moustache dripped.

'Maisie!' cried Alice, staring at the stranger. 'Is everything . . . all right?'

'Yes, yes.' Maisie frowned at the little pools of water forming on her freshly cleaned floor. 'I'm just not used to seeing this young man with a moustache.'

Tancred put a hand up to his moustache and Maisie said, 'No, no, don't take it off. Grandma Bone might see you.'

Pressing his moustache firmly to his upper lip, Tancred said, 'Sorry about the mess, Mrs Jones. I've been practising.'

'Thought as much,' muttered Maisie, reaching for the mop. 'Alice, this is Tancred Torsson, friend of Charlie's. Calls himself a weather-boy.'

'Ah, the rain!' Alice glanced at the window. 'Not at school then,' she commented.

'I'm supposed to be dead,' Tancred said gloomily. 'A boy called Dagbert Endless drowned me – almost.'

'I see.' Alice understood immediately.

'I'm so bored,' went on Tancred. 'There's no one to talk to during the week. I've no idea what's going on at school, and I just feel so out of it. I live miles away, you see. Up in the –' He suddenly stopped and frowned at Alice, as if he was worried he'd said too much. 'Excuse me,' he said, 'but who are you?'

'I'm Olivia Vertigo's godmother,' said Alice. 'Olivia is in trouble. That's why I'm here.'

'Really?' Tancred leant forward eagerly. 'That's just it, you see. I never know anything now. What sort of trouble has Olivia got herself into?'

'She didn't get herself into it,' Alice said reprovingly.

'She was trapped by my opposite number.'

Tancred sat back and digested this. 'Ah,' he said at last. 'You must mean Mrs Tilpin.'

Alice sighed. 'I fear so.' All at once she looked over her shoulder. 'Someone's coming. Tancred, be prepared.'

Tancred sat up very straight and laid a hand on his bag. The door opened and Grandma Bone came in. She was wearing her dressing gown and looked very sleepy. 'Tea?' she asked with a yawn. 'Is it teatime?'

'Yes, I think it is, Grizelda,' said Maisie, putting the kettle on.

Grandma Bone turned and stared at Alice and Tancred. 'You don't live here,' she said.

'I'm staying for a while.' Alice gave Grandma Bone a radiant smile. 'I'm Alice Angel. Remember?'

'I suppose I do.' Grandma Bone yawned again. 'And who are you?' she asked Tancred.

Tancred sprang to his feet and opened his bag. It was full of broken china, half-heartedly wrapped in tissue paper. Tancred had gathered up all the broken china his mother had put aside, ready for gluing. Poor Mrs Torsson now used only plastic cups and saucers, her husband and son having broken every single piece

with the violent weather they produced.

'So?' Grandma Bone poked at the china with her bony finger. 'Are you trying to sell this stuff? It looks broken.'

'Exactly, madam,' said Tancred in an odd, gravelly voice. 'I'm mending it. Do you have any broken china?'

Grandma Bone stared glumly at Tancred. 'No. And I wouldn't give it to you if I had.'

Tancred chewed his lip and sat down.

'Here you are, Grizelda,' said Maisie. 'I've popped two Marie biscuits on the saucer.'

Grandma Bone took her tea and biscuits and left the room without another word.

'Is Mrs Bone all right?' asked Tancred in a low voice. 'She doesn't seem to be all there.'

Maisie laughed. 'She's been like that ever since Alice came. I think you've cast a spell on her, Alice.'

Alice regarded her long, elegant fingers and said, 'I probably have. Oh look, the rain has stopped.'

Tancred grinned sheepishly and stood up. 'I was going to wait for Charlie,' he said, 'but I don't suppose he'll be back for another hour, so I'll head off. Tell him I'll see him tomorrow, maybe at the bookshop.'

Maisie saw Tancred to the door. 'I'd better warn Charlie about your . . .' She tapped her upper lip and gave Tancred a wink.

'Bye then, Mrs Jones.'

Tancred marched confidently up Filbert Street. He noticed that several people were filling their cars with cases, bedding, bags and even plants. People often left the city on Friday, for a weekend away. But the amount of stuff that was being crammed into some of the cars made it look as though their owners were going away for months, or even years.

The High Street was almost deserted. What was going on? Curiosity got the better of Tancred. 'Excuse me,' he said to a harassed-looking mother with a baby in a pushchair. 'Has something happened? I mean, where is everyone?'

'Fog,' said the woman.

'Fog?' Tancred looked up and down the street. 'I don't see any fog.'

'It's coming.' The woman walked on.

'Coming?' Tancred called after her. 'How do you know? What sort of fog?'

'Bad. It's coming off the river.' The woman was

actually running now. 'Listen to your radio.'

Tancred stood still. He looked around him. Shops were closing. Cars were roaring down the High Street, breaking all the speed limits. Tancred changed his mind about going home. The bookshop was closer. He began to run.

It was Tancred's intention to go straight to Ingledew's Bookshop, but as he passed the end of Piminy Street something made him turn into it. He decided to visit Mrs Kettle. He hadn't seen her for some time and wanted to make sure she was safe in the street of tricksters and scoundrels.

There was no sign of anyone leaving Piminy Street. If anything, there were even more people about than usual. Oddly dressed people in fashions long gone. Unshaven men who laughed unpleasantly and walked right into Tancred, knocking him aside. There were women in shawls and greasy bonnets, their long skirts trailing in the gutter.

Angry and nervous, Tancred caused a blast of wind to sweep across the street. His electrified hair blew his hat off and rain began to fall again in bucketfuls.

In the Stone Shop carved creatures with grotesque

faces stared out into the street, their eyes glimmering behind the rain that streamed down the windowpane.

Tancred shuddered and made a dash for the Kettle Shop. A group of teenagers with white faces, velvet coats and plaited hair glared at Tancred as he put his finger on the bell, and rang and rang and rang. His false moustache slipped off his wet face and mocking laughter erupted from the teenaged gang. He turned to send a blast of wind in their direction but was distracted by the sight of Norton Cross standing on the other side of the road, his gaze fixed on Tancred.

The door was opened at last by Mrs Kettle, tall and jolly, her red hair as shiny as polished copper. 'Come in, young man,' she said, hauling Tancred over the doorstep. 'As for you lot,' she glared at the teenagers, 'you can push off!' She slammed the door.

Tancred stood in the shop, gazing at the bright kettles. Only a few weeks ago, almost every kettle had been smashed by a vicious stone troll, brought to life by Eric Shellhorn. 'You've mended them all,' he said. 'Everything looks just great.'

'Come into my parlour,' said Mrs Kettle, leading the way through an arch into her private part of the shop.

She stopped suddenly and, putting her hand to her chin, said, 'I think I should warn you . . .'

But Tancred had already seen the boy, carefully polishing a big copper kettle. It was Dagbert-the-drowner.

The two boys stared at each other in horror, and then Dagbert uttered a low wail and shook his head. 'You're dead,' he moaned, 'dead, dead, dead!' and dashing past Tancred, he ran out of the shop.

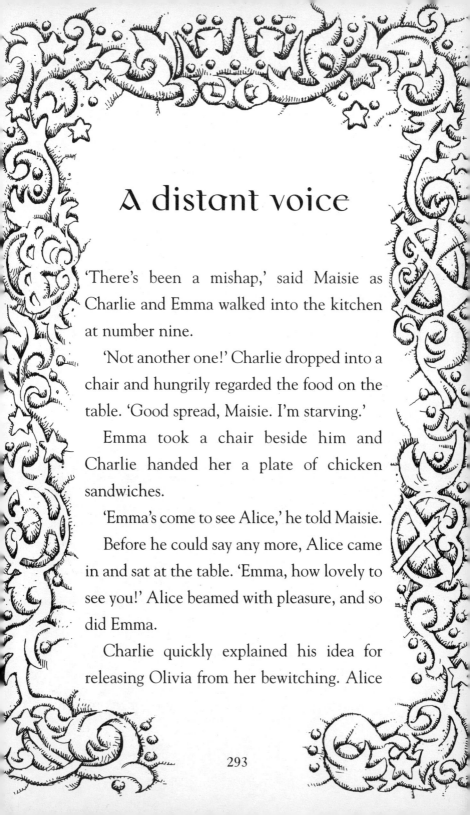

A distant voice

'There's been a mishap,' said Maisie as Charlie and Emma walked into the kitchen at number nine.

'Not another one!' Charlie dropped into a chair and hungrily regarded the food on the table. 'Good spread, Maisie. I'm starving.'

Emma took a chair beside him and Charlie handed her a plate of chicken sandwiches.

'Emma's come to see Alice,' he told Maisie.

Before he could say any more, Alice came in and sat at the table. 'Emma, how lovely to see you!' Alice beamed with pleasure, and so did Emma.

Charlie quickly explained his idea for releasing Olivia from her bewitching. Alice

looked at him with great interest, her head on one side, before saying, 'Charlie, that's an excellent idea.' She turned to Emma. 'So can you describe this waistcoat for me – the little details, the placing of the sequins, the size of armholes, the length, the buttonholes?'

'Every night, when Liv takes it off in the bathroom, I take a good look,' said Emma. 'She snatches it up very quickly, hardly looks at it when she puts it back on. So I don't think she'll notice if it's not an exact match.' She reached into her pocket and brought out a folded piece of paper which she flattened out and laid in front of Alice.

'A sketch! Emma, this is wonderful!' Alice bent over Emma's drawing of the waistcoat and studied it intently.

'So, what's the mishap?' asked Charlie, not very enthusiastically.

'I thought you'd never ask.' Maisie put a plate of scones on the table and sat down. 'Your friend Tancred was here and –'

'Tancred?' said Charlie through a mouthful of chicken.

'Yes, in a moustache,' said Maisie.

'A moustache,' said Emma. 'I hope no one saw

him. I hope he's all right. I mean, I hope he hasn't been caught.'

'Well, *they* probably know he's alive by now.'

When Maisie said this, Emma's hand flew to her heart, her eyes wide and glistening.

'Because,' Maisie went on, 'he went up Piminy Street and lost his hat and moustache. Probably due to the weather he'd brought about. So he's only got himself to blame. But, anyway, he went into the Kettle Shop and saw that drowning boy, Dagbert something-or-other. The boy rushed out, but luckily Miss Ingledew saw him hovering outside the bookshop in a bit of a state, so she coaxed him in.'

'How do you know all this, Mrs Jones?' asked Emma.

'Your auntie rang me just before you got here. I asked her if she wanted to speak to Paton, but she gave me a definite no.'

'She's given up on him,' said Emma.

'Given up?' Charlie looked anxious. 'She can't have. I think Uncle Paton wants to marry her.'

'He should have thought of that before.' Emma sounded very cold and practical. It was almost as if Uncle Paton had upset her personally.

To make matters worse, at that moment, Uncle Paton walked into the kitchen. He had obviously overheard Emma's remarks and no one could fail to notice that he appeared to be very upset. Without a word, he walked over to the worktop, put on the kettle and got a bottle of milk from the fridge.

Even Maisie was lost for words. Emma, however, was indifferent to Uncle Paton's feelings. 'So is Tancred all right?' she asked. 'Where is he now?'

'They're all at the bookshop.' Maisie glanced uneasily at Paton. 'Mrs Kettle and Tancred are there, trying to put things right, Julia said.' She gave Paton another quick glance. 'Whatever that means. But she rang because Dagbert will only speak to you, Charlie. He says he doesn't trust anyone else.'

'Me?' Charlie swallowed a large piece of scone and washed it down with a mug of tea. 'I'd better get over there, then.' He jumped up and, going to his uncle, tapped his arm, saying, 'Hi, Uncle P. I'm glad you're here.'

Uncle Paton gave Charlie a half-smile and said, 'We'll talk later, Charlie.'

All this time Alice had been quietly contemplating Emma's drawing. Although she hadn't spoken she had

been listening intently to the conversation and now, all at once, she looked keenly at Charlie and said, 'Go with the dog, Charlie. Things are not right out there.' She nodded at the window.

Charlie was about to ask her what she meant by 'the dog', when the bell rang and, running to open the front door, Charlie found Benjamin and Runner Bean on the doorstep.

'That's odd,' said Charlie. 'Someone else was thinking about you, before I was.'

'Eh?' Benjamin wrinkled his nose. 'You all right, Charlie?'

'Mm.' Charlie managed to swallow the last piece of scone that had lodged in his throat. 'I was just going to the bookshop. Want to come?'

'That's why I'm here,' said Benjamin. 'I think.'

Emma appeared in the hall behind Charlie, and when they had both flung on jackets and scarves, they joined Benjamin on the pavement and all three began to walk up Filbert Street, preceded by a very energetic dog.

'Have you noticed?' said Benjamin. 'Lots of cars have gone from the road.'

'People too,' Charlie observed. On his way down

from the school bus, he hadn't noticed how empty the street had become, because he was thinking of tea, but now he saw the big gaps between cars that were normally parked bumper to bumper all along the road. 'Where's everyone gone?'

'It's the fog,' said Benjamin. 'Our neighbours on both sides have left the city. They said on the radio that it's going to be so thick, it won't be safe to travel in or out. But we're not going. Dad says if everyone leaves, the villains will have a free hand.'

'A free hand for what?' asked Emma.

Benjamin shrugged. 'Looting and pillaging I expect.'

This sounded rather too medieval. Charlie had never heard of a fog so thick it couldn't be penetrated. Surely there would always be at least one way in or out of a city. He was relieved to see a police car cruising down the deserted High Street.

As they approached Cathedral Close, they could hear snatches of music drifting towards them. The music grew louder and when they passed the end of Piminy Street, they saw that a party seemed to be in full swing. People were dancing in the middle of the road, while a group of musicians in velvet coats and tall stovepipe

hats played wild jigs and polkas. Some sawed at the strings of small violins, while one beat a drum and others played pipes adorned with coloured ribbons that fluttered in the air, as the players swayed to the rhythm and tapped the ground with their pointed boots.

Charlie and Benjamin watched open-mouthed as the dancing grew faster and wilder. And then Runner Bean barked, and heads were turned in their direction. The dancers' faces were distorted with malice and Emma plucked Charlie's sleeve, saying, 'Come on, quick!' They ran for the bookshop.

Tancred, looking quite himself again, was re-stacking some of the books Miss Ingledew's customers had taken out during the day, but not replaced. Since it was the end of the week, Miss Ingledew was doing her accounts beside the till.

Emma ran down the steps, crying, 'Tancred, you're safe! I heard about your moustache and everything.'

'Well, they all know I'm alive by now, because Norton Cross saw me, so there's no point in hiding any longer,' he said, giving Emma an especially welcome smile.

'Where's . . .?' Charlie looked around the shop.

'Dagbert?' said Miss Ingledew. 'He was exhausted, so

I put him in Emma's room for a little nap.'

'Oh!' Emma wasn't quite sure how to take this news.

The curtain behind the counter billowed alarmingly and Runner Bean gave a howl of anxiety as Mrs Kettle pushed her way into the shop. 'Ah, Charlie, there you are,' she said. 'You'd better go and have a word with that poor lad upstairs. He's in quite a state.'

'Poor?' said Emma indignantly. 'He's not poor. He tried to drown Tancred.'

'He seems pretty harmless now,' said Tancred, fitting the last book into place. He turned to the others. 'I think he's changed. There's nothing weird about him any more. He doesn't even smell fishy.'

'Have a word with him, Charlie,' said Mrs Kettle. 'Just calm him down. There's enough trouble in this city already. We need all hands on deck.'

A funny way of putting things, thought Charlie as he walked round the counter and into Miss Ingledew's sitting room. He was surprised to see Dagbert standing on the other side of the room. He was clutching the glass sea-storm, and Tancred was right, he looked quite ordinary, just a boy who was scared and worn out. He gave Charlie a weak smile and said, 'I heard a dog.

300

What are they going to do to me, Charlie? I know Tancred's alive. I thought I was seeing a ghost.'

Charlie took a few steps towards Dagbert and said quietly, 'They're not going to do anything, Dagbert. You're safe here. Tancred didn't drown, as you've seen. And he's forgiven what you did. There's no point in being angry with someone who doesn't exist.'

Panic showed in Dagbert's blue-green eyes. 'But I do exist. Don't I?'

'Of course,' said Charlie emphatically. 'But that other boy, the mean, drowning, selfish boy that *was* you, is gone. Isn't he?'

Dagbert turned the sea-storm over and over in his hands. 'Seems to be gone,' he murmured. 'I'm not frightened that my life is going to end any more.' He held up the sea-storm and watched the silvery shower of foam fall from top to bottom. And then he gave Charlie a very ordinary, happy grin.

'You're one of us now, Dag,' Charlie said. 'And you'll be needed. Things are happening in this city.'

Charlie was aware that a small tide of people had begun to fill the room. First came Mrs Kettle, then Emma and Miss Ingledew, Benjamin and Runner Bean,

and lastly Tancred. They eased themselves into seats around the room and, trying not to be too obvious, had been watching Dagbert to see if Charlie was having an effect. Runner Bean, sensing the gravity of the situation, gave not one bark.

'Charlie's right,' said Miss Ingledew. 'Something is happening. I think we shall all be tested in the next few hours. You must have noticed that half the inhabitants of this city have left. I predict that over the next few days even more will go, until only a few remain. It will be tempting to leave, before the fog finally encloses us.'

Mrs Kettle stood up and began to pace about the room, her copper hair looking more like a helmet than ever. Even her shiny bomber jacket gave the appearance of armour. 'But we must stay and fight,' she said, 'or the shadow will drag this city into the past, and the Red King and all he stood for will not even be a memory.'

'Fight?' said Emma in a small voice. 'What with?'

'With whatever comes to hand, my dear.' Mrs Kettle gave her an encouraging smile. 'Unfortunately we have no way of knowing when or how Count Harken will make his move. But it will be soon. The swelling ranks

of the residents of Piminy Street, the increase in stone creatures, the fog, all these things suggest that he will arrive very soon. His conduit, the Mirror of Amoret, is cracked, that is true, but he will find a way. We may be sure of that. He is an enchanter, after all.'

Miss Ingledew got up and patted her cushions. 'Mrs Kettle and I have made some arrangements. She will stay here with me and Emma; Dagbert, you too. We'll make up some beds down here. Piminy Street is too dangerous now.'

'There's something I have to do,' Charlie said suddenly, 'before it's too late.'

They all looked at him. Mrs Kettle wore a forbidding frown. 'I hope it's not a dangerous task,' she said.

Charlie shrugged. 'Not really. I have to get Billy out of Badlock. I promised Cook.'

Frowns turned to disconcerting stares.

'It's not a very good time, Charlie,' Miss Ingledew remarked.

'I think it's kind of now or never,' he replied. 'But I've got to find that painting of Badlock or I'll never get in. Mrs Tilpin has moved it from the old chapel, but I don't know where she has put it.'

'It'll be in the Academy,' said Miss Ingledew.

Charlie shook his head. 'Nope. I've looked everywhere. Everywhere I can, that is. The Bloors don't like it, so it won't be in the west wing.'

'It could be in Darkly Wynd,' Tancred suggested. 'In fact, I'll bet that's where it is. In one of your great-aunts' dingy basements.'

Charlie reckoned that Tancred could be right. But which great-aunt had the painting, and how was he to get into any of those awful houses without being seen? 'I'll sleep on it,' he said.

Night was falling. It was time for Charlie and Benjamin to go home. They didn't want to pass Piminy Street in the dark, even with Runner Bean.

Tancred volunteered to walk with them as far as the High Street. Emma stood outside the shop and watched the three boys make their way down Cathedral Close. 'Take care,' she called. Tancred turned and waved. He almost blew her a kiss, at least that's what it looked like to her, but he obviously thought better of it.

When they parted, on the High Street, Charlie anxiously watched Tancred stride out alone towards the

Heights. He had a long way to go. And then he took something from his pocket and a flash of silver told Charlie that the weather-boy was phoning his father. In a few minutes, Mr Torsson's roaring whirlwind of a car would be swooping down from the Heights. But before that happened, three bright forms leapt out from a dark alleyway and encircled Tancred's legs, so closely that he almost tripped over them.

'The Flames,' said Benjamin. 'He'll be OK now.'

'And so will we.' Charlie grinned at Runner Bean, who gave an appreciative bark.

Although the boys felt safe, they were both aware of the curious whispers that seemed to float through the air above them. And they could feel sounds through the soles of their shoes, as though underground creatures were moving beneath the pavement. The fog seemed to have crept closer, and the houses on the other side of the road looked blurry and distant.

It was almost dark when Charlie got home. Maisie was watching the road from the kitchen window. Benjamin and Runner Bean ran across to number twelve, and Benjamin shouted, 'See you tomorrow.'

Filbert Street seemed to be completely deserted.

Numbers twelve and nine were the only houses where a light showed.

'I'm glad you're back, Charlie.' Maisie shut the front door behind him and leant against it. 'It's bad out there.'

Charlie knew what she meant. There was no other way to put it. 'Bad,' he agreed.

'Alice wants to see you,' Maisie told him. 'She's up in the box room.'

Charlie took off his jacket and hurried up to the top of the house. A row of candles stood on the box room windowsill, and Alice explained that Uncle Paton had been helping her to tidy. Charlie noticed a small black waistcoat lying on the sewing machine.

'It'll be finished by Sunday,' Alice told Charlie when she saw him looking at the waistcoat. 'First I have to find enough silver sequins. This room is a real treasure trove.'

Charlie guessed that the waistcoat wasn't the real reason for Alice wanting to see him. He was right.

'Something rather . . .' she paused, 'strange would be a way to describe it, but it was more than strange. Wonderful would be better. Yes, something wonderful happened up here, just before you came back from

school, Charlie. There wasn't time to talk about it then, but I think you should know, someone has been . . . calling you.'

'Calling?' Charlie sat down rather quickly on the edge of the rocker, and a thread of cane snapped beneath him.

'I touched the window, just here,' Alice laid her hand on a pane close to her shoulder, 'and I felt another.'

Charlie waited for her to continue, but she merely gave him an enigmatic smile. 'Another what?' he asked.

'Another person, Charlie. And then I heard her voice. She asked me if you were here, and I had to tell her no, but that you might be later on.'

'What sort of voice?' asked Charlie, hardly daring to breathe.

'Faint, but very sweet. I believe I was speaking to someone many hundreds of years distant.'

'Matilda!' Charlie's voice was almost as faint as that faraway girl's.

Alice stood away from the window, so that Charlie could touch the same pane of glass. He took a breath

and laid his hand on the window. The glass felt hard and cold. But he let his hand rest there for several minutes.

After a while, Alice said gently, 'I must warn you, Charlie, that you may never feel the girl's touch. I am peculiarly sensitive to the past.'

'I'll wait,' he said. 'I'll wait until she comes back.'

Alice left him leaning against the window, his hand beginning to turn blue on the cold glass. As she closed the box room door she felt a pang of guilt. Perhaps she had given Charlie false hope, telling him about that distant girl, and yet how could she have kept it from him?

An hour later Alice brought Charlie a mug of cocoa and some biscuits. He made her put them on a rickety table beside him, so that he could reach them with one hand.

'The girl might be asleep now, Charlie.' Alice carefully lifted his hand and laid her own on the glass. 'Perhaps your Matilda can't reach the gate between our worlds just now,' she suggested. 'I think you should go to bed, Charlie, and try again tomorrow.'

Charlie shook his head. 'I'll wait,' he insisted.

When Alice had gone he sipped his cocoa and

quickly changed hands. 'Matilda!' He spoke close to the glass, his breath steaming up the window. 'I'm here. It's Charlie. I'm coming to Badlock.'

But how could he get there?

Charlie sat back in the rocker and, with one hand still touching the window, he fell asleep.

Eagle thief

Emma had gone to bed feeling useless. She lay awake for a long time, her thoughts divided between Olivia and Tancred. And then she began to worry about her aunt. Paton Yewbeam had woefully neglected her with his sudden changes of plan, his lack of attention and his forgetfulness. As for the enchanter, could that ancient book be right? Was it possible that Count Harken could surround the city with a mist of enchantment and drag it back into the past?

Already the city was beginning to change. Parts of it were deserted, while the inhabitants of Piminy Street appeared to have doubled in a week.

Emma thought of Billy, alone in that

bleak and dangerous place, and she suddenly sat bolt upright. There was something she could do. She could help Charlie to rescue Billy before it was too late. They should all be together, they stood a better chance that way. She resolved to wake up very early and set off for Darkly Wynd. Tancred had suggested the painting of Badlock might be there. And Tancred was always right. Emma chose not to think of the occasions when he had been wrong.

Her mind made up, Emma slept soundly for a few hours and then woke at dawn, refreshed and determined. She decided to get dressed before leaving, even though she would be travelling as a bird. When she opened the window an unpleasant, musty smell drifted into the room. A thick, grey-green cloud lay just beyond the edge of the city. Was this the fog the radio had been warning them about?

Emma climbed on to the windowsill and closed her eyes. She thought of a bird, small, brown and inconspicuous. Feathers rustled at her fingertips and she felt herself beginning to shrink. Smaller and smaller. The tiny feathers swept up her arms and covered her head. In a few seconds a small brown wren was perching on

the windowsill. It lifted its wings and flew into the grey, dawn sky.

The city beneath was silent and still. A few cars were parked in some of the outlying roads, but otherwise the place appeared to be deserted. No milk floats, no post vans, no refuse collectors. Nothing moved except the birds in the sky and a few cats, hunting in parks and gardens.

Emma swooped down towards Greybank Crescent and fluttered along the cul-de-sac called Darkly Wynd. The sight of the three tall houses always made Emma shudder. Which one should she choose to investigate first? Perhaps Charlie's great-aunt Venetia was keeping the painting. She had a lot in common with Mrs Tilpin. Yes, Emma could imagine a poisoner and minor sorceress living happily beside that grim, forbidding landscape.

The little bird flew back and forth across the three houses. The curtains were closed in every window and she couldn't see any that were open. She would have more luck at the back, she thought. But here, too, the curtains were drawn across and the windows shut. Refusing to give up, Emma flew into Venetia's garden.

No one had bothered to mow the lawn, ever, by the look of it, and the dry grass grew waist-high, completely concealing the lower part of the house. To a tiny bird this didn't present a problem. Hopping through the stalks, she came to a low basement window. It was un-curtained but not open.

Emma fluttered down to the sill and peered into the room beyond. The pane was grimy with dust and cobwebs, but she could just make out a long table covered in material of every description. Bottles of coloured liquid stood at one end; poisonous potions, thought Emma, twisting her head from side to side to get a better view. Now she could see piles of sequins at the other end of the table; beside them were reels of cotton, needles and scissors of different sizes. Bunches of herbs hung from the ceiling and dark shiny plants snaked their way across the walls. But there was no sign of a painting.

Something glinted at the back of the room. The bird's sharp eyes made out another table, small and round. And there, sitting on a pile of silk, was a mirror. Even from a distance Emma could see that it was very beautiful. The circle of glass was set in a golden frame

and the handle was an oval of twisted gold and silver. Intricate patterns and tiny jewels were set into the frame, and even though the mirror was in shadow it had a vibrant glow. It was definitely Amoret's mirror, stolen by Mrs Tilpin and broken by Joshua. Venetia was obviously trying to mend it for them.

How can I reach it? Emma hopped along the windowsill. She was too small to break a pane. If only she had chosen to be an eagle, or a vulture. Think, she told herself. See what you wish to be. And she saw an eagle, its dark wings spread like a cloak against the sky, a white head and golden talons as sharp as knives.

Emma shivered and stretched. She could hear her feathers crackling as they grew and multiplied. She was now so tall she could see further into Venetia's workroom, and so wide she could no longer perch on the narrow sill. A hoarse cry came from her white throat and she lifted in the air. Hovering for a moment, high above the dismal garden, she measured the basement window with her faultless sight, and then swooped, so fast she could hardly draw breath. Her feet smashed through the windowpane with a bang that resonated like a rifle shot.

Folding her wings, Emma sailed through the broken window, thrust out her talons and seized the mirror. With a lightning-swift turn she was through the room and out into the air. Success made her give a triumphant cry, and as she flew up into the sky she saw windows opening in the three number thirteens.

'Eagle!' screeched Venetia from the top of her lofty house. 'It's got Titania's mirror.'

'Eagle thief!' shouted Eric from the window below her. 'Kill it!'

'I'll get it!' cried Eustacia, appearing with a crossbow in a window in the middle house. And an iron bolt came whizzing past Emma's head. She screamed in terror and almost dropped the mirror.

'Missed,' yelled Lucretia from a window in the third house.

Before the next bolt could hit her, Emma was out of reach and flying high over the city. Charlie's house was easy to spot because of the chestnut tree that grew in front of it. Emma came down in a whoosh of air, right at the top. The eagle is a heavy bird and the branch that Emma landed on creaked under her weight as it swung down beside a window underneath the eaves.

Spread flat against the window was a hand. Behind the hand was Charlie Bone. He was sitting in a chair, half-asleep by the look of it. Emma tapped the windowpane with her beak and Charlie's eyes flew open. He stared at the huge bird framed in the window, its feathers covered in shards of glass, and then he saw the mirror clasped in the talons of its left foot.

Charlie opened the window very carefully, so as not to push the eagle off the branch. 'Em, is that you?' he said, astonished at the size of the huge bird.

Emma thrust her foot through the open window and Charlie gingerly took the mirror from the lethal-looking talons. Before he had time to thank her, the bird took off from the shuddering treetop and soared into the air.

Charlie sat back in the chair and gazed at the mirror. He wondered how Emma had managed to find it. The eagle was covered in glass. Had she risked her life to get the mirror? He hoped not, for it was still cracked, still useless. He would never get into Badlock with this broken mirror.

From outside there came a shout. 'Charlie, let me in.' He looked out of the open window and saw Emma,

standing on the pavement and looking quite herself again, if a little dishevelled.

'Hang on!' called Charlie. He ran down to the bottom of the house and opened the front door.

Emma quickly stepped inside. Little pieces of glass were caught in her long hair and there were scratches on her forehead.

'You OK, Em?' Charlie asked, still amazed by what she had done.

'I thought I could find the painting for you,' she said, gulping for air. 'Phew! Sorry, couldn't get my breath back.'

'It's very . . . well, thanks, Em.' He didn't know how to tell her that the mirror was useless. 'No one's awake yet. Do you want to come up to the box room?'

'The box room? Have you been sleeping there, Charlie?'

He reddened. 'Sort of.'

'Why?' she asked. 'And could I have a drink or something?'

'Um, yes.' Charlie shifted from foot to foot. 'Can you make it yourself? I've got to get back upstairs.'

'Why?' Emma was disappointed. Charlie didn't

seem very excited about the mirror.

'Because I'm kind of waiting for someone.' Charlie dashed upstairs, saying, 'I'm sorry. It's hard to explain. See you up there.'

Mystified, Emma went into the kitchen and made herself some hot chocolate instead of tea. Having got up so early she felt desperately hungry and helped herself from a tin of biscuits sitting on the dresser.

By the time Emma had climbed up to the box room, Charlie had settled himself back in the rocker and placed his hand on the window. It was in exactly the same position as before, all five fingers splayed out on the glass. The mirror lay on a table beside him.

'Charlie, what are you doing?' asked Emma, becoming more and more puzzled.

'Alice started it,' Charlie said awkwardly. 'She felt Matilda's hand, just here, and heard her voice.'

'Matilda?' Emma didn't know anyone of that name.

'The girl in Badlock,' Charlie said with slight impatience.

'Sorry, I'd forgotten her,' Emma confessed.

Charlie obviously hadn't forgotten.

'I mean it's not as if I've ever seen her,' Emma said

defensively. 'But why have you got to keep your hand there? It's going blue.'

'She wanted to talk to me,' Charlie explained, 'and Em, I really want to see her again.'

'Ooooh.' Emma understood at last. 'So that's why you want to get into Badlock.'

'I want to get *Billy*,' Charlie stressed, 'but I'm hoping to see Matilda as well.'

'Try the mirror.'

'It's broken, Em. I'm sorry, but I don't think it will work.'

Emma's look of dismay made Charlie feel guilty and then, suddenly, her face lit up. 'Charlie, look!' She pointed at the mirror.

Throughout the night Claerwen had kept Charlie company, nestled on a duster that Alice had left on a shelf. But now the moth was busily skimming over the cracked glass. The rapid movement of her silver-white wings began to cause shafts of brilliant reflected light to stream out of the mirror. The glass became so bright they could barely look at it.

'She's mending it!' Forgetting the windowpane for a moment, Charlie screwed up his eyes and stared at the

mirror. But it was too bright. He got up and rubbed his tired eyes.

Emma's sight was still as sharp as a bird's. She couldn't tear her gaze away from the dazzling glass. 'It's fading, Charlie,' she said. 'The crack. It's disappearing.'

'Claerwen, you've done it,' marvelled Charlie as the moth, her task complete, left the mirror and settled on to his shoulder.

The blinding light became a manageable shine and Charlie's eyes could, at last, rest on the mirror. There was nothing there, of course. No reflection of his face or the room behind him. The Mirror of Amoret didn't work like that.

'Can it help you to travel now, Charlie?' Emma asked hopefully. 'Like Amoret?'

Charlie nodded. 'I used it once and saw my father. I nearly reached him, but because of the spell laid over him, I couldn't quite. And then Olivia took the mirror from my hand because I made a dreadful sound, and she thought that I was dying.'

'I won't do that,' Emma promised. 'Unless you think I should.'

'No, no. Don't touch the mirror, whatever happens. Claerwen will bring us both back, me and Billy.'

Emma watched Charlie's face. If anyone looked spellbound, he did. She wondered if she should let him go into Badlock, looking the way he did; shocked and already almost gone.

'Look into the mirror,' Charlie chanted, remembering Uncle Paton's words. 'Look into the mirror, and the person you wish to see will appear. If you want to find that person, look again, and the mirror will take you to them, wherever you are.'

'So all you have to do is to think of Billy, and you'll see him in the mirror, and then . . .' Emma took a breath, 'and then, you'll be travelling.'

'Yes.' Charlie's voice was so quiet, Emma could hardly hear him.

Charlie wasn't thinking of Billy. He kept seeing the face that he had wanted to see ever since he had returned from that first journey into the past.

'Is he there?' asked Emma, who could only see a misty glow on the surface of the mirror.

'Mmm,' Charlie muttered absently, but the face beginning to appear in the glass wasn't Billy's. It

belonged to a girl; a girl with large tobacco-brown eyes and soft black curls.

'Matilda,' Charlie murmured.

An electric shock passed through Charlie's fingers and he almost dropped the mirror. The handle became red-hot and he had to use both hands to cling to it.

'What is it?' cried Emma, alarmed by Charlie's grimace of pain.

And then he was gone.

Emma stared at the space Charlie had occupied only a minute ago. She hadn't expected him to vanish quite so quickly. Once before she had seen him travel, but then his body had remained exactly where it was, and it was only his mind that had travelled.

Charlie had progressed. His endowment must be stronger, thought Emma, for his travelling to have become so fast.

But for Charlie it wasn't like that at all.

Rembrandt's fly

A journey with Amoret's mirror was nothing like travelling through a painting. By the time Charlie had reached his destination his head had been filled with images that would never desert him: golden sand-hills as smooth as velvet, a camel racing through trees with a tiny boy riding him, domed cities and a sea the colour of sapphires.

And then Charlie was standing in a castle of white stone where a duel was taking place between an African boy in crimson and a yellow-haired youth in emerald green. The clash of swords rang in Charlie's ears as he was torn from the scene and drifted in a vast grey ocean; above him an orange sail flapped in the wind. He glimpsed white

cliffs, an endless forest and a blood-red castle.

And now Charlie was falling, tumbling, twisting in an avalanche of rocks; flying across a barren landscape where black towers leant into a stormy sky. 'Badlock,' Charlie cried as the wind tossed him through the air. He was hurtling towards a mountain that rose before him like a curtain of stone. But before he hit it Charlie was lifted above a palace of black marble where flames streamed from iron brackets set into the wall. And then he was falling, falling, falling . . .

Someone screamed. Charlie shook his head and rubbed his eyes. He was sitting on a very soft carpet patterned in rich colours.

'Charlie Bone!' said a shocked voice.

Charlie turned his head. And there was Matilda, sitting on the end of a four-poster bed. She was wearing the same buttercup yellow dress that she had worn before.

'Hello!' Charlie found himself grinning happily, even though his head still ached and he felt bruised all over.

Matilda slipped off the bed and gently helped Charlie to his feet. 'I am so very pleased to see you,' she

said. 'But I thought you would arrive through my grandfather's painting.'

Charlie held up the mirror. 'I used this.'

'Oh!' Matilda looked astonished. 'But I've seen that here, in my grandfather's spell room. It was a long time ago, and I was very small.'

Charlie frowned at the mirror. 'How can it be in two places at once?'

'No, no.' Matilda shook her head. 'The enchanter took it back to your world. He told me he had buried it there, for the future. How did you find it?'

'It's a long story.' Charlie turned the mirror over and over in his hands. 'I'd like to know its history.'

'Perhaps you will one day.' Matilda took Charlie's hand and pulled him down beside her on the bed. 'I can't tell you how happy I am to see you,' she said, looking deep into his eyes. 'You didn't hear me, did you, when I touched a window in the picture of your house?'

Charlie shook his head regretfully. 'There's a woman called Alice in our house. She's a kind of guardian angel. She heard your voice. She senses things, and she has an effect on people. My grandma's a bully and a

grump usually, but since Alice came she's been all slow and sleepy.'

'The enchanter can do that,' said Matilda, 'but he doesn't often bother. My grandmother has a temper and so does my brother. But the enchanter watches with amusement when they rant and rave.'

They smiled at each other and Charlie wished the moment would last forever. He imagine himself living here, in this incredible room with its green marble walls, its soft, bright carpets and gleaming black furniture.

'You've come for Billy, haven't you?' Matilda said. 'I knew you would.'

'For Billy, yes,' Charlie hesitated. 'And maybe you. D'you think it would work, Matilda? Could you come back with me?'

She beamed at him and then quickly turned away, as if she were trying to hide the sudden sadness in her face. 'The enchanter can read my mind,' she said at last. 'He knows that you came here before, trying to rescue Billy. And he knows that I have been thinking of you often.'

'Often?' said Charlie happily.

Matilda gave him a haughty glance. 'Who else am I

to think about, living in this vast lonely palace? Outside the wind roars and nothing exists but dark crawling things.' She nudged his arm. 'So you mustn't think too much of yourself.'

Charlie grinned. 'You were saying . . . about the enchanter,' he reminded her.

Her smiled faded and she said, 'One day the enchanter told me that he knew my future, and that I would never travel nine hundred years ahead, and live in the Red King's city. I will marry my cousin, who lives in a place called Venice. He is rich and handsome, and I will travel there by boat and carriage when I am sixteen. So you see, I cannot come with you even though,' she dropped her voice, 'I might wish it.'

'Just because he sees your future in some crystal ball, it doesn't mean that it can't be changed,' said Charlie gruffly.

Matilda slid off the bed. 'There is no crystal ball, Charlie. It is my fate. Now let us go to Billy. If luck is with us, the gaoler will be taking his ale in the kitchens. He lingers there for longer than he should, knowing that Billy cannot escape.'

'Escape?' said Charlie. 'Where is Billy?'

'In the dungeons, where they kept your ancestor, the giant.'

Charlie leapt off the bed. 'Why is he there? I thought he was happy here, being treated like a prince.'

'It was the rat's fault,' Matilda told him. 'He made a fuss.'

Charlie had to smile. 'Trust Rembrandt.' And then, all at once it struck him that he had travelled thoughtlessly. He had left the boa behind, the snake that made him invisible. He clutched his hair, moaning, 'Oh, Matilda, I've been so stupid. I forgot the snake. How am I going to get through the palace without being seen?'

Matilda didn't look in the least perturbed. From inside her gown she produced a large iron key. 'A copy,' she told Charlie, 'made by a friend.' And raising her voice she called, 'Dorgo, are you there?'

The door opened and a small being shuffled in. Charlie couldn't help a slight intake of breath, not a gasp exactly, but loud enough to make Matilda smile. 'Billy tells me that there are none like Dorgo in your city,' she said, patting the being's shoulder.

Charlie gulped. 'None.' Indeed, he had never seen

such a small, square, lumpish thing. Its hair, if it had any, was hidden in a big woollen cap, and its body was covered, rather than dressed, in a long brown robe. But it had a gentle face and kind grey-brown eyes.

'Dorgo, give your clothes to Charlie,' said Matilda.

Showing no surprise or embarrassment, Dorgo pulled off his cap and held it out. A head of brown bristles was revealed, rather like a hedgehog's spines. Charlie took the cap and put it on, then Matilda helped him to tuck all his hair inside. This wasn't difficult as the cap was so large it covered his ears and eyebrows. While they were dealing with Charlie's hair, Dorgo lifted the brown robe over his head and dropped it on the floor.

Charlie was relieved to see that Dorgo's square body was still hidden in yellow underwear. Seizing the brown robe, Matilda put it over Charlie's head. 'Bend your knees,' she commanded. 'Now, let's go.'

Charlie obediently followed Matilda to the door. But before he shuffled out, he looked back and thanked the small being whose clothes he was wearing.

Dorgo beamed. 'Is good,' he said.

'Quick!' hissed Matilda. 'We must hurry. I can hear movements below. The guards are leaving the kitchen.'

Charlie shuffled after her. It was not easy to hurry with bent knees.

'Lower,' whispered Matilda. 'You are still too tall.'

Charlie groaned and crouched even lower. Now it was impossible to walk properly. He lurched from side to side as he moved his bent legs forward.

Matilda put her hand over her mouth but failed to stifle a giggle. 'You really do look like Dorgo now,' she whispered.

They were making for a marble staircase that led down to the lower regions of the palace, but before they got there, a woman appeared at the top of the stairs. 'M'lady Matilda,' she said. 'The Countess wants to see you. The shoe-smith has come with some fine leather. You are to have your feet measured.'

'Oh!' Matilda stopped in the middle of the passage, her hand resting on Charlie's shoulder. 'Must I come now?'

The woman came towards them. She had a pale, stern face and her brown hair was pulled back severely into a silver net. Her dress was the colour of dark ivy and coloured beads glittered at her neck. 'Who is this servant?' The woman's cold, grey eyes rested on Charlie. 'I have not seen him before.'

Matilda gave a nervous laugh. 'Of course you have, Donata. But they all look the same, don't they? This one is young. I am instructing him.'

'The countess will not be kept waiting.' Donata turned on her heel and swept down the staircase.

Matilda and Charlie stared at each other in dismay.

'Can you remember the way to the dungeons?' Matilda asked softly. 'I dare not come with you now.'

'I think so,' Charlie said dismally. 'Oh, Matilda, I can't believe I'll never see you again.'

'Nor I,' she said. 'It is sad to part like this.'

'M'lady!' Donata called from the foot of the stairs.

'I'm coming!' Matilda put one foot on the stair, then turned back to Charlie. 'The key,' she whispered, putting it into his hand. 'Wait a few minutes after I am gone. And keep Dorgo's clothes with you when you go. He will be in trouble if you leave them in the dungeon. I can easily find another outfit for him.'

Charlie nodded and slipped the key into his pocket, beneath the brown robe. 'Goodbye, Matilda,' he murmured.

'Fare thee well, Charlie.' She bent and kissed him, and then she was gone, her fine leather shoes tap-

tapping on the marble staircase and then receding into the distance. Somewhere deep within the palace, a heavy door clanged shut. And then all was silent.

The mirror seemed to move beneath Charlie's fingers, warm and smooth. He must hurry. Deciding not to attempt a descent on bent legs, Charlie straightened up and ran down the staircase. At the bottom he crouched again and shuffled forward. It took him some time to get his bearings.

Count Harken's palace had few windows. The wide corridor that Charlie was lurching along was carpeted in furs and lit by flaming rushes. Peering into the passages that led off the corridor, he saw one that he recognised and, straightening his knees, dashed into it. Here there were no rush lights, and it became darker and darker. Claerwen crawled from inside Charlie's collar and flew ahead, her soft light showing him rock walls and a floor of brick and rubble.

Deeper and deeper they went. The air was thin and stale. At last Charlie reached a familiar half-circle of iron railings. Behind the railings a stairway of rocky steps twisted down into an even greater darkness.

Was the troll gaoler already there, waiting to grab

him? Charlie had no way of knowing. He cautiously began to descend the steep steps. He was only halfway down when he heard footsteps approaching, and then a deep, hoarse voice echoed along the passage above him. Someone, the troll probably, was attempting to hum a monotonous tune.

Charlie tore down the rest of the steps, stumbling and slipping on the rocky surface. He arrived, at last, in a cave-like room where a candle spluttered on a table. Beyond the table Charlie could see the bars of a cell. He leapt towards the cell and, looking through the bars, saw a small figure curled on a rough bed of straw.

'Billy!' Charlie whispered. 'It's me, Charlie!'

Billy sat up. He stared at Charlie, aghast. 'W-what?'

Charlie briefly lifted Dorgo's cap. 'See! It's me. I've come to take you back.'

'CHARLIE!' cried Billy.

'Sssh!' warned Charlie. 'Someone's coming.'

The footsteps above had increased their pace. Now they were descending the rough steps.

Charlie fitted Matilda's key into the lock on the cell door, and it swung open. He leapt inside.

'How . . . how are we going to . . .?' Billy began.

Charlie held up the mirror. 'With this, and with Claerwen. Hold my hand.'

'Wait!' cried Billy. He ran over to his rat, who was crouching beside a small hole in the wall. 'He's waiting for his friend,' said Billy. 'But, Rembrandt, we've got to go.' He clutched the rat, who gave a loud squeal and began to struggle violently.

'Quick!' said Charlie, grabbing Billy's hand. 'We must go, NOW!' He looked into the mirror and thought of Emma, waiting for him in the box room at number nine. He could see her face now, pale and anxious. Charlie wished himself there, beside her. 'Claerwen, let's go,' he cried.

Feet appeared, stumbling down into the gaoler's room. And there was Oddthumb, the troll, leaping towards the cell, his hand with its great thumb extended towards them.

All at once Charlie was rocked off his feet and tugged upwards, the mirror burning one hand, and Billy's fingers clutched in the other.

The second journey was nothing like the first. How many tricks could the mirror play? Charlie wondered, as they tumbled through the dark. Wind howled in

their ears and hailstones beat into their faces. Their legs kicked aimlessly, reaching for a solid mass to land on. And still they whirled, over and over, round and round.

'Aaaah!' groaned Charlie. His knees hit the floor and he fell in a crumpled heap, unable to brace himself with either hand, as one still held fast to the mirror and the other clung to Billy Raven.

'That was quite something,' said a voice.

Charlie let go of Billy's hand and rolled on to his back.

Emma peered down at him. She was smiling. 'You've got him,' she said. 'Well done.'

Charlie turned his head. Billy was lying beside him. One of the lenses in his spectacles had cracked and he looked quite sinister with a starburst covering his eye.

'You didn't have time to change, then,' Emma remarked.

Charlie slowly got to his feet. He was still wearing Dorgo's woollen cap and ill-fitting gown. Billy was dressed in a blue velvet jacket braided in gold at the collar and cuffs, and blue velvet trousers. The outfit looked somewhat the worse for wear. The front was

stained and the trousers torn. On one foot he wore a very long pointed shoe. His other foot was bare.

Rembrandt was sitting on Billy's chest, squealing endlessly. Billy sat up. 'I'm sorry about Gloria,' he told the rat in a series of small squeaks. 'But it was then or never. Anyway, we couldn't have brought her back.'

'Huh!' Rembrandt turned his back on Billy, and a fly buzzed out of his fur. 'How come we managed to bring a fly back, then?' the rat asked sulkily.

Billy couldn't answer that one. 'Hi, Em,' he said. 'It's good to see you.'

'You too,' she said. 'Nice outfit.'

'It was.' He looked down at the stains on his jacket. 'I hope there's something to eat. I'm really, really hungry.' He got up and made for the door, but Charlie held him back.

'You'd better stay in here, Billy,' Charlie said. 'Grandma Bone might see you, and if the Bloors know you're back they'll be after you.'

Billy sighed, sat down on a box and rubbed his tummy.

'I'll get you something,' Emma rushed off.

As Charlie pulled off Dorgo's clothes he glanced

out of the window and noticed that the rooftops he could normally see were now completely obscured by the fog.

By the time he had tidied himself up, Emma was back with a tray of cakes and orange juice, and also Alice Angel. When Billy saw Alice, the eye behind his good lens widened in terror and he pushed himself and his box back into a corner. But Alice knelt beside him, not too close, but near enough for him to take her hand if he needed to. 'Billy, you must be so frightened,' she said. 'What a journey you've had. You're safe now. My name is Alice Angel and I won't let anything happen to you.'

Billy relaxed and a smile touched the corners of his mouth. 'I'm Billy Raven,' he said, clasping her hand. 'And that's Rembrandt.' He pointed at the rat, who was sulking in a corner, facing the wall. 'He had to leave his girlfriend behind in Badlock and he's very cross about it.'

Alice covered her mouth with her hand, but she couldn't hold back a peal of laughter. Emma joined in, and even Billy started to giggle. But Charlie thought of Matilda, and couldn't find the joke funny.

'I'm glad I'm back,' Billy said, 'and Rembrandt will be too, when he's found another girlfriend. I suppose I was silly to like it so much in Badlock. But the count was nice to me at first. He made all those animals for me, and even if they didn't have hearts, they let me stroke them, and the tiger purred. But then I was put in that dungeon. I think the count got bored with me. Maybe he thought I'd be useful, and then he found out that all I could do was talk to animals.' Billy took off his glasses and touched the frame of the shattered lens. 'And that wasn't good enough.'

'Count Harken trapped you in Badlock because the Bloors wanted it,' Charlie said.

'Why?' asked Billy.

Charlie didn't think that now was the right time to tell Billy that he would inherit the Bloor family fortune if a certain will in a certain box could be found. Uncle Paton had been reluctant to discuss the hidden will just lately. Perhaps he had changed his mind about it.

The doorbell rang and voices could be heard, down in the hall. Charlie went out on to the landing and called, 'Who is it, Maisie?'

Maisie came to the foot of the stairwell and said,

'Miss Ingledew's come for Emma.'

'Miss Ingledew?' said Charlie. 'Why?'

Emma ran out on to the landing, crying, 'I'm sorry, Auntie, so sorry. I should have come straight home.'

'She can't hear you,' shouted Maisie. 'She won't come in, but she doesn't want you to walk home alone. The fog's getting thicker.'

'Emma, take this, it's finished.' Alice handed Emma a white plastic bag.

'The waistcoat,' said Emma, peeping into the bag.

Alice nodded. 'Good luck.'

'Thank you, Alice!' Emma kissed Alice's cheek and ran down the stairs. She reached the landing below just as Grandma Bone came out of the bathroom.

'What are you doing here?' Grandma Bone demanded, seizing Emma's shoulder.

'Paying a visit,' said Emma, wriggling free and bounding down the next flight.

'At this time of the morning?' Grandma Bone leant over the banisters and stared down into the hall. 'Maisie, why's the front door open? What's going on?'

Before Maisie could reply, Alice Angel appeared at the top of the stairwell and called down to Grandma

Bone, 'There's nothing to worry about, Grizelda. Go back to bed and I'll bring you a nice cup of tea.'

'Oh.' Grandma Bone looked confused. 'All right, then.' She padded back to her bedroom and closed the door. Emma left the house at the same moment, and Maisie shut the front door. Half a second later, Uncle Paton opened his bedroom door and, looking up at Charlie, asked, 'Was that . . .?'

'Miss Ingledew, Uncle P,' said Charlie.

'She didn't come in, then?' his uncle enquired tentatively.

Feeling a little uncomfortable, Charlie replied, 'No, Uncle.'

'I see.' Uncle Paton withdrew his head, and Charlie felt even worse.

In the box room, Billy had coaxed Rembrandt out of his corner with a piece of fruitcake, the rat's favourite. The fly that had travelled from Badlock in Rembrandt's fur was now buzzing round the window.

'I don't like the look of that fly,' said Alice, trying to swat it with a duster.

Charlie noticed that, in a certain light, the fly looked green. Claerwen fluttered after it, but the fly dropped

behind a pile of books on a shelf, and went quiet.

Alice went to tell Maisie what had been going on, and to fetch Grandma Bone a cup of tea. Charlie ran down to his bedroom to look for some clothes for Billy. It was decided that Billy should stay in the box room until other arrangements could be made. What those arrangements might be nobody could work out just yet. Even Alice was stumped. And when Charlie asked his uncle for advice, Paton just stared at Charlie as if he'd been told that a Martian was sitting in the box room.

'I don't know what to suggest,' Uncle Paton said at length. 'Yes, keep him in the box room for a while, by all means. But he can't stay there forever.'

'It won't be forever, will it, Uncle P?' said Charlie. 'Because something is going to happen very soon. Something that will change *everything* forever.'

'Indeed,' agreed his uncle, without much enthusiasm.

It was an odd day, quiet and still. The fog had crept closer and the city was holding its breath. Benjamin and his parents came over at teatime and, with the exception of Grandma Bone and Billy, they all gathered in the kitchen to hear what Mr Brown had to say. Being a private detective meant that he had

managed to discover the truth of some of the rumours that had been flying around.

The mayor and some of the councillors had left the city. Part of the police force could not be located, though PC Singh and PC Wood had been spotted patrolling the High Street. All the schools would be closed on Monday, except for Bloor's Academy. The post office and all the banks would be closed. One or two buses might run. There were no taxis to be had.

'So we're on our own, more or less,' said Mrs Brown cheerfully. 'I've got enough food for a fortnight, and fogs never last longer than that.'

No one liked to say that this particular fog might carry something that could last forever.

The Browns stayed on for supper, and when they had gone home, a bed was made up for Billy in the box room. With Rembrandt on his pillow, he was soon fast asleep.

In the middle of the night a deafening explosion ripped through the house. The building shook to its very foundations; china slid off the dresser and furniture groaned and slithered out of place.

Tumbling out of bed, Charlie met his uncle,

clutching the railings on the landing. Maisie and Alice appeared on the landing above, and ran down to meet them. The front door was open and a cold wind swept through the house.

'Was it an earthquake?' cried Maisie.

'More like a meteor strike,' said Uncle Paton.

'A bolt of lightning?' Charlie suggested.

Alice said quietly, 'Or the sound of a fly turning into something much larger.'

They looked at her in horror, and Charlie whispered, 'Rembrandt's fly!'

Rescuing Solomon

There were few to see the dark figure striding up the road; his magnificence was wasted on the creatures of the night, who quickly fled. Emeralds glinted at the stranger's neck, his gold cloak rippled like a waterfall, his black tunic was encrusted with pearls and his hair was dusted with gold.

From the roof of number nine the bright eyes of three cats watched the enchanter's progress through the fog. When he reached the end of the road, the cats climbed down and began to follow him. Soon he sensed their presence and turned, with a hiss that would have chilled the blood of any ordinary cat. But these flame-coloured cats were not ordinary. They had the hearts and

minds of leopards. As soon as the enchanter had resumed his course, they followed, keeping to the shadows, but never losing sight of their prey.

It quickly became clear that the enchanter was making for Bloor's Academy. The cats watched him climb the steps between the two towers and cross the courtyard to the entrance. The cats ran past the steps and along the side of the building until they reached a high stone wall. Up they went, the three bright forms. They paced along the top of the wall, watching the frosted field below, and the woods beyond, where the great red arch led into the castle ruins.

A stirring in the naked winter trees alerted them. They moved closer together, as though each cat knew his senses would be enhanced by the nearness of the others. They saw the white mare first, and then her rider: a knight in a silver helmet, his suit of chain mail glimmering in the frail light of a fogbound moon. A deep purr rose in the throats of the three cats. They leapt from the wall and ran to the mare's side.

The enchanter didn't wait for an answer to his knocking. He seized the bronze handle in fingers

ringed with emerald and gold, and with one twist he
shattered the lock, letting loose a shower of sparkling
splintered wood.

The heavy doors crashed open and the enchanter
swept into the hall.

A heavyset man in tartan pyjamas flung himself,
trembling, to the floor in front of the enchanter. 'I was
coming, my lord . . . sire . . . Count Harken,' he
declared. 'Forgive . . . I didn't know . . .'

'Get up, Weedon.' Count Harken kicked the
prostrate body in the ribs, causing a violent shudder to
run through it.

Weedon stumbled to his feet. He couldn't quite
bring himself to stand upright, but remained bent at the
waist, in an untidy sort of bow. 'We didn't know,' he
muttered, 'though Mrs Tilpin told us to be ready.'

'Where are they?' the count demanded.

'In the west wing, my lord, asleep.'

'Not for long,' said the enchanter. 'Take me there.'

Weedon straightened up a fraction and tottered
over to the door to the west wing. Holding back the
door, he let the enchanter sweep past him, the gold
robe scratching his knuckles as it brushed against his

hand. Weedon suppressed a sob of pain and hurried after the count.

'I'll have to wake them, my lord,' the porter mumbled. 'Forgive me, but it's well past midnight. It might take a while to gather them.'

'Ring a bell. Bang a gong!' the count commanded. 'There must be one.' He began to mount the stairs to the first floor.

'Oh, indeed, there is,' said Weedon, scrabbling after the scratchy gold-threaded cloak.

The huge brass gong hung in an oak frame outside the headmaster's study. A hammer with a round leather head lay beneath it. Weedon had never beaten the gong. He wouldn't have dared. In fact, he had only heard it once, when Manfred, in a teenaged tantrum, had pounded it so hard the head of the hammer had split in two. The sound had been deafening. It had reached into every part of the building and took fifteen minutes to subside. The hammer had been mended, and Manfred forbidden ever to touch the thing again.

The enchanter regarded the gong with interest, pronouncing it excellent for his purpose. 'I'll do it myself,' he said, rubbing his hands together in

anticipation. Lifting the hammer, he drew back his gold-spangled arm and beat the gong with such force Weedon's left eardrum was permanently perforated.

The sound reverberated through the building, even reaching Cook in her underground rooms. And for Cook that sound spelled the end of an era. For many years she had kept the balance in Bloor's Academy. She called herself the lodestone of the house, keeping a watchful eye on the endowed children and doing whatever she could to make sure those who used wickedness did not overcome the others: the children who refused to let the Bloors corrupt them.

Cook knew no one who would strike the massive gong in the middle of the night. Something told her that the Shadow of Badlock had broken into the city again. And this time it would be hard to banish him. This time he had made sure he had followers in the city. Even as Cook sat there, wondering what to do, an army from the past was coming to life.

'So why am I sitting here?' Cook muttered to herself. She pulled her suitcase from a cupboard and began to pack.

Up in the west wing a motley group had assembled

in the headmaster's study. They were all standing, except for the enchanter who sat behind the headmaster's desk, and Titania Tilpin, who had fainted at the sight of her ancestor, the count. Dr Bloor wore a tweed dressing gown that wouldn't have looked out of place on a golf course. Manfred had appeared in purple silk pyjamas, much to his father's disapproval, and Ezekiel wore a red nightcap, a tartan jacket and a too-short nightshirt (another embarrassment for Dr Bloor). Titania, prostrate beside the door, was wearing a black kimono, while Joshua, in an ordinary green dressing gown, was trying to revive his mother by patting her cheeks.

'Foolish boy,' said Count Harken. 'That will do no good.'

'Weedon, get some water,' said Dr Bloor.

Clutching his left ear, Weedon staggered out.

'It's lucky he's still got one good ear,' said Manfred, chuckling at his own joke.

No one else chuckled. This was a serious moment and the sooner Manfred cottoned on the better. Everyone waited for the enchanter to speak, while he waited for Weedon to return. He arrived at last, with a

jug of water and his wife, in curlers and a pink shawl.

'Put it on her face,' the enchanter commanded, pointing at Titania.

'Put it?' Weedon, looking uncertain, held up the jug.

'Pour it!' thundered the enchanter.

'Pour? Of course.' Weedon turned the jug and let a stream of water splash on to Titania's face.

She sat up, gulping for air. 'I'm drowning!' she screamed.

'You are not,' said the count. 'Calm yourself.'

'My lord, it really is you!' Clinging to her son, Titania pulled herself to her feet. 'I knew you would come, but with the mirror broken and –'

'I came another way,' the count said, with a private sort of smile.

'Tell us how,' begged Ezekiel. 'We'd love to know.'

'With the boy,' the count said carelessly. 'Charlie Bone. I knew he would come to Badlock. My granddaughter has a fondness for him. She tried to reach him through my painting, but he used the mirror.'

'The mirror?' cried Titania. 'The Mirror of Amoret? But it's broken.'

'Not now. I allowed the boy to arrive, I even

watched him use a ridiculous garb to rescue his friend, Billy, and I travelled back with them.'

A babble of complaints and questions broke out and, raising his hand for silence, the enchanter said, 'How did I travel? As a fly. And why did I allow Billy to return to your city? Because he was of no use to me.'

'But what about the will?' Ezekiel screeched. 'That kid stands to inherit everything if the will is found. We had a bargain, sir. You keep Billy, and we help you to get back into the city.'

Leaning across the desk, the enchanter roared in Ezekiel's face, 'But you didn't help, did you?'

'What, what?' Ezekiel spluttered. 'She tried.' He pointed at Titania. 'And Venetia Yewbeam attempted to seal the crack in the mirror.'

'I called to your shadow in the Red King's portrait,' Titania whined. 'But all in vain. I brought back my ancestor, Ashkelan Kapaldi, to help, but the Red Knight killed him.'

'Red Knight?' The enchanter sat up, his ringed fingers drumming the desk. 'What Red Knight?'

'A killer, a rogue, a dressed-up devil –'

Dr Bloor's calm voice cut through Titania's

hysterical outburst. 'A knight on a white horse has been seen, now and then, riding through the city. He appears to be protecting some of the endowed children, Charlie Bone among them. This knight has a plume of red feathers on his helmet, a red cloak and a shield with a burning sun.'

'The king!' Count Harken leapt up, his eyes blazing. 'So he has returned to give me the ultimate satisfaction. All my life I have relished the thought of this encounter.'

'I hesitate to disagree,' said Dr Bloor, 'but surely it cannot be the Red King himself, the man who built this city nine hundred years ago?'

'*I* am here,' the enchanter reminded him, 'so why should he not be here?'

Manfred, who had been listening to the conversation with increasing impatience, suddenly spoke up. 'The Red King is a tree, always will be, so we have heard. If he could have returned as a man, then he would have done it years ago.'

The count began to look uncertain. At last he said, 'If he is not the king, then he is someone who has taken on the king's mantle. Whoever he is, he must be

destroyed before I can take this city into the past.'

'The past?' said Ezekiel. 'But . . .'

'Oh, you can keep your house, your garden, your treasures.' The enchanter waved his hand disdainfully. 'But they will all be taken into the past.'

The Bloors stared at the enchanter, not quite comprehending what they had heard. Even Titania looked anxious.

'You will hardly notice the difference,' the enchanter said airily. 'The city will be in the world of Badlock, that is all. Now, can someone find me a horse? Preferably a stallion. And I'll need some of the armour that I saw displayed in your hall. We will do battle on the morrow!'

'We?' croaked Ezekiel.

'Battle?' said Dr Bloor.

The family at number nine Filbert Street were on their way back to bed when the doorbell rang.

'It's going to be a long night,' sighed Uncle Paton. He went down into the hall and called, 'Who's there?'

'It's me. Cook!' said a voice.

'Cook?' Uncle Paton drew back the bolts and

unlocked the door. When he opened it a small figure darted in. She was carrying a large suitcase in one hand and a leather bag in the other.

'My word,' she puffed, dumping the suitcase and the bag on the floor. 'It's dark in here, Mr Yewbeam.'

'There's a reason,' said Paton.

'Oh, of course.' Cook noticed the candle burning on the landing above.

'Cook!' cried Charlie.

Cook blinked at the three figures on the stairs, the smallest of whom was now bounding down towards her.

'What's happened?' asked Charlie. He had rarely seen Cook outside the school.

'I've left Bloor's,' she said. 'The balance is gone. You can't go back there, Charlie. None of you. It's all over.'

'What's all over?' Paton ushered Cook into the kitchen, where he lit another candle. 'Sit down and tell us what's happened.'

Charlie followed them, and when Alice came in Cook exclaimed, 'Alice Angel! I'm so glad you're here. What a difference it will make.'

Alice smiled and sat beside her. 'Tell us, Cook!'

'*He's* come back.' Cook couldn't control the tremble

in her voice. 'Count Harken. It's all over for us. We'll have to leave before it's too late.'

'It *is* too late.' There was anxiety in Alice's tone, but not despair, and Charlie took comfort from this.

'The fog is very thick,' Cook agreed. 'I could barely see my way here. Some of the street lights are out, and I heard looters in the High Street. I came the back way.'

Maisie, who'd been making yet another pot of tea, said, 'What's going to become of us all? What can we do?'

'Plenty,' said Paton firmly. 'I wouldn't want to leave this city, even if I could. It's worth fighting for, I'm sure you all agree.'

They did agree, but a sudden thought caused Charlie to gasp, 'Mum and Dad! If we can't get out, they can't get in, and they're on their way here.' He paused. 'At least I think they are.'

Alice touched his hand. 'They *will* be here, Charlie.'

It was like a promise, and although Charlie tried hard to ignore the uncomfortable doubts that kept tormenting him, all at once they became too much to bear, and he burst out, 'Why did he run away, just when we needed him?'

358

Nobody spoke and Charlie realised that even Uncle Paton had been worried by the same distressing doubts.

'We'll know soon enough,' said Maisie, handing Cook a cup of tea. 'I'll make up a bed in the sitting room,' she told her. 'The sofa's very comfy, and I'm sure we'll all be thinking better in the morning.'

'Indeed,' said Uncle Paton. 'I'm off. Sleep well, everyone.'

Charlie followed his uncle upstairs. He was about to go into his room when he saw a small figure sitting on the second flight of stairs.

'Charlie,' Billy whispered. 'Is he here?'

'The enchanter?' Charlie was reluctant to alarm Billy, but he would have to know the truth eventually. 'Yes, he is,' he admitted. 'But Cook's here, and we think everything's going to be all right.'

'Oh, good.' Billy gave a huge yawn. 'Night, Charlie.'

In the bookshop, Mrs Kettle had been given Emma's room, while Dagbert took the sofa downstairs. Emma shared her aunt's bed. None of them slept very well. Voices from Piminy Street carried through the air in

disturbing waves of sound: raucous laughter, rough deep singing and wild strains from a fiddle that played on and on, the fiddler seeming never to tire. But it was the smell of burning that finally drove Mrs Kettle to the window.

From the rear of the bookshop you could see the backyards of the houses in Piminy Street and Cathedral Close, and the narrow alley between them. The alley was deserted at the moment, and it would not be too difficult to creep across without being seen. Smoke was billowing from behind the roofs of Piminy Street, and Mrs Kettle began to feel anxious for the blue boa. In her haste to find Dagbert and get him to safety, she had forgotten her precious snake.

'He can't stay there, poor love.' Mrs Kettle dressed hastily. She was about to leave the room when the door opened and Emma crept in.

'You gave me quite a fright, m'dear,' said Mrs Kettle, patting her chest.

Emma explained that she had left something in one of her drawers: a waistcoat that Alice Angel had made for Olivia. 'She's been won over,' Emma told Mrs Kettle. 'Someone gave her a waistcoat that's made her

one of *them*. She's changed completely, will hardly speak to me. And she absolutely won't be parted from the awful thing.'

'So you want to swap them. The one that troubles her must be exchanged for one that brings her peace.'

'It is a bit like that.' Emma smiled. Mrs Kettle had put it so well. Olivia was troubled. Even though she struggled to keep the bewitching waistcoat with her, it appeared to be draining the life out of her. Emma went to her drawer and lifted out the waistcoat that Alice Angel had made.

'It's beautiful.' Mrs Kettle touched the silver circles. 'It's easy to see why Olivia would want to wear a thing like this.'

'It's as light as a feather,' said Emma, 'and yet Olivia seems to sink under the other one as though it's weighted with stones.'

'Evil is heavy,' Mrs Kettle declared, 'goodness a pleasure to wear.'

Mrs Kettle looked so strong and solid, any qualms that Emma might have had were instantly swept away, and she found herself describing how she would go to

Olivia's house in the morning and change the waistcoats, while Olivia was dressing. 'That's the only moment in the whole day when she'll take it off,' said Emma.

'Good luck, m'dear.' Mrs Kettle laid a hand on Emma's shoulder, and Emma could feel the strength of all those smith-magicians who had gone before, and it gave her a rush of courage.

'Thank you, Mrs Kettle. Goodnight!'

'Goodnight to you, m'dear. I'll be off now, to get my lovely snake.'

While Emma went back to bed, Mrs Kettle slipped down the stairs. She tiptoed through the sitting room where Dagbert Endless was moaning in his sleep, and into the kitchen. The back door opened into a small yard. Mrs Kettle stepped out into the foggy air and closed the door behind her. Then she made a sudden dash across the alley to her own backyard. On the way she had to pass behind the Stone Shop, and what she saw there made her blood run cold.

The yard was crammed with huge stone creatures, hideous things with tusks, broad noses, eyes hidden in wrinkled stone and pointed teeth protruding from their

lower jaws. What warped imagination had conjured up these dreadful beasts? she wondered. One turned its head, and Mrs Kettle ran. Eric Shellhorn, she thought. He's bringing them to life.

When she reached her shop, Mrs Kettle dared not turn a light on. The blue boa was curled beneath a table at the back. He had obviously tried to get as far away from the window as possible. Flames from the street fires bathed the shop in an angry orange glow, and the silhouettes of prancing figures passed constantly across the window.

'Come on, my love!' Mrs Kettle reached down and coaxed the snake from his hiding place. He crawled up her arm and wrapped himself around her neck. 'We'd best be quick,' she whispered.

As she stepped into the alley, two figures appeared in the Stone Shop yard: Melmott, the stonemason, and a burly figure in a string vest. Mrs Kettle hoped they hadn't seen her, but Melmott heard the rattle of a pebble under her foot, and looked her way.

'Ah! What have we here?' he said in his cold, rough voice.

'Oh, lor,' whispered Mrs Kettle. 'Solomon, do

something!' She pulled the boa's tail, hoping he'd understand.

Solomon did. In two seconds he had slithered from Mrs Kettle's head right down to her shoes, and both he and Mrs Kettle vanished.

'What the heck!' Melmott exclaimed.

'Where did they go?' shouted String Vest.

Mrs Kettle held her nerve. While the men turned their heads this way and that, she stealthily crept past them.

A cat jumped from a wall further up the alley and the men ran towards the sound, shouting, 'Gotcha! You can't fool us!'

Mrs Kettle hitched the invisible boa back on to her shoulders and hurried to the bookshop. Bounding into the kitchen, she ran straight into Dagbert Endless, who was getting himself a drink of water. He was just about to scream when an invisible hand was clamped over his mouth, and a familiar voice said, 'Sssh, m'dear! It's only me, Mrs Kettle. You can see for yourself in a tick.'

Dagbert watched the space in front of him gradually fill up with the broad figure of Mrs Kettle. Across

her shoulders lay a huge blue snake with feathers on
its head.

'This is Solomon,' said Mrs Kettle. 'Isn't he a beauty?'

Dagbert nodded. He was too astonished to speak.

On the heath

During the night the fog crept right over the city in a smothering grey cloud. The merry-makers of Piminy Street slept where they had dropped, on pavements littered with broken glass and drifting ash. The cathedral clock chimed seven across a city that waited, in fear, for the day that was to come.

In Ingledew's Bookshop, Dagbert had fallen into a deep sleep. The cathedral chimes never woke him, and nor did Emma, creeping past with the waistcoat in a white plastic bag. When she'd fortified herself with a glass of milk, she tucked the bag under her arm and left the house by the back door. Outside, she stood for a moment in the yard. The smell of the fog and burning rubbish hit

the back of her throat and she put a hand over her nose and mouth. She would have to fly through that noxious air and she needed a moment to prepare herself.

Deciding, at last, on a jackdaw, she hastily changed her shape behind the yard wall, and then picked up the bag in her beak. Olivia's house was in Dragon Street, only two blocks beyond Charlie's. If the Vertigos wouldn't let Alice into their house, Emma stood no chance, so she had resolved on an alternative to the front door. Mrs Vertigo had often complained about the mess that jackdaws made, dropping twigs down her chimney. Twice a jackdaw had been found flapping sootily round their sitting room.

As Emma winged her way above the rooftops, she could hear voices in the cloud of fog: hoarse whispers, distant laughter and even the clink of weapons. She ducked her head and tilted down to Dragon Street.

Olivia's house stood back to back with Alice Angel's old home, and no one could fail to recognise the orchard that grew between them. White buds were already appearing on some of the plum trees.

Alighting on the Vertigos' chimney, Emma was surprised to find a jackdaw already in residence. Her

eggs hadn't yet been laid, but a fine nest was already half-built. She seemed more surprised than angry to see Emma perching at the edge of her home.

'Excuse me,' Emma murmured and she dived through the tangle of twigs and straw, before plummeting down the dusty chimney. She landed in the Vertigos' sitting room fireplace, with the plastic bag still held in her beak. The remains of last night's log fire were warm but luckily not alight.

After a few moments of feather riffling, Emma stepped out of the fireplace, a girl once more. It wasn't until she began to tiptoe up the stairs that she noticed her feet were leaving sooty marks on the carpet. Can't be helped, thought Emma. Perhaps they'll blame the jackdaws!

There was a large airing cupboard on the landing, and Emma quickly crawled under the lowest shelf, pulling the door shut behind her. Now she would have to wait.

Mr and Mrs Vertigo always slept late on Sunday mornings, so Olivia would be the first one up. Emma hoped she wouldn't need anything from the airing cupboard on her way to the bathroom.

Time passes slowly when you're waiting in the dark in a rather uncomfortable position. Emma was just beginning to think that she couldn't bear it another minute, when she heard a door open. Someone walked past the airing cupboard and went to the bathroom. Emma heard the bathroom door close, but the lock didn't click. She crawled warily out of the cupboard and listened. Someone was taking a shower. It had to be Olivia.

Emma crept over to the bathroom door. She slowly turned the handle until it opened, just wide enough for her to see a pile of clothes on a low chair. There was no sign of the waistcoat. Perhaps it was under the pile? Or in Olivia's bedroom? Emma darted to the bedroom. She couldn't see the waistcoat anywhere. Frantically she lifted the bedclothes and the pillows. She looked under the bed, pulled out drawers, searched the wardrobe. Nothing. Was Olivia wearing the waistcoat in the shower?

Emma ran back to the bathroom. Olivia was now humming monotonously as she washed her hair. Seizing the pile of clothes, Emma turned it upside down. And there was the waistcoat. As she pulled the

new waistcoat out of the bag Emma's hand began to shake. She couldn't afford to stop now, even though she had no idea what might happen if Olivia discovered her precious waistcoat had been switched. Grabbing the enchanted garment, she stuffed it into the bag, replaced it with the new one and laid the clothes back on the chair.

'Is someone there?' Olivia called from behind the shower curtain. 'Mum, is that you?'

Emma dropped to the floor behind the chair. Olivia peeped round the curtain. Her eyes were misted with soapy water and she failed to see the hunched figure behind the chair. When she went back to her showering, Emma crawled out of the bathroom and got in the airing cupboard, where she stuffed the bag behind the boiler. It was too late to go back and close the bathroom door. Olivia had turned off the shower.

Emma waited. Waited and waited. How long did it take a person to dry themselves and get dressed? There was a sudden long wail and then a thump. Emma ran back to the bathroom. Olivia, fully dressed, was lying on her back. Her eyes were open and her hands rested on her chest. She seemed to be finding it difficult to

breathe. 'Ah! Ah! Ahhh!' she moaned. Beneath her fingers the silver discs on the new waistcoat were turning all the colours of the rainbow. They sparkled and crackled and sang, while Olivia cried, 'Help me! Oh, help me! I'm dying.'

Emma dropped to her knees beside her friend. 'You're not dying, Liv,' she said. 'You're coming to life again.' She took Olivia's hand and held it tight in both of her own. It wasn't easy to escape wickedness, she realised, and she couldn't imagine the pain that Olivia must be feeling.

Olivia began to thrash about, kicking her legs, flinging one arm out and banging the floor with her free hand, while Emma still clung to the other.

'Whatever's going on?' Mrs Vertigo ran into the bathroom and bent over her daughter. 'Liv, what is it? What's the matter?'

Emma wondered how she could tell Mrs Vertigo the truth. She was afraid the waistcoat would be torn off Olivia before she had been healed. But Olivia suddenly became still. Her eyes closed and she appeared to be in a deep and peaceful sleep.

'Has she fainted?' Mrs Vertigo asked Emma.

'She's smiling. Emma what's been going on?'

'I'm not sure, Mrs Vertigo,' Emma said a little guiltily. 'But I think Liv's OK now.'

Olivia opened her eyes. 'Hi, Em,' she said. 'Wow! I feel weird.'

'You fainted, darling,' said Mrs Vertigo. 'I expect you got up too early.'

'I expect I did,' said Olivia. She sat up. 'Silly me.'

It was too much for Emma to behave as if nothing extraordinary had happened. She suddenly hugged her friend tight, crying, 'Oh, Liv, I'm so glad you're better.'

'Me too,' said Olivia, looking somewhat puzzled.

Nobody thought to ask how Emma had got into the house, and the sooty marks were put down to yet another chimney jackdaw. Soon Emma and the Vertigos were eating a hearty breakfast. When the doorbell rang, the girls continued their conversation about fashion, while Mrs Vertigo went to the front door in her white bathrobe.

When Mrs Vertigo came back, she looked anxious. 'There are three young men here,' she told the girls. 'Friends of yours.'

Before she could go any further, Tancred Torsson

poked his head round the door and said, 'Hello, Em. I'm glad I found you. Charlie said you might be here.'

Emma's face turned pink as she gave Tancred a profoundly welcoming smile.

'I'm here too,' said Olivia. 'In fact, I live here.'

'And you look quite your old self to me,' said Tancred. 'I heard you'd been acting a bit peculiar.'

Olivia frowned. 'I was tricked,' she said. 'It won't happen again.'

By now Lysander had pushed Tancred further into the kitchen and walked in himself, followed by Gabriel Silk. At this moment Mr Vertigo chose to come galloping down the stairs in jeans and what might have been a pink pyjama top, but you couldn't always tell with him, as he was a famous film director.

There was now quite a crush in the Vertigos' smart kitchen, but they managed, somehow, to get everyone round the table, and luckily there was enough orange juice left for the three boys. Lysander waited until Mr Vertigo had helped himself to a banana before explaining why they had arrived so early on a Sunday morning.

'It was Mr Silk,' he said, glancing at Gabriel. 'You

can imagine what it's like up on the Heights in this fog. We can hardly see an inch in front of our faces. Mr Silk rang my dad and Tancred's, and he said . . . well, he said something odd, although it made sense to us, to me and Tancred anyway.'

'Well, none of it makes sense to me yet.' Mr Vertigo knitted his brows. 'Everyone seems to be leaving the city, which is a dumb thing to do, if you ask me.'

'Something has happened, Mr Vertigo,' Lysander said earnestly. 'I expect you've heard of Count Harken?'

Olivia's parents might have been in the movie business, but that didn't mean they weren't aware of the city's history. In fact, they knew a great deal about it, and they had certainly heard of Count Harken the enchanter. They also knew that a day would arrive when their daughter's extraordinary talent would be needed for something more vital than scaring a few misguided children.

'I imagine that he's got back, somehow,' said Mr Vertigo, looking at the mist creeping through their garden.

'That's about it.' Lysander was relieved to find that he wouldn't have to explain a rather complex situation.

'The thing is, Gabriel's dad has advised us to walk up to the heath.'

'Why?' asked Olivia's father.

Her mother was more interested in, 'Who?'

'Us.' Lysander looked at Gabriel.

Taking his cue, Gabriel said, 'Erm, my family has always kept the Red King's cloak but, just lately, my dad passed it on to someone else, a . . . er . . .' he cleared his throat. 'A . . . um . . . knight. The knight has been protecting us, but now my dad says we must do something for ourselves. All of us.' He glanced at Emma and Olivia. 'All of us children of the Red King. The knight needs our help to save the city.'

'Who is this knight?' Mr Vertigo demanded. 'He could be leading you into a trap.'

'I don't think so, sir,' Gabriel said firmly.

Mr Vertigo leapt up. 'I'll get my jacket. We'll come with you. I can't allow the girls to go alone.'

'They'll be with us, sir,' said Tancred, 'and we think it's best if you stay here.' He allowed a slight breeze to blow across the table to emphasise his point. 'We have talents. We can protect ourselves better than you can, if you don't mind my saying so. Mr Yewbeam will be

there, and Mrs Kettle and Alice Angel.'

'Alice?' Mrs Vertigo looked at her daughter.

'Alice Angel? Why didn't you say?' cried Olivia. 'I'll be absolutely fine, Mum, if Alice is with me.'

'If you say so.' Mrs Vertigo clasped her face in her hands. 'And I suppose we must just sit here and wait?'

'That's about it, Mrs V,' Tancred said cheerfully. 'I think we'd better be off now, so if you two girls . . .'

'Ready in a tick.' Olivia pranced out of the room and up the stairs. She returned a few seconds later wearing a silver-grey bomber jacket, black boots and a white faux fur hat with earflaps. 'Ta-da! I'm ready!' she announced.

Emma smiled. It was so good to have the old Olivia back again.

With brief kisses for her parents, Olivia followed the others out into the fog. Their next stop would be at number nine Filbert Street.

Charlie was waiting for them in the open doorway. As soon as he saw the group arrive through the fog, he called up the stairs and his uncle appeared, wearing his black fedora and long coat. He was carrying a stout walking stick that Charlie had never seen before.

Alice Angel came down the second flight, followed closely by Billy. When she reached the hall Olivia caught sight of her and leapt up the steps, crying, 'Alice! Alice! I'm so happy to see you!'

Alice gave her a hug. 'I'm happy too, Olivia, dear.'

Maisie and Cook came out of the kitchen, and Maisie said plaintively, 'What are *we* going to do, Cook and me? Just wait, and wonder? And what about Grandma Bone?'

'She won't give you any trouble,' Alice told her. 'We'll be back, dear Maisie. Please don't worry.'

'I'll be with you.' Cook took Maisie's arm. 'We'll keep the balance together.'

Maisie looked briefly reassured. Nevertheless she watched anxiously from the door as the two groups met at the foot of the steps, and then proceeded up Filbert Street together.

'Good luck!' called Maisie and Cook.

Seven children and two adults turned and waved to her.

They walked on in silence, an unusual state for some of them. Even Olivia had nothing to say, though she clung to Emma's hand. The gravity of the situation had

finally struck home, and all of them were preoccupied with their own thoughts.

Halfway up the High Street two figures loomed out of the fog, one large and one small. Mrs Kettle and Dagbert had been waiting for the others. As they drew closer, the sight of Mrs Kettle's cheerful face and strong, broad shape brought a sudden babble of chatter from the group, and they increased their pace.

'Is Julia all right?' Uncle Paton asked Mrs Kettle.

'Just fine,' she replied. 'Piminy Street's deserted. There's no one there to worry her now.'

'That means they're all on the heath,' said Paton.

'It does indeed,' Mrs Kettle agreed. 'But we can cope, can't we?' She pulled back her coat and patted her hip, and they all saw the bronze hilt of a great sword, sheathed in a leather scabbard attached to her belt.

Charlie realised that, apart from Mrs Kettle, none of them had a weapon of any kind. 'Shouldn't we have one of those?' he asked, staring at her sword.

'You have your endowments, m'dear,' said Mrs Kettle.

'They don't amount to much,' Charlie muttered. He was thinking of himself. Travelling into pictures wasn't much use in a fight, nor were Gabriel's psychic powers.

And what about Billy? Communicating with animals wouldn't help, when there were no animals about.

'Listen, m'dear,' Mrs Kettle said gravely. 'You are children of the Red King. That's all you will need, when the time comes. Isn't that so, Alice?'

Alice gave one of her enigmatic smiles. 'Of course!'

And so they set off again, Dagbert falling into step beside Charlie. What should we call him now? Charlie wondered. Because Dagbert no longer had the fishy smell that made people hold their noses whenever he was near. His skin had lost its green tinge, although it was very pale. Charlie couldn't imagine what it must be like to lose your father in such a dramatic way. 'Water-boy,' he murmured to Dagbert, 'can you still . . . you know?'

Dagbert nodded. 'I haven't lost *that*!'

There was a distant shout. Looking back, Charlie saw Runner Bean bounding towards them. Benjamin and Fidelio were following fast behind.

'Uncle!' Charlie called to Paton who, together with Mrs Kettle, was leading the group. 'There are two more of us – and a dog.'

Uncle Paton stopped and the group behind him

came to a sudden halt. They all turned to the two boys racing up to them. Fidelio and Benjamin arrived, gasping for breath and grinning, while Runner Bean bounced round, joyfully barking his head off.

'You left without us!' Benjamin complained.

'Maisie told us where you were heading,' added Fidelio. 'You might have let us know.'

Lysander stepped forward and said, 'Sorry, guys. You can't come. You're not endowed.'

'So what?' said Fidelio.

'You won't be safe,' said Tancred. 'You need protection.'

'We've got Runner Bean,' Benjamin said stoutly, 'and we won't be left out.'

'What about your parents?' Alice asked gently. 'Did you tell them what you were about to do?'

'We left notes.' Fidelio glared at them defiantly. 'And we're coming. So that's that.'

'I'm sorry, boys,' Uncle Paton began, 'but you –'

He was cut short by an explosive crash from behind. The traffic lights had toppled over and now straddled the pavement. The lights themselves had broken off the pole and lay in the middle of the road. The misty

figures of Mrs Branco and the twins could just be made out, standing beside the lights.

'We can't go back now,' Fidelio said happily. 'So you'd better let us join you.'

The three adults accepted this and Benjamin and Fidelio tagged on behind Charlie. He had to admit that he was glad to have his two best friends with him, on what he guessed might be the longest day of his life. They were now a group of fourteen, if you counted Runner Bean.

On they went. Everyone had fallen silent again, but at their backs the Brankos were doing their worst. Chimneys toppled, signs fell from shop windows, doors fell in. Charlie tried to ignore the sounds. And then suddenly one of the lamp posts just ahead fell to the pavement, its glass shattering into thousands of tiny shards. This was too much for Uncle Paton. Leaping into the road, he glared at the Brankos before lifting his gaze to a lighted window, high in a building beside the telekinetic family. With a deafening explosion, the windowpane burst, showering the Brankos with glass. Yelling and cursing, they retreated down the street.

'We'll get a bit of peace while they're licking their

wounds,' said Uncle Paton, resuming his steady march
up the High Street.

When they passed the square that led to Bloor's
Academy, Charlie half-expected Manfred and Mrs
Tilpin to come racing out. But no one appeared. A little
later he became aware that two more people had joined
their ranks. Looking over his shoulder, Charlie was
astonished to see Dr Saltweather and Señor Alvaro.

'Dr Saltweather, I didn't know . . .' said Charlie.

Lysander, Gabriel and Tancred turned and stared at
the two teachers. Emma and Olivia just gaped.

'March on!' Dr Saltweather commanded. 'Don't stop
for us.'

Señor Alvaro smiled at Charlie, saying, 'Forward,
Charlie Bone.'

Their pupils ran to catch up with Paton, Mrs Kettle
and Alice, who were all striding purposefully onward,
though Billy had stopped, for a moment, to speak to
Runner Bean.

The heath lay on their left, just beyond Bloor's
Academy. It was a wide stretch of tough grass and low
windblown shrubs, over a mile long. In the distance a
line of rocks protruded from the earth like the spines of

a great serpent. The fog made them appear almost to float above the ground. The whole place seemed to be deserted. There was no sign of the Red Knight. The group stood at the edge of the road, watching and waiting.

A warning growl rumbled in Runner Bean's throat, and then they saw the dogs. Two Rottweilers were bearing down on them from the direction of the Heights. They looked the most bloodthirsty dogs Charlie had ever seen. He imagined their great teeth tearing into his flesh, into everyone who stood there, too stunned to move. Behind the dogs came Dorcas Loom and her two large brothers.

'Go on, Brutus! Go on, Rhino! Get 'em!' urged the brothers.

Runner Bean snarled bravely, encircling his people protectively, but they all knew he didn't stand a chance against the Rottweilers. For a moment, no one could think what to do. Mrs Kettle had drawn her sword, and Tancred was already calling up a storm, but even as the rain began to fall, Billy Raven suddenly stepped forward, whining, barking and howling at the two savage dogs.

The Rottweilers stopped abruptly, dropped to their haunches and began to whine back at Billy.

'What is he saying?' Dagbert whispered.

'Haven't a clue,' said Charlie. 'But it seems to be working.'

The Looms were furiously egging on their dogs to attack but, all at once, the Rottweilers turned and leapt at their owners. Their strong teeth sank into bone and sinew. With piercing screams Dorcas collapsed, and then her brothers fell to the ground, one on top of the other. The Rottweilers paced round the three forms, growling dangerously. When they were satisfied that their victims no longer posed a threat to their new master, they trotted up to Billy and licked his hands.

'Well done!' said Billy, first in his own language, and then in theirs.

'Well done, Billy,' said Uncle Paton, and the group echoed his words, cheering, 'Well done, Billy! Well done!'

Billy grinned and patted the dogs' heads.

'Three down and two to go,' Charlie said, almost to himself.

'You're thinking of Manfred and Joshua,' said

Tancred, 'but don't forget Mrs Tilpin.'

'And Eric. We can't forget him. Look!' Lysander pointed at the fog that swirled above the heath. And they saw that the shapes they had taken for rocks were now moving forward. As they came closer, the floating forms solidified into what appeared to be huge, lumbering creatures.

'Eric!' said Charlie. 'What do we do now?'

'Stop them,' said Tancred.

There was a violent clap of thunder and a bolt of lightning shot through the fog, cracking into the skull of one of the stone beasts. It made no difference. The creatures came on, and now they could see a small figure prancing before the line of beasts, drawing them forward, animating them to such a degree that they were not lumbering but running, their great feet sending shock waves through the earth.

Tancred had taken off his jacket and was now whirling it above his head. His yellow hair sparkled as a gale-force wind tore into the fog. It thinned and lifted, revealing something they would rather not have seen.

The fog had hidden a ghostly army of trolls and beings that could only be half human. Every one of

them was armed. Spears, pikes and axes glinted in the weak sunlight. Some swung clubs, others slingshots.

'Harken's mercenaries,' Paton muttered, and from his walking stick he withdrew a slim, rapier-like sword. As soon as the sword met the air, a flash of electricity spun from Paton's hand down the narrow length of steel. 'That should work,' he said with satisfaction. 'Let's go.'

'Why, Paton Yewbeam, you've grown another foot,' Mrs Kettle declared, stepping up beside him.

Indeed, Uncle Paton did appear to be something of a giant – a rather thin one, Charlie thought, but a giant nevertheless, with a weapon that could surely deal death to anyone it touched.

Tancred's storm was now raging above the stone beasts and, although the creatures still advanced, they had slowed down considerably, and the troll army was not finding it easy to move through the icy wind that howled into their faces.

The group formed a ragged line behind their two leaders and Charlie saw a determined smile on some of the grim faces around him. They had begun to believe that they could win.

And then, from somewhere behind them, a rock came hurtling through the air and with a moan of pain, Dagbert fell to the ground. The others appeared not to have noticed, but as Charlie dropped to his knees beside Dagbert, he saw a row of wild figures on the road. The Piminy Street gang. An old woman with red ringlets was brandishing her slingshot and cackling with glee. Others held clubs, knives and even hammers.

Charlie didn't know what to do. If he alerted his friends they would turn back and the troll army would fly at them. But it was already too late. Olivia had seen the gang on the road. 'Look!' she screamed. 'We're caught.'

As the group turned, the gang on the road rushed to meet them. But before Charlie could get to his feet, he was knocked aside by a heavy club and he fell face forward on to the stony turf.

The battle

When Charlie opened his eyes, he could hardly take in the scene around him. He'd read descriptions of battles, but nothing came close to this. Everywhere he looked a savage fight was taking place.

He saw Lysander's spirit ancestors surround a group of roaring trolls; he saw Olivia conjure up a monster army, only to have it vaporised by a gleeful Mrs Tilpin. The witch was sending showers of ice from her long white fingers. He saw Gabriel fighting Joshua, and a huge bird sweeping down, seizing Joshua by his neck and carrying him off the heath. Mr Torsson had arrived and together he and Tancred were raining bolts of lightning upon the stone beasts.

Charlie dragged himself through the screaming, grunting, roaring crowd. He had lost sight of Dagbert, and then he saw a leopard crouching by a boy's body. Was it Dagbert? He saw another two leopards attacking the stone beasts, and then Runner Bean and the two Rottweilers came flying past, with Billy Raven close behind, barking out orders.

Mrs Kettle was laying into everything that crossed her path. Her heavy sword struck at heads, legs and bodies. Beside her, Benjamin, Fidelio and Gabriel used their fists and their feet to help subdue her victims.

Charlie stood up. His legs were shaking uncontrollably and he felt useless without a weapon. A hideous being with one eye lumbered towards him, wielding an axe. Charlie backed into the crowd, waiting for the axe to fall. But a man with a white cloud of hair seized the fellow by the waist and swung him round. The one-eyed man growled in fury and raised his axe again, only to have his hand severed by a blow from Señor Alvaro's slim silver sword.

Charlie blinked. 'Th–' he began, but the two masters had run back into the battle. Charlie looked round for a friend to help. But his friends were

hidden in the tangled mass of the battle.

There was a sharp tap on his shoulder, and he turned to face Mrs Tilpin. Or was it Mrs Tilpin? For this woman's features were all askew and he could hardly bear to look at her.

'This is the end for you, Charlie Bone!' the witch shrilled. She dug her claws deep into his shoulder. Deeper and deeper. And when the pain stopped, Charlie thought he must be dead, only he wasn't too dead to see Alice Angel reach over him and send a shaft of pure white light into Mrs Tilpin's dreadful eyes.

The witch covered her face with her hands and reeled back, shrieking. A second later she was lying very still on the ground, and Alice had moved on.

'Charlie!' The call came from Uncle Paton, who was striding through the crowd towards Charlie. His uncle's sparking sword appeared to stun everything it touched and in his wake his victims lay withering on the ground.

With a surge of hope, Charlie rushed towards his uncle, crying, 'We're winning, Uncle P! We're winning!'

The arrow came from nowhere. One moment his uncle's triumphant smile was there before him, the next

it had gone, and Paton was lying at Charlie's feet with an arrow in his chest.

Charlie's scream rang out above the sounds of battle, on and on and on. The sound wouldn't stop, even when Charlie had closed his mouth and dropped beside his uncle's motionless body. But when the scream finally ended a deathly silence fell across the heath. And he sensed an eerie, soundless movement all about him. When he looked up, the trolls and beasts, the Piminy Street gang and all the enchanter's mercenaries had retreated. Charlie was surrounded by his friends, or most of them. He couldn't see Fidelio or Mrs Kettle or Dagbert or Señor Alvaro. And where was Gabriel?

'Have we won?' Charlie asked miserably, for how could they have won if his uncle was dead?

'Not yet, Charlie,' said Lysander.

And then Charlie saw, on the other side of the heath, a mounted knight in shining armour. He wore a green cloak and the plume on his helmet swirled in the air like the fronds of poisonous green hemlock. His mount was a great black stallion that snorted with a fiery breath and cleaved the air with hoofs of white-hot iron.

The enchanter's army stood in a row behind him. But the stone creatures lay in motionless heaps between the two groups. Felled by whom? Charlie wondered. Had the Torssons' lightning bolts pummelled them to pieces, or had Eric, their animator, finally been struck down?

'Come, Charlie!' Alice raised him to his feet.

'What's going to happen?' he asked, his eyes never leaving the prancing stallion and its green swathed rider.

'We're finished, that's what,' said Olivia.

Alice darted her a fierce look. 'No.'

But Olivia looked at the huddled shapes lying about the heath. The leopards were moving between the bodies, pawing and crying to them. 'Without Mrs Kettle and Mr Yewbeam . . . and without . . . without . . .' She choked on her words, and the great bird beside her rubbed its head against her sleeve.

'We must do our best,' said Alice. 'We cannot permit him to take the city so easily. We cannot allow him to carry us back to a life not worth living. We cannot.'

'Never,' said a determined-looking Dr Saltweather.

'No!' Tancred and Lysander agreed, their faces stern and resolute.

But Charlie could see tears glistening in Alice's eyes, and he knew that she was not entirely certain of the outcome of the battle.

An awful laugh rolled across the heath; a victorious and deathly rumble. The enchanter's voice boomed in their ears as though he were standing beside them.

'Go home!' he roared. 'It's finished. The city is mine.'

'No,' Alice whispered.

'No,' they all whispered in unison, though they had each begun to wonder why they stood there, waiting to die.

The enchanter kicked his horse and the great beast came galloping towards them. They tried to hold the line, but Runner Bean and the Rottweilers began to howl. They sank on to their bellies and wriggled away. And who could blame them?

On came the enchanter, his army moving after him. The group took a step back, then another.

Why? Charlie asked himself. Where were the bolts of lightning and the spirit ancestors? Why did the giant bird crouch beside her friend? Why wasn't Billy talking to the dogs? Why were the tears falling freely down Alice's cheeks?

They were paralysed, Charlie realised. So we are lost.

All at once a brilliant shaft of light struck a path across the heath. The leopards leapt up, their ears pricked forward, and the black stallion reared as though the light was a lethal thread of wire before him.

The leopards were now bounding towards the source of light and Charlie saw, on a hill at the edge of the heath, the bright flash of a sword held by a knight on a white horse. The leopards reached the horse as it began to gallop down the hill; the knight's red cloak flew out behind him and the leopards came leaping after it.

The enchanter turned his horse. Again came the chilling laugh. 'At last!' he roared. 'We'll put an end to this.'

At the bottom of the hill the Red Knight reined in his mount. And now they confronted each other, the Red Knight and the Green, with a few hundred metres between them. They drew their swords and began to advance.

Suddenly Charlie found he was running, propelled by the worst fear he had ever known. He could hear his friends calling him back, but he couldn't stop. He had to get between the two horses. For he knew that the

Red Knight was a man. He might have a magic cloak and an unbeatable sword, but he was not a magician, so how could he defeat a being whose very fingers were laced with deathly enchantments?

Charlie was too late. With a clash of steel the knights met and the battle began. Charlie dropped to his knees and the leopards surrounded him, nudging his shoulders and purring into his ears. Did they know something that he didn't?

The fighting was fast and furious. Every trick, every bit of sorcery was dredged from the enchanter's mind and used against his adversary. His weapon was by turns red-hot and ice-cold; he rained spikes on the Red Knight's helmet and sharpened bolts on his chain mail, while the black stallion snorted fire into the white mare's eyes.

The Red Knight was beginning to tire. His head fell forward and he swayed from side to side, lowering his sword. The Green Knight prepared to come in for the kill.

'No!' cried Charlie and again he ran. With all his strength he leapt for the stallion's harness, dragging at its head. The enchanter lifted his weapon. 'Cursed

boy!' he roared. And then, suddenly, he gasped as the unbeatable sword struck home, clean through the thick breastplate and into the Green Knight's heart.

The stallion reared and the enchanter rolled off its back. He hit the ground with a noise like the clash of giant cymbols, the sword still buried in his heart.

Charlie lay back in the grass. Above him the fog was rising and he could see blue sky and a brilliant sun. The ghostly army seemed to have vanished with the fog, and the Piminy Street gang were limping away; their heads were low and their gaudy costumes in rags. They looked so pathetic Charlie felt almost sorry for them.

When he sat up he saw that his fallen friends were not fatally injured. Alice Angel was lifting his uncle's head. Fidelio had got to his feet. The leopards were moving round the injured, purring and nudging them back to life.

Lysander and Tancred came racing over to Charlie. 'He's gone!' cried Lysander.

'Not a trace,' said Tancred. 'Truly dead!'

It was true. There was no sign of the enchanter, though the unbeatable sword lay where he had fallen, and a black stallion chomped the grass beside it.

'But the Red Knight!' said Charlie, standing up.

He lay on his back, only a few metres away. The white mare stood over his body. Now and then she nuzzled the battered helmet, snorting encouragingly. Blood seeped through the chain mail on the knight's chest and arms. It trickled from beneath his helmet. Was he dying already when he made that fatal thrust into the enchanter's heart?

Charlie ran over to him. 'What shall we do?' He looked at his friends.

'Better take off the helmet!' Lysander suggested.

Charlie was afraid. Suddenly he didn't want to know the identity of the Red Knight. The spell would be ended. And if the knight was dead? But I must know, he thought. He knelt in the grass and gently pulled off the helmet.

A familiar face smiled up at him.

Charlie couldn't speak. His astonishment, his joy was too great. He could feel the others gathering behind him, murmuring, 'It can't be!' 'Is it, really?' 'Why didn't we know?'

'Dad!' Charlie breathed.

The seat of evil

The city had not been entirely deserted. PC Singh and PC Wood arrived at the heath soon after the battle had ended. More police arrived. Ambulances parked at the edge of the grass and medical teams ran over to the injured.

Lyell Bone was lifted on to a stretcher and carried to an ambulance. Charlie was allowed to travel with him. Just before the doors were closed PC Singh approached Charlie and asked how he felt. 'You've got a lot of nasty bruises, lad,' he said. He looked intently at Charlie, as though he had a particular interest in him.

'I'm OK,' said Charlie. 'I'm just worried about my dad. And my mum, she ought to

know what's happened.'

'She does,' said PC Singh. 'I've just given her a call'

Charlie was puzzled. 'You know where she is? But how?'

'Ah,' said the policeman. 'She'll have to tell you that herself.'

Charlie's mother was waiting for him at the hospital, and after hugging him half to death they went to wait in the corridor, while Lyell's wounds were dressed.

'I don't understand,' Charlie kept repeating. 'Where have you been? When I thought of you, I always saw a little boat far out on the sea. And then there were all those postcards with foreign stamps.'

'Charlie, I'm so sorry.' His mother hugged him again. 'We hated doing this to you, but we had to make sure that the Bloors never guessed who the Red Knight was. We couldn't let them find out by hypnotism, clairvoyance, or any of their dreadful tricks.'

'What difference would it have made?'

Amy Bone touched her son's bruised face and looked into his eyes. 'They would have held you for ransom, Charlie. They would have kidnapped you, imprisoned you, perhaps even have threatened to torture you if

Lyell didn't give up his quest. So they had to believe it was someone else wearing the red cloak and riding the white mare.'

'I thought it was Bartholomew Bloor,' said Charlie, 'because he wears a blue duffel coat and Gabriel saw his father give the cloak to a man in a duffel coat.'

His mother smiled. 'Ah, Mr Silk knew the truth. He was the only one apart from Bartholomew.'

'Why did *he* have to know?'

'Because he was on that boat, Charlie. There really was a boat called *Greywing*, and it was sailing up the Australian coast. Bartholomew had always wanted to go whale-watching. He's a great sailor and was quite confident that he could survive Lord Grimwald's storms. He and his family are on their way back to the city right now.'

'Phew!' It still didn't make sense to Charlie. 'Whenever I thought of you and Dad I saw the boat. But why, if you weren't on it?'

Amy shook her head. 'I'm sorry, Charlie. We had to make you believe that we were there, in case you were hypnotised, and Manfred got at the truth.'

'I *was* hypnotised,' said Charlie, frowning. 'So

someone must have got into my head and made me believe you were there on that boat. Hmm. I wish I knew who it was.'

His mother hesitated. She seemed to be in a dilemma, so Charlie kept his eyes on her face, determined to get an answer.

'It was Señor Alvaro,' she said at last. 'He's very gifted in that way.'

'I'll say.' Charlie could hardly believe it.

A doctor approached them. His cheerful smile told them that Lyell wasn't in any danger. They were shown into a small ward where Lyell was sitting up in bed. His head had been wrapped in a bandage, and one arm was in a sling. Charlie wanted to hug him but he couldn't see how, so he kissed his father's cheek and clung to his free hand.

'Forgive me, Charlie.' Lyell's dark eyes glistened. 'I don't deserve you.'

'Mum told me everything,' said Charlie shyly. He felt ashamed that he had doubted his father who, after all, was a hero.

Lyell squeezed his hand. 'You have every right to be angry with us.'

Charlie shook his head vigorously. 'The enchanter had to be killed, didn't he? So he'd never, ever try to take the city again.'

'I so nearly didn't succeed. You saved my life, Charlie.'

'Did I?' It hadn't occurred to Charlie until now.

'There are a few more things to do before the city is completely purged,' his father said wryly.

'Bloor's Academy?' Charlie suggested.

Lyell gave a grim smile. 'In a few days I'll be myself, and we'll put everything to rights, you and I, won't we?'

'You bet,' said Charlie.

Charlie and his mother stayed with the patient for another hour, and Charlie learnt where his mother had been staying, while her husband roamed the city as the Red Knight.

'Do you remember the hundred heads' ball?' asked Amy.

How could Charlie forget. 'It's when I found out about Mrs Tilpin and the enchanter,' he said.

'There was a man in a blue turban.'

'Yes. He saw me and Billy hiding under the table, but he didn't give us away.'

'His name is Mr Singh,' said Amy. 'He's PC Singh's father, and he let me stay in his house in the south. I wanted to stay with you, Charlie, but it would have looked suspicious if Lyell and I parted when we had only just been reunited. Mr Singh is, of course, a descendant of the Red King.'

'Then so is PC Singh!'

A nurse came in with a trolley of pills, and Charlie and his mother said goodbye to Lyell, promising to return the next day. On their way out they caught sight of Miss Ingledew leaving another ward. She looked rather flustered. Charlie ran up to her, crying, 'Where's my uncle? Have you seen him?' And then he remembered their disagreement and said hesitantly, 'Or was it someone else you were visiting?'

Miss Ingledew smiled. 'It was Paton,' she said. 'He's not badly injured. He said something about leopards helping, which I didn't really understand. But there's been a spot of bother with the lights. They've had to move him twice, but of course the same thing happened every time.'

Charlie tried to hide a grin behind his hand. 'Was anyone hurt?'

'Luckily, no,' Miss Ingledew said. 'But there was an awful mess. Glass everywhere. He's been put in a little room by himself, just inside the door. He'll be out tomorrow, to everyone's relief, I should imagine.'

Charlie didn't wait to hear any more. Pushing through the swing doors, he found his uncle's room and flung his arms around the long thin man who was scratching at a bandage that poked out of the top of his pyjamas.

'Blasted thing, itches like mad,' Paton complained when Charlie released his grip. 'Hello, Charlie. Well done all round, I say. What a day, eh? We learnt a few secrets at last. My word, your father's a dark horse.'

Charlie kept nodding. When he thought his uncle had finally said all he wanted, he asked, 'Have you and Miss Ingledew . . .?'

'Made up our silly quarrel? Yes, we have. She was very kind. Blames herself, though it was all my fault, no doubt, rushing about the country, poking into family affairs.' He gave a false sort of cough and added, 'Being injured does wonders, when it comes to . . . er, relationships, you know. You look a bit the worse for wear yourself, Charlie.' Paton gave another odd cough.

'Ah, nurse is coming. Visitors out, Charlie. But before you go,' he grabbed Charlie's hand, 'I want you to be the first to know . . .'

His cheeks turned a healthy pink.

'Know what?' asked Charlie.

'Miss . . . erm . . . Julia . . . uhum . . .' Paton seemed to be having trouble with his throat today, though his wound was in his chest. Charlie waited patiently for the spasm to pass. 'Yes. She . . . er . . . has agreed to marry me.'

'WOW!' yelled Charlie. 'That's a turn-up.'

A nurse accelerated towards him, calling, 'Out, young man!'

By the time Charlie and his mother got home, a great deal had happened at number nine. Grandma Bone had left, for one thing.

'She's gone to live with her sisters,' Maisie told them. 'Though I don't know how long that will last.'

Alice Angel was putting her old house to rights. She had decided to sell her shop in Steppingstones and come back to live in her old home.

On Sunday evening, people began to return to the city. They behaved as though they had just left

for an ordinary weekend away. The pernicious fog that had covered their homes was considered a mere coincidence. No mention was made of the battle on the heath. It was an event that most people couldn't really take in. Everyone agreed that it was going to be a beautiful Easter. Daffodils and irises were already blooming in borders and the avenues were filled with fragrant cherry blossom. A curious optimism pervaded the streets.

The wild strangers that had invaded Piminy Street seemed to have vanished as mysteriously as they had arrived. Mrs Kettle was now the only resident. She was sure that more congenial neighbours would arrive in time. Her great sword now hung back in its place on the wall of her smithy and the blue boa once more roamed around the kettles; now you saw him, now you didn't. Mrs Kettle had offered Dagbert Endless a home, which he had joyfully accepted. He contemplated a long and happy life making beautiful iron objects. 'Not necessarily weapons,' he told Mrs Kettle, 'but maybe ceremonial swords and ornamental gates and stuff like that.'

'And iron kettles?' asked Mrs Kettle.

'Naturally,' said Dagbert.

Not one student attempted to go back to Bloor's Academy on Monday. Word had spread that it was not a good place to be right now.

On Monday afternoon Lyell Bone and Uncle Paton came home to Filbert Street. Cook took Grandma Bone's room temporarily. There was much to do, for Lyell and Amy wanted to move into their old house, Diamond Corner, as soon as possible. But before this happened there was one more mystery to clear up. Maybelle's will.

The next evening, Lyell took Charlie and his uncle up to the cathedral, where Lyell was still the official organist. They walked along the wide aisle and round the choir stalls to the great organ, its long pipes reaching right up to the vaulted dome. And Charlie wondered where his father could possibly have hidden the pearl-inlaid box. Lyell gave a mischievous smile and lifted the cushioned top of the organist's seat. In a neat compartment just beneath sat the box.

'Well I never!' Uncle Paton exclaimed. 'What a hiding place. Who would have guessed?' He lifted it out. 'But without a key, how is it to be opened?'

'We could force the lock,' Lyell suggested, 'but the pattern would be destroyed in the process.'

Charlie took the box from his uncle. He turned it over and studied the intricate patterns: tiny mother-of-pearl stars, birds, leaves and flowers adorned the lid and the sides. He stared at the stars and found himself travelling very slowly, very gently, into a candlelit room, where a craftsman was pressing tiny pieces of mother-of-pearl into the back of the box. The man turned and looked at Charlie, holding up his finger. And Charlie gasped, for it was his old friend, Skarpo the Sorcerer, and on his finger sat a small pearl cat.

'Charlie!' His father was shaking his arm. 'What is it? Where are you?'

Charlie blinked. Skarpo had gone. 'His finger,' Charlie gasped. 'His finger.'

Uncle Paton and his father stared at Charlie in concern.

'It was a cat!' Charlie looked at the back of the box. He saw leaves and flowers, birds and stars, but no cat. He brought the box up close to his face. And then he saw it. There was a cat. Its ears poked from behind a star, its tail ran beneath a flower. Charlie gently pressed

the slim tail. And the lid of the box clicked open.

'Charlie! How extraordinary!' said Uncle Paton.

'How clever!' said Lyell.

Charlie kept his secret travelling to himself.

Inside the box was not one will but many, beginning with Septimus Bloor's. He had left everything to Maybelle. There was also a will made by Maybelle when she feared her life was in danger. She left her entire estate to her son, Daniel Raven. And then there was Daniel's will, leaving all he possessed to . . .

'His daughter, Ita?' said Lyell. 'Who on earth was she? I thought Daniel left everything to his son, Hugh, who gave the box to Billy's father, to prove that he would inherit the Bloor estate, if Septimus's true will could be found.'

'Which it has been,' Paton agreed. 'I want you both to come and look at something.' He led them down to the front pew, and they sat either side of him while he drew a folded paper from his pocket. 'This is what I have discovered during my weeks of research,' he said, flattening the paper on his knee.

Charlie and his father bent their heads over the

paper. There was nothing to see but a vertical line of names, beginning with Daniel Raven's eldest child, Ita, who, in 1899, had married a Simon Bone.

'Bone!' said Charlie and his father.

And there, beneath Ita and Simon, was the name of their son, Eamon, who had married a Clara Lyell. And beneath Clara and Eamon was the name of *their* son, Montague Bone, who had married Grizelda Yewbeam in 1961, and died the following year.

'My father,' said Lyell slowly.

'Who left everything he owned to you,' said Paton.

They sat a while longer in the quiet cathedral, trying to take in this momentous news.

'So Bloor's Academy belongs to you, Dad,' said Charlie at last.

His father frowned. 'I suppose it does. But how do we prove it?'

'Quite easily, I hope,' said Uncle Paton. 'I've made an appointment to see Judge Sage tomorrow morning.'

The following day, Lyell Bone and Paton Yewbeam took the box of papers to Lysander's father, Judge Sage. He was known as one of the wisest and most open-

minded members of the judiciary, and it didn't take him long to declare that Lyell Bone was the indisputable heir to Septimus Bloor's fortune. He would have to take the matter to court, of course, but the judge thought that Lyell stood an excellent chance of winning his case.

'We'll have to warn the present owners of Bloor's Academy,' Uncle Paton remarked wryly.

Charlie wanted to accompany his father and uncle on their visit to the Bloors, but Lyell was reluctant to let him. 'All the recent woes of this city have come from that family,' Lyell said, laying a hand on his son's shoulder. 'It's the seat of evil, Charlie, and there's no knowing what they will do when they discover that Septimus's will has been found.'

'Please!' begged Charlie. 'I want to be there. After all, I was the one who opened the box.'

Lyell laughed. 'So you were. You've won me over, Charlie, but please do everything I say.'

Charlie made a solemn promise and in the late afternoon, before the street lights had come on, Uncle Paton, Charlie and his father made their way up to the Academy. They were approaching the square when a

black car drove out. It stopped a moment before turning into the High Street, and Charlie saw Weedon at the wheel. Beside him sat his wife, and in the back was the unmistakable figure of Norton Cross in his elephant jacket. Beside him was a hunched figure, veiled in black. Charlie didn't see the fourth passenger until the car was driving away from them. A small white face looked out of the back window, and then hastily bobbed out of sight.

'Joshua,' muttered Charlie.

'And his mother most likely,' said Paton. 'They're all leaving.'

'Rats and a sinking ship come to mind,' said Lyell drily.

Weedon hadn't even bothered to close the Academy doors behind him. The three visitors stepped into the shadowy hall without bothering to knock. And for the last time in his life, Charlie shivered in the cold wickedness that seemed to pervade the building. It was truly a seat of evil, and the prime cause of all that evil was sitting in his wheelchair, staring down at them from the landing at the top of the staircase. It was almost as if he had been waiting for them.

'I suppose you've come to gloat,' he shouted. 'But you haven't won yet. You've finished off Count Harken, but I'm still here, and I'm not budging.'

'We have the will, Ezekiel,' said Lyell. 'The true will. It's all over for you.'

'Never!' screeched the old man.

'I'm afraid, Ezekiel,' said Uncle Paton, 'you'll have to spend your last days in a nice home for the elderly.'

'No, I won't. I'm staying put!' Ezekiel began to giggle uncontrollably. 'Manfred's going to make sure of that. If you make another move, he's going to burn the place down, and you wouldn't want that, would you now?'

At these words Manfred walked out of the shadow behind the stairs. He held his hands in the air, every finger blazing like a torch. 'Don't come any closer,' he warned. The awful power of his ancester, Borlath, the Red King's eldest son, had at last materialised in Manfred.

Lyell took a brave step towards Manfred.

'Dad, no!' cried Charlie, staring at the flames leaping from Manfred's fingers.

'Woooo!' shrilled Manfred, and the flames leapt higher. 'Scaredy cats!'

What happened next was so astounding, Charlie could hardly believe his eyes. For old Ezekiel came flying down the stairs. The wheels of his chair hit the treads once, twice, and then he was in the air. Too shocked to move, Manfred could only stare at the airborne thing in horror. When it landed on him he emitted a single high-pitched scream that would echo in Charlie's head for years to come.

Old Ezekiel rolled out of his chair, gave a long gurgle and fell silent. The flames, smouldering on a hand that protruded from the tangled heap, spluttered and died.

The three visitors were momentarily too shocked to speak, and then Paton murmured, 'How on earth?'

Charlie had seen the culprit, or rather their saviour, depending on how you looked at it. A short, fat dog stood at the top of the stairs, wagging his meagre tail. 'Blessed!' cried Charlie. 'Dog of the day!'

Paton brought out his mobile and began to ring for an ambulance. While he was doing this, Charlie noticed a solitary figure standing by the door to the west wing. Dr Bloor moved towards the dreadful pile of wood and bones. It was difficult to read his expression, but he didn't touch either of the bodies.

'It was the dog,' said Lyell. 'He must have pushed the chair.'

'I knew he would do that one day,' Dr Bloor said bleakly. He looked up at Blessed, still happily wagging his tail. 'I gather you've found the will.'

'We have,' said Lyell.

Dr Bloor gave a huge sigh. 'I won't give you any trouble,' he said. 'There's no point now. I'll go and pack.'

'Thank you,' said Lyell.

The Easter holiday arrived, and Paton Yewbeam and Julia Ingledew were married in a small church at the edge of the city. It was packed to the door; there were even people singing outside, under the cherry blossom. After the ceremony the newly-weds went to live in candlelit harmony above the bookshop. Emma was very happy with the new arrangement.

Billy Raven was unaware that he had almost been the heir to the Bloor fortune. While Charlie and his parents were packing up their belongings in number nine, Billy stayed with Benjamin. But after a few days of being chased round the house by Runner Bean, Rembrandt said that he couldn't stand another day in

the place. So Billy went up to the Silks' smallholding on the Heights. He enjoyed talking to the Silks' many pets, but Gabriel's sisters kept complaining that they needed more room, even though Mr and Mrs Onimous had moved back to the Pets' Café. Fidelio Gunn's house was Billy's next temporary home. The Gunns were such a large family, they decided that one more child would hardly make any difference, and they asked the social services to start drawing up some adoption papers.

Was Billy happy with this arrangement? It was difficult to tell. He smiled at the appropriate time, and nodded his head when he was required to. But was he happy?

He had taken to visiting the cathedral when Lyell Bone was practising the organ. He would tuck himself in a pew behind one of the great pillars, close his eyes and listen. But his presence didn't go unnoticed. One day Lyell called to Billy and asked if he would like to learn how to play the organ.

Billy crept shyly out of his hiding place and approached the great organ. Lyell helped him to place his fingers in the right places, and Billy thrilled to the sound that came from the tall pipes. After the lesson

they walked out of the cathedral together. It had begun to rain. It was only a light spring shower, but enough to make them stop in the porch for a while.

As they watched the rain bouncing on the shiny cobblestones, Lyell put a hand on Billy's shoulder and said, 'Billy, would you like to come and live with us?'

Billy frowned. He took off his new spectacles and rubbed the lenses with his thumb. 'How long for?' he asked.

Lyell smiled. 'Forever.'

Billy replaced his spectacles and stared straight ahead. He could hardly believe what he had heard. He felt breathless, his throat closed up and he wondered if he was going to die.

Worried by Billy's silence, Lyell said, 'I would do my best to be a good father.'

In a small, choked voice, Billy asked, 'What about Charlie?'

'It was his idea,' said Lyell. 'And Amy and I thought, well, we thought we'd really like another son.' Lyell peered down at Billy's rigid face. 'So how about it?'

Billy couldn't believe it. The kindest, bravest man in all the world had just offered him life with a family he

loved. Speechless, he clasped his arms round Lyell's waist and clung to him.

'I'll take that as a yes,' said Lyell.

'There's just one thing,' said Billy in a whisper, and he reached into his pocket. He felt that his life depended on Lyell's answer. 'What about my rat?'

Lyell took the proffered glossy black creature into his hands. 'I'm particularly fond of rats,' he said. 'Welcome, Rembrandt.'

'Many thanks,' squeaked Rembrandt.

A week after the Easter holidays, Bloor's Academy opened under new management. It also had a new name – The Bone Academy. Dr Saltweather's appointment as headmaster proved to be very popular, and Señor Alvaro took his place as Head of Music. A few of the staff left, old Mr Paltry and Mr Pope among them. They were considered no great loss. Cook moved back into her old apartment beneath the kitchen, but this time she said her cupboard door would always be open to children in need of cocoa and sympathy. Blessed spends most of his days lying beside her stove, and Dr Saltweather visits her often.

Cook brought her friend, Maisie Jones, back to the Academy with her. And Maisie is now Queen of the green canteen, in place of grumpy Bertha Weedon. It took only a few days of the new regime for every student to declare that The Bone Academy was the best and happiest school for miles.

Today the city is a very different place. It has a permanently spring-like atmosphere. The three number thirteens in Darkly Wynd are deserted. No one knows where the four sisters and Eric have gone. The Loom family have left the city, and the Brancos' shop and café lie empty. Not so the Pets' Café. It reopened with a grand party. So many animals attended there was scarcely any room for their owners. Gabriel arrived with enough gerbils for everyone, even Dagbert. Lysander came with his parrot, Homer, his girlfriend, Lauren, and her parrot, Cassandra.

The three Flames watched the proceedings from the counter. No one dared to suggest they should move.

Charlie and his friends had managed to grab their favourite place beside the window. Altogether there were twelve pets and eleven children. Mrs Onimous had outdone herself and six plates piled high with

delicious pet food and assorted cakes sat in the middle of the table.

After rather too much food, Rembrandt fell asleep and slipped off Billy's lap. Billy quickly ducked under the table to rescue him from Runner Bean. When Billy came up again his eyes were very wide and he had a big grin on his face. Leaning close to Charlie, he whispered, 'Tancred and Emma are holding hands.'

Descendants of the Red King

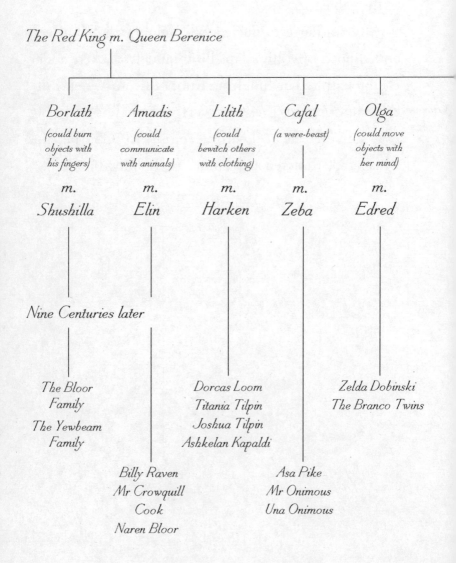

The Red King m. Queen Berenice

Borlath	Amadis	Lilith	Cafal	Olga
(could burn objects with his fingers)	*(could communicate with animals)*	*(could bewitch others with clothing)*	*(a were-beast)*	*(could move objects with her mind)*
m.	m.	m.	m.	m.
Shushilla	Elin	Harken	Zeba	Edred

Nine Centuries later

The Bloor Family

The Yewbeam Family

Dorcas Loom
Titania Tilpin
Joshua Tilpin
Ashkelan Kapaldi

Zelda Dobinski
The Branco Twins

Billy Raven
Mr Crowquill
Cook
Naren Bloor

Asa Pike
Mr Onimous
Una Onimous

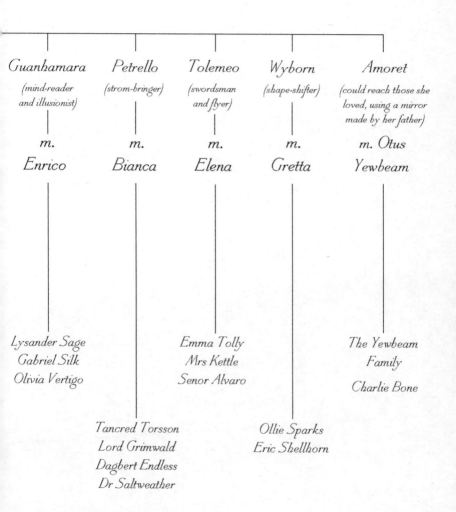

Guanhamara	Petrello	Tolemeo	Wyborn	Amoret
(mind-reader and illusionist)	(strom-bringer)	(swordsman and flyer)	(shape-shifter)	(could reach those she loved, using a mirror made by her father)
m.	m.	m.	m.	m. Otus
Enrico	Bianca	Elena	Gretta	Yewbeam

Lysander Sage
Gabriel Silk
Olivia Vertigo

Emma Tolly
Mrs Kettle
Senor Alvaro

The Yewbeam
Family

Charlie Bone

Tancred Torsson
Lord Grimwald
Dagbert Endless
Dr Saltweather

Ollie Sparks
Eric Shellhorn

Charlie Bone

Have you read the other books
in the Charlie Bone series?

CRACKLING WITH MAGIC

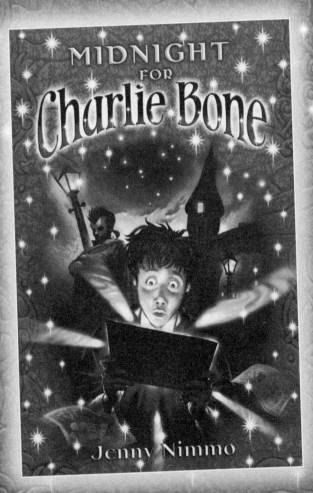

Midnight for
Charlie Bone

978 1 4052 2543 4

Charlie Bone
and the
Time Twister
978 1 4052 2544 1

Charlie Bone
and the
Blue Boa
978 1 4052 2545 8

Charlie Bone
and the
Castle of Mirrors
978 1 4052 2465 9

Charlie Bone
and the
Hidden King
978 1 4052 2820 6

Charlie Bone
and the
Wilderness Wolf
978 1 4052 3317 0

Charlie Bone
and the
Shadow of Badlock
978 1 4052 4586 9

www.charlie-bone.com

EGMONT PRESS: ETHICAL PUBLISHING

Egmont Press is about turning writers into successful authors and children into passionate readers – producing books that enrich and entertain. As a responsible children's publisher, we go even further, considering the world in which our consumers are growing up.

Safety First
Naturally, all of our books meet legal safety requirements. But we go further than this; every book with play value is tested to the highest standards – if it fails, it's back to the drawing-board.

Made Fairly
We are working to ensure that the workers involved in our supply chain – the people that make our books – are treated with fairness and respect.

Responsible Forestry
We are committed to ensuring all our papers come from environmentally and socially responsible forest sources.

For more information, please visit our website at
www.egmont.co.uk/ethical

Egmont is passionate about helping to preserve the world's remaining ancient forests. We only use paper from legal and sustainable forest sources, so we know where every single tree comes from that goes into every paper that makes up every book.

This book is made from paper certified by the Forestry Stewardship Council (FSC), an organisation dedicated to promoting responsible management of forest resources. For more information on the FSC, please visit **www.fsc.org**. To learn more about Egmont's sustainable paper policy, please visit **www.egmont.co.uk/ethical**.

Beatrice Bloor
b.1835
Witch.

Bertram Babington Bloor
b.1840
Having read Mary Shelley's Frankenstein, Bertram, a scientist-magician, tried to make a human being. He was not successful.

m.

Donatella da Vinci
b.1845
Daughter of an Italian magician. She assisted Bertram but was electrocuted during one of his experiments.

Maybelle Bloor
b.1833
Endowed.

Gideon
b.1875
Mathematician. Knighted for tutoring a royal prince. Sir Gideon was not endowed or interested in magic.

m.

Gudrun Solensson
b.1876
Amateur singer.

Ezekiel
b.1902
Spoiled, cunning, flawed magician. Continued his grandfather's experiments.

m.

Hilda Hansoff
b.1902
Botanist. Fatally poisoned by a rare plant.

Bartholomew
b.1930
Unendowed. Mountaineer. Lost in the Himalayas.

m.

Mary Chance
b.1930
Dancer. Danced herself to death when Bart disappeared.

Maisie Jo
b.1935
Widow.

Note:

Charlie Bone can hear the voices of people in photographs and paintings. In certain circumstances he can meet them.

Harold
b.1955
Unendowed, but interested in his grandfather's experiments.

m.

Dorothy de Vere
b.1957
Violinist.

Manfred
b.1985
Hypnotist.